D0499422

CHRONICLES OF THE HOST 4

FINAL
CONFRONTATION

CHRONICLES OF THE HOST 4

FINAL CONFRONTATION

D. BRIAN SHAFER

© Copyright 2004 — Doug Shafer

All rights reserved. This book is protected by the copyright laws of the United States of America. This book may not be copied or reprinted for commercial gain or profit. The use of short quotations or occasional page copying for personal or group study is permitted and encouraged. Permission will be granted upon request.

Destiny Image Fiction
An Imprint of
Destiny Image® Publishers, Inc.
P.O. Box 310
Shippensburg, PA 17257-0310

ISBN 0-7684-2174-8

For Worldwide Distribution
Printed in the U.S.A.

2 3 4 5 6 7 8 9 10 / 10 09 08 07 06 05 04

This book and all other Destiny Image, Revival Press, MercyPlace, Fresh Bread, Destiny Image Fiction, and Treasure House books are available at Christian bookstores and distributors worldwide.

For a U.S. bookstore nearest you, call
1-800-722-6774.
For more information on foreign distributors, call
717-532-3040.
Or reach us on the Internet:
www.destinyimage.com

In the Beginning was the Word,

And the Word was with God,

And the Word was God.

Dedication

It is with gratitude in my heart that I dedicate this book to the three women and one little man of God in my life who make it complete:

Lori, who puts up with my late nights at the computer and my early morning runs to Starbucks; Kiersten, who has been after me to bid on something on eBay and has the gift of giving and daddy's wallet to try and make it happen; Breelin; my Little Bit who always makes me laugh and who will knock the fashion world over one day with her designs; and to my as yet unborn but here when this book comes out son Ethan—Your name means "strong" in Hebrew—may you be a warrior for the Kingdom! I love you all!

P.S. OK girls, now let's REALLY get that Monopoly game out!

"Some Thoughts From the Author About Book Four"

This last book of this series has been both a challenge and a joy. I have loved receiving emails from people all over the country who have enjoyed reading Chronicles of the Host. I hope it has been both a blessing and a fun read. I look forward to starting my next book. But first, some housecleaning issues for Book Four:

I recognize there has been an adjustment made in the calendar then and now, and that according to our calendar Jesus was probably born around 4 B.C. That could be confusing when reconciling Jesus' death to a likely time of 33 A.D. as corroborated by other historical references, Pilate's time as governor, Herod Antipas' rule in Galilee and Matthias' authority in the priesthood. So this book uses a year one to year 33 chronology in order to simplify matters. Check it out sometime and you'll find what I mean.

I also chose to use the traditional names for the wise men rather than make them up. And even though the Bible doesn't number the wise men, again I stuck with tradition for the sake of clarity and readability. Besides—they're great names!

In the transformation of Simon Peter, I have used the name Peter immediately after Jesus' first meeting with him. Hopefully this will alleviate confusion of too many Simons, as Simon the Zealot becomes involved later on. By the way, any scriptural usage and/or reference is from the NIV version.

Again, I have to repeat this is biblical fiction. It is an attempt to blend the Bible story with fictional accounts of angelic activity. I know in some cases you will find things that are "not in the Bible," but the truth is I wrote this entire series with a Bible in front of me as a guide. Yes, you'll find places where I make up names and events—but I think you will also find that the truth of the Bible is never intentionally violated in as much as I know. Have a great read!

Finally, I have included study notes at the end of the book. There is so much rich teaching and Bible information implied as well as stated in the series that I decided to include some thought-provoking questions.

Check out the Chronicles of the Host Web site for more study notes and information at: www.chronhost.com

Contents

Final Confrontation Cast of Characters:

Holy Angels

Michael	an archangel
Gabriel	an archangel and Chief Messenger
Crispin	a wisdom angel
Millas	a wisdom angel
Alamar	an aide to Michael
Serus	an aide to Michael
Bakka	an angel assigned to Serus
Rufus	a wisdom angel

Unholy Angels

Lucifer	chief of the fallen angels
Kara, Pellecus, and Rugio	Lucifer's three chief angels
Lucifer's Council	Vel, Nathan, Prian, Fineo, Drachon, Sar, Rega, Tinius, Lenaes
Berenius	aide to Kara
Demas	spirit assigned to Herod the Great
Rhedi	one of Kara's spys
Jerob	an aide to Rugio
Achsan	one of Kara's angels, assigned to Galilee
Lucien	an angel over the city of Gadara
Korah	a demon in possession of the Gadarene man
Drachus	a demon of infirmity
Brusial	a demon of infirmity assigned to Lazarus

Humans

Caspar	a wise man
Melchior	a wise man
Balthasar	a wise man
Zacharias	a priest and father of John the Baptist
Elizabeth	mother of John
Eli	a priest and friend to Zacharias
Mary and Joseph	mother and father to Jesus
John	the forerunner of the Christ

Priests, Sanhedrin, Sadducees and Herodians

Zairus	a Sanhedrin
Nicodemus	a Pharisee
Zichri	a Pharisee determined to discredit Jesus
Shallah	a Pharisee and an aide to Zichri
Zeruiah	a priest
Zereth	a Sadducee
Ethan	a priest
Achish	envoy of Herod Antipas

Rulers

Herod the Great	king of Judea at time of Jesus' birth
Matthias	his high priest
Zereth	Herod's chief assassin
Herod Antipas	Herod the Great's son—ruler of Judea during Jesus' ministry
Herodias	his wife
Caiaphas	his high priest
Malchius	servant to Caiaphas
Pontius Pilate	Roman governor in Palestine
Claudia	his wife
Lucius	aide to Pilate
Augustus	Roman emperor at time of Jesus' birth
Tiberius	Roman emperor at time of Jesus' death
Sejanus	Tiberias' chief aide

Disciples of Jesus

Andrew
Peter
Philip
Bartholomew
Simon the Zealot
Thomas
Judas Iscariot
James
Nathaniel
James the elder
Matthew
Thaddeus

Others

Gehazi	a disciple of John the Baptist
Jadok	a disciple of John the Baptist
Justus	a man baptized by Jesus
Lazarus	a friend to Jesus
Mary and Martha	sisters to Lazarus
Mary Magdalene	a woman delivered by Jesus of evil spirits
Barabbas	a convicted man

Chapter 1

"It was in Eden that the Seed was first mentioned."

2 A.D.

The sky seemed a little brighter than usual, the stars shimmering like sharply focused dots dancing on an inky black canvas. The moon, too, was glorious, ever showing its gray face to the earth in solemn and solitary dignity. Of all the lights in Heaven, the greatest was the new star that had only recently appeared and hung suspended over the city itself. It was a perfect night for traveling; it was an even better night for completing a journey.

Three figures on camels followed the little road leading to the city. Dusty, tired, and happy to see the lights of Jerusalem flickering in the distance, the men did not speak as their camels plodded down the highway. Not far behind them came the rest of the group—servants atop camels weighed down with the trappings of a long sojourn.

The caravan halted on a rise in the road. The three men looked at each other and then at the bright star hanging low on the horizon. The star was set above the city, as if its light alone ruled the evening sky.

The men were obviously of some importance. Their traveling clothes were distinctly Babylonian. They wore headgear in the eastern style, and carried costly jewels hidden in their clothing. Each was like the other in appearance, although they were different in character. All three seemed poised and purposed as they made their way through the desert night.

"The gods be praised," said Caspar. "This must be the city."

"This is Jerusalem," answered Melchior. "The holy city of the Jews. Perhaps we are mistaken?"

"Nonsense," retorted Caspar, as he took a drink from his water pouch. He wiped his mouth. "No, this is it. I'm sure of it."

"Who rules in these parts?" asked Melchior.

"Herod the king of the Jews," came the voice of Balthasar. "Or king so long as Rome permits it. He's a crafty one though, and not to be dealt with lightly."

"No doubt," said Caspar. "Yet we must seek him out and inquire where the Child might be found."

The three continued toward Jerusalem, wondering what the end of their adventure would hold for them. They had known for some time theirs was a sacred task. Called out of Chaldea to pay homage to a newborn King, Caspar, Melchior, and Balthasar had left their exalted positions as magi to find the Child whose birth had unmistakably beckoned them. All of their calculations pointed to this place—and the star had guided them the entire journey. Now it was rewarding their efforts with precision.

"It is good to know we shall soon be in the presence of the One foretold," said Melchior. "We will be forever blessed with this memory."

"Yes," said Caspar. "Tomorrow we shall visit King Herod. I'm sure he will be interested in our mission."

Unseen by the humans, two large dark figures watched as the caravan passed by. They grinned at each other.

"Do you also suppose Herod will be interested in their mission?" asked one of the angels.

The other smiled and nodded, his reddish eyes gleaming, then responded, "I believe I can guarantee it!"

"All right, all right. Come to order!"

The din of the energized gathering of angels quickly abated as Michael and Gabriel took the dais that stood in front of the largest assembly hall in the Academy of the Host. Some of the students, who had never spoken with either of the archangels, watched the two rulers whose exploits on earth were becoming well known in Heaven. A few even hoped to pose a question to them, or catch a brief conversation with them after the meeting.

For Michael, this was a familiar setting. He had become accustomed to sitting in on Crispin's classes—even doing some teaching now and then. Most of these were unfamiliar faces—some of the myriad of angels the Most High had created. Whenever he saw a face he knew, however, he nodded and smiled. He thought back to his own time at the Academy—he was like these eager candidates, many of whom were hopeful to be under Michael's personal command as warriors of the Host.

Gabriel was not as comfortable in the role of instructor as he was in the role of messenger. He much preferred repeating words already reasoned out than presenting his own information—even in a friendly environment like this. But his great respect for Crispin brought him to the Academy with Michael to discuss the events unfolding on earth. Michael glanced over at his friend and laughed at his predicament.

"Come now, Gabriel," he said in mock concern. "Surely one who carries the revelations of the Most High to the corners of creation will not be upended by some bright angels in one of Crispin's classes?"

Gabriel gave Michael an incredulous look.

"Of course not," he retorted. "After all, Michael, I am privy to the greatest revelations in Heaven. Why, I've even given information to the Chief Elder." He looked up in mock surprise. "And even to you, Michael."

Michael grinned at the response.

"I love the Academy," Gabriel continued, glancing around the room. "And these angels. But I prefer delivering messages—not creating them."

"Come to order, please," repeated Crispin. The angels settled into hushed silence as the archangels continued their banter. He stared at Michael and Gabriel. "Ahem! I'm speaking now to our guests who are intent on their own conversation," he added playfully.

"Good master, we beg your forgiveness," said Michael. "Gabriel cannot restrain his enthusiasm for this occasion. I was instructing him to stop chattering."

"Yes, so I see," said Crispin, who nodded at Gabriel with the hint of a grin.

Crispin looked over the class with a scholarly expression and authority that captured the room. He then glanced in the direction of Michael and Gabriel.

"My dear angels," he began, "This is a wonderful moment in the history of this academy. I know you have awaited this moment for some time now as have I. Before we open the discussion for questions, I would like to read a brief statement which I have prepared, and, with the indulgence of our esteemed guests, the archangels Michael and Gabriel, I will commence reading."

An aide to Crispin handed a scroll with a wide golden band around its center to the revered teacher. He unrolled the scroll with little ceremony. Michael glanced at Gabriel and gave him a "here we go" look. Crispin began reading:

"To the students of the Academy of the Host—an account of those events which have been both witnessed and experienced on earth since the

dark rebellion began and which have revealed in some measure the wonder-ful and mysterious and ultimate intention of the Lord our God, the Most High Creator.

In as much as the Lord in His wisdom ordered the recording of the greater portion of the events we are about to recount to you in the Kingdom Chronicles as well as in the Chronicles of the Host, it is our intention to give those details we believe are instructive and of interest to those of you whose future ministry on earth will depend on your ability to deal with the fallen wills of both humans and angels alike.

Indeed, there are two wills with which we contest on both earth and in the heavenlies, and yet they are of the same mind, the same dark source. The mind of man has, since the great disaster in Eden, been twisted and bent on selfish industry. The once glorious earth has been transformed into a blood-stained planet of hopelessness and hate. It thus becomes the ministry of the Host to secure with the Most High the final outcome of His great and glori-ous plan something we still don't understand, but in which we shall play some part as ministering spirits."

Crispin handed the scroll back to the aide, who bowed his head, and rolled it up as he walked away. Crispin then returned his focus to the capacity-filled room. He motioned for the two archangels to join him at the dais.

"You all are a part of the greatest contest ever to have presented itself," he began. "You have witnessed or heard of events great and small in the brief but brutal history of the earth. These events, when taken in total, begin to paint for us a picture that becomes both clear and murky with the birth of the Child at Bethlehem."

At the mention of Bethlehem, many of the angels in the room looked at Gabriel, who had played such a visible role during that event. Michael smiled discreetly at his friend whose message to Mary had been so shattering.

"I think you're a hero," he whispered playfully.

Gabriel grumbled something back, causing Michael to grin.

"And so while we have these two ruling angels among us, we shall take advantage of them," Crispin continued. "But go easy on them. It has been a while since they were my students in the Academy!"

The room burst into laughter.

"Perhaps before we open the class for questions we should hear from Michael and Gabriel, our great archangels!"

The room broke out in cheers and applause as the two powerful angels looked at one another as if deciding who should speak first. Finally Gabriel came to the platform and began addressing the assembly.

"Thank you Crispin," he began. "But we all know that there is only One who is great in Heaven."

Crispin nodded his head in agreement and glanced toward the Great Mountain of the North where the Lord's Presence rested.

"We angels," Gabriel continued, "warriors and ministers of the Most High God, have been given a sacred task to serve the Lord by entering the world of humans—those curious creatures made in God's very image whose rebellion has cost them everything and for whom our Lord is planning some great work through the new-born Child. What this Child shall accomplish, or what shall be His end, only the Most High knows. Ours is not to raise questions—ours is merely to obey the Lord in matters great and small. I will be more than happy to answer any question this body might have."

He looked over at Crispin. "But I, for one, am looking forward to hearing from the greatest teacher in Heaven!"

The room again broke out in praises to the Lord and applause for the archangel, and the wise angel who was their instructor. Michael then began speaking.

"As you are learning, the human question is a complicated one. As angels and servants of the Most High God, it is our task to accomplish the Lord's will in Heaven and on earth as He deems necessary. I heard a number of you before this session questioning the Lord's longsuffering in dealing with such capricious spirits as human beings—the creature-turning-on-its-Creator sort of thing. But, beware. Angels were guilty of this before humans."

Quiet held the room, as the angels clung to Michael's words.

"Still, humans have, by their own choice you may recall, established a world that is essentially anti-God. It was not meant to be that way from the beginning. But this is the outcome of a free will that has tasted sin and gathered an appetite for it. We cannot question the Lord's motives for loving creatures who treat Him in such unloving ways. As Gabriel said, we serve the Lord's purposes, not our own."

"Thank you Michael and Gabriel," commented Crispin, who now took over the presentation and broke the silent spell of the room. "I'm certain your ministry on earth will be of great interest to these eager angels. And having once sat under my teaching, I'm also quite certain a portion of my instruction carried you in some of your more challenging moments."

Michael and Gabriel laughed, nodding their heads in agreement. The room also fell to laughter.

"In all seriousness, I appreciated the sharp observation made by Michael concerning the 'capricious' nature of humans. It is quite true. Humans are a strange mixture of behaviors. Ever since the disaster in Eden, the one-time innocence that was known to those first humans has been distorted and mired in the darkness of pride and rebellion— a behavior we all witnessed in this very Kingdom in the distant past.

Crispin began to pace, clearly in his element.

"Our Lord had determined that in Eden He would create a people with whom He would fellowship in a way even angels cannot appreciate. Remember the speculations and the wonder leading up to that dramatic day when the first man was created? We didn't know what the Creator was doing but we understood it would be glorious, whatever He did."

Crispin closed his eyes as if drinking in the day in Eden so long ago.

"A'dam was a beautiful creature—almost god-like in his perfection. He was given the freedom to rule and govern the earth in the Lord's name. He was given authority over all the creatures and even allowed to name them. He was to become the father of a great nation of humans who would live in fellowship with the Lord and would steward His world forever. He was given a mate..."

Upon these words a quiet rumble among the angels began. The word 'Eve' could be heard here and there in the room. Crispin looked over the sea of faces.

"Ah now," Crispin continued, wagging a finger. "Eve is only a part of this problem. Many angels accuse Eve for the current state of affairs. I submit to you that the rebellion in Eden was the responsibility of A'dam—not Eve!"

The reaction in the room was one of surprise.

"You see, Michael, angels can learn something!"

Michael and Gabriel smiled.

"Yes! Hear me! A'dam was the responsible party in Eden. It was to A'dam that the law was given—not to Eve. It was A'dam to whom the responsibility for upholding the law was delivered—not to Eve. Now, Eve was a catalyst, to be sure. But A'dam? Did he attempt to stop her as she fell into the trap of our enemy? Where was he? He was standing there when it happened and complicit in the crime!

"So instead of remaining true to God's one great prohibition to him and possibly atoning for her sin by obeying the Lord, he himself disobeyed the very law God Most High had delivered to him personally! Eve fell prey to her own senses and the subtle cunning of a far greater intellect. But A'dam? He fell prey to himself—a far deadlier adversary."

"Good teacher!" an angel shouted. "Are you saying that A'dam might have prevented the current state of affairs had he remained true—even after Eve ate?"

Crispin was annoyed at the interruption.

"I would prefer to wait on your questions until after the presentation, but as this has always been a point of sharp debate among the Host, I will answer your question by simply saying we shall never know. But wouldn't it be interesting to discover what the outcome might have been had A'dam stayed true—despite Eve's disobedience?"

He looked to the archangels standing near him.

"You were both there in Eden, as were some of these in attendance. It was a tremendous contest of wills. I like to think that perhaps A'dam's obedience might have made all the difference. Perhaps not. In any case we shall never know."

Michael's mind sped back to that bitterly disappointing day when the plan of God fell victim to the pride of man. He recalled Eve's discussion with the serpent. Lucifer certainly was in top form that day. He used the cunning and intellect of a beast to tempt Eve into failure.

The memory of thousands of angels—wicked and holy—swooping in and watching the drama untold in the center of the garden was especially poignant. The evil angels under Lucifer's control were baiting and hostile, laughing, cajoling, and encouraging the trap. The holy angels, horrified at the humans' disgrace, could only watch in silent shame as A'dam and Eve walked from innocence into death.

"I mentioned two minds at work on earth. For there is indeed another mind that is active and engaged—far more cunning than that of man—and one that has seeded in mankind a destructive nature driven by pride and destined for destruction. It is this carrier of iniquity—this depraved and fallen spirit that has overtaken the world and who, through the assistance of other like-minded spirits, fosters the insanity now flourishing in the one-time paradise."

"Lucifer," someone whispered.

"Yes, of course," said Crispin with a sense of resignation. "Lucifer, called Satan by our Lord through some of the human prophets—the adversary. Our one-time brother who, with his horrible group of compliant and ambitious angels—low spirits all and demons by designation—kindle in men the very passions now holding them prisoner.

"These base spirits fill the minds and hearts of humans with all manner of wickedness, and sensuality; with a lust for power and an appetite for wealth. And then, assuming the role of earthly gods, they swagger for the men who swear by them, priests and prophets in unholy alliance with fallen angels, fostering meaningless religious ceremony that finds salvation in itself, but whose end is only death."

"Good master, why would humans who have rejected the Living God serve this or that god on earth?" asked Alamar, a warrior whom Michael had recently pegged to join him on earth.

"Excellent question, Alamar," said Crispin, who had decided to open the teaching up to discussion. "The reason for such behavior is quite evident—and is a great paradox. Since their disobedience in Eden, humans became essentially anti-God, as you have reminded us. Yet they also possess a God-ward thrust—an inner spirit that careens them through life in search of meaning—to link up with that which has been lost in antiquity, so to speak. Of course, devoid of truth, and left to their own devices, and encouraged by dark spirits and their own base instincts, they find refuge in things carnal and earthly, dark and forbidden..."

He paused then added, "This is the price of rebellion...the fruit of pride. For they long for truth and connection with their Creator, yet have settled for something far inferior. And in their blind quest they pursue the very truth they have rejected while rejecting the very truth they pursue!"

"So what hope do humans have?" Alamar continued. "I will of course serve the Lord my God in any task. But it seems humans have lost their ability to relate to the Lord in a holy way. Why does He continue this ministry to them?"

Crispin looked at Gabriel, who nodded and began speaking.

"Because the Lord, ever willing that humans regain that pre-fallen state, is at work on earth and has been since Eden," remarked

Gabriel. "Remember, while Eden was the site of great misfortune, it was also the beginning of great hope. It was at Eden that the Lord prophesied the One who should come and undo the work of darkness begun by Lucifer."

"And it was in Eden the Seed was first mentioned," added Michael. "The Seed that has recently been delivered in Bethlehem."

"And thus it becomes our ministry to serve mankind by serving the Child," continued Crispin. "Oh I don't pretend to understand how the Child Jesus will do it. But the fact He is the Son Incarnate, born of a woman, must be giving Lucifer something worrisome to think about."

"Remember the circumstances of the Child's birth," said Gabriel.

"And what are we to do to serve the Son?" asked another.

"I suspect the Son comes to do what A'dam was unable to do," said Crispin. "To remain true to His Father. And in so doing, He will crush the head of Lucifer. It's all been foretold."

"Ah!" exclaimed Alamar. "So through obedience the Son will crush the serpent!" He paused for a moment. "But what is so extraordinary about that? Can mere obedience undo the darkness of sin?

Crispin looked at the angel intently.

"There is nothing 'mere' about obedience," he said. "No human has been able to maintain an obedient relationship with the Most High—some angels have not. Obedience has been a catalog of failure where humans are concerned. But I assure you this, if obedience is the key to the Son's crushing of Lucifer, then it shall be an extraordinary obedience indeed. And at great cost."

He motioned Gabriel to be ready.

"But now, we shall hear from the one whose ministry was so closely aligned with the Seed's delivery on earth. And I trust that you will see, Alamar, even mere obedience has its place in the plans of our Lord."

King Herod observed the dedication of a newly completed building he had ordered to be constructed. He watched an official from his court stand by as a priest prayed over the site—which was to be a charitable office governed by the temple wards. As the priest prayed, his eyes scanned the horizon of the dusty, noisy, and always-agitated city of Jerusalem. There in the distance, just to the right of the new building, the Temple could be seen.

The Temple project, an ambitious work and Herod's pride, had been going on for some 22 years. It was truly a marvel. In hopes of an obvious and favorable comparison, Herod made sure to use the same type of soft white stones used for Solomon's Temple. Called "the Great" largely because of his magnificent buildings, amphitheaters, sporting centers, ports and the mighty fortress of Masada, Herod now employed some 10,000 workmen to build the Temple, including over 1,000 priests, whose presence was necessary since laymen could not enter the Temple proper. It was to be his crowning achievement, one that would secure his legacy in the minds and hearts of this cantankerous people.

But now, with the sun bearing down, he grew impatient over the long prayer of the priest. As the prayer droned on he thought backwards in time to his ascension to power through the political connivance of his father. He recalled the early days of consolidating power and partnering with Rome; he looked toward the Temple and thought of the future he was building for his children. But mostly he thought of his own immortality.

Herod was getting old, and saw every minute as precious. For all his intrigue and political skill he could not manufacture more time for his life. So he guarded his life very carefully. Suspicious by nature, Herod had obtained his throne through subtlety and murder and had retained it the same way. Anyone he considered a threat to his throne was immediately dealt with—up to and including his own wife and children. It was an uneasy kingdom over which Herod reigned.

Finally the priest finished. The ceremonial party looked up at the sedan chair in which Herod sat, borne by four large Egyptian slaves that had been a gift from the Roman governor. Herod stepped down from his perch and walked over to the site. He took the golden goblet from the hand of the priest and poured wine along the doorstep of the building.

"I hereby call you as witnesses that this office is now officially open," Herod said with great reverence. "May it be a blessing to the poor in this nation of ours. And may the Lord always bless our nation."

"So be it," said the officials.

Then the priest took the cup and poured wine onto the pavement in front of the entrance. Several drops of the dark red liquid splashed on Herod's robe. The priest gasped in terror and stepped back, as did several of the other officials. Herod looked down at the robe and then back at the trembling priest. He smiled and the tension broke.

Herod quickly turned and stepped back into his chair, ordering the slaves to take him on to the Temple. He would inspect its progress. He motioned for the Temple Warden to approach him. The man nervously came to Herod's sedan.

"Yes, sire?" said the warden.

"Wonderful ceremony," Herod said, swatting at a fly with a horse-tail baton.

"Many thanks, my king," said the man. "Your presence here is always inspiring."

"Yes. Today it was exceedingly inspiring." He lifted up the skirt of his ruined robe. "See to it this priest is removed to a less public duty."

"At once, sire," returned the warden as the sedan began moving.

The guard who accompanied Herod went ahead and cleared a path for him. Herod hated traveling with an armed unit, but the Romans insisted on it and besides, there were many living relatives of those executed under his orders. As he moved through the narrow street he sat back in the chair, the curtains drawn so no one could see inside.

Suddenly the sedan was knocked to one side. Herod slipped onto the floor, caught off guard. He could hear screaming outside. It was a man ranting about the cowardice of Herod and how he was a Roman lapdog unfit to rule in Judah. The guards cleared the area, calling for reinforcements as a crowd gathered. In minutes, Roman sentries arrived and dispersed the crowds.

Once the situation was under control Herod stepped out. The crowd gasped in astonishment as their king emerged from the sedan. He looked at the hate-filled eyes of a man of about 30. The man looked like any other Jew, except he had a fire in his eyes that was unnerving, even to Herod. An officer produced a dagger the man had concealed in his cloak and had intended to use on the king. Herod walked over to the man who was held securely by his guards.

"Did you mean this for me?" asked Herod.

"Yes" answered the man. "I intended it for your black heart."

"But what have I done to you?" asked Herod, now clearly in control and aware of his audience. "Do I know you? Have we ever met?"

"You are a murderer and a fraud," the man continued, turning his head this way and that, speaking to the silent crowd "I know I shall die for this, but it will have been worth it for my son to remember that I resisted you. If only he would have remembered me killing you!"

Herod looked over at a woman under Roman guard who was crying. She held the hand of a small boy about four years of age. Herod looked at the boy.

"Is this your son?" Herod asked, with chilling gentleness.

"Yes," said the man, nervous as Herod made his way over to the boy. "My wife knew of my intentions and came to stop me. But I'm glad my son saw this. He will remember this day. And one day he will grow up and perhaps bring freedom to my people."

"No doubt, no doubt," said Herod, stroking the young boy's head. "I'm not sure if he will ever grow up to be a freedom fighter. Perhaps he won't even grow up at all."

The boy's mother began crying and begging for her son's life. Herod waved her off as if to say that the boy would be spared. "But he will indeed remember the day he saw his father die. Take this man to the place of execution! And the boy."

The crowd gasped once more and Herod was satisfied that this display of swift justice should remind them whose authority they were under.

"You will die one day, Herod!" screamed the man as he was led away. "You will stand before the Judge of Heaven and Earth! There is a King coming who will take your place—the place of all authority in Israel!"

The last words were cut off by a severe blow to his mouth, administered by one of the guards. Herod watched as the mother followed after, pleading for her husband to be quiet and begging for his life. The boy broke away and looked back at Herod.

"Simon!" she screamed at the boy. "Stay with me!"

Then the two disappeared in the crowded street. People began talking in hushed conversation, looking and pointing and watching Herod. For his part, Herod became uncomfortable with the situation and quickly climbed back into his chair.

"Get me back to the Antonia! At once, you fools!" he shouted.

The guards closed in tightly around Herod as they hastily made their way back to Herod's fortress palace in Jerusalem. He had decided to visit the Temple construction site another day.

As the band moved through the street on its way back to the Antonia, a messenger approached the party. Herod's personal aide waved him through. The courier bowed low and handed the note to the aide, who in turn handed it to Herod. Herod took the dispatch and read it.

"Well, now, this is interesting," he said, handing the message back to his aide. "It seems we have visitors in Jerusalem—three of them to be exact."

CHAPTER 2

"How can this be? I am a virgin!"

"Tell us about the birth," someone spoke from the back.

Others began to chime in immediately.

Gabriel smiled and looked at Crispin, who nodded his assent.

"Go ahead," Crispin said. "They all know the story, but it will be refreshing for them to hear it directly from the angel who actually experienced the glorious event!"

"Thank you Crispin," Gabriel began. "The event was indeed glorious. But to be sure, the glory is the Lord's. Remember this—the Most High shares His glory with neither men nor angels. It is not for angels to glory in what they do."

The angels listening, nodded in agreement.

"As to the events surrounding the birth of the Christ, it is true this was a marvelous spectacle. To be witness to, and take a small part in, the greatest prophecy given by our Lord was quite humbling."

"Was Mary truly unafraid when you appeared to her?" asked an angel seated in the front of the room.

"Not quite," answered Gabriel. "She was in fact quite frightened, as most humans are when first we appear to them. Of course we *never* appear to a human unless the events are extraordinary and warrant such an appearance, and usually only as commanded by the Lord Himself."

Gabriel stepped into the center and stood directly in front of the assembly, near enough to touch them if he had extended his hand.

"Of course, the story didn't begin with Mary," he continued. "It began after the final prophecy was recorded by the prophet Malachi—some hundreds of human years earlier. During that time the words of the Lord were precious and few and only held in esteem by a remnant of Israel. The people of God had lost their way and their nation. But there was a man named Zacharias, of the house of Levi, who loved the Lord. He and his wife Elizabeth greatly desired children, but were unable to conceive. And now they were old in years.

"His name meant 'the Lord remembers,' for it was to him the Lord remembered His promise of the Seed after hundreds of years of silence; it was to him the first whisper of the Christ Child was to be told while serving at the Temple—a whisper that included a son of his own, a boy to be named John…".

1 B.C.

"Such a day, such a day!" exclaimed Zacharias.

He hurried about the little house he had shared with his wife Elizabeth for many, many years. Elizabeth smiled at her husband, a man in his seventies, who today was acting like a young man. Zacharias was distinguished in his community, known for his faith and reverence for the Most High. His reputation for piety and devotion carried great weight in a time when such devotion was uncommon.

Elizabeth was likewise held in great esteem. She, too, was of the house of Aaron, and was a righteous daughter of Israel. They were indeed a couple who honored the Lord with their lives. It was therefore a mystery as to why Elizabeth had remained barren all these years.

Chronicles of the Host

Zacharias' Honor

It had been King David who had ordered the priesthood into 24 divisions, each to take turns serving in the Temple. Zacharias was of the division of Abijah, and to be chosen by lot among so many was a once-in-a-lifetime honor. Zacharias had rehearsed the procedure in his mind over and over again in preparation for the event, and even as he bade his wife good-bye in the predawn hour, he thought about the heritage that he would live out today.

Zacharias entered the Temple, as was his custom, and awaited the morning sacrifice offered on the altar outside the Holy Place. After the priest had dipped the blood on the horns of the altar, Zacharias began making his way up the steps leading to the Holy Place. Many eyes were upon the old man who had served the priesthood for so long.

He was accompanied by two other priests who would assist in the ministry. They were to remove the old coals and place live coals in the censer and then leave. And so while hundreds of priests awaited Zacharias in the Court of Israel, Zacharias was quite alone in the Temple...or was he?

"Zacharias!"

The old man looked up and cocked his head. He waited a moment and then realized he must have heard the priests outside. He went back to his prayers.

"Zacharias!"

He looked up again. In the eerie glow of the room he could not make out anything. He was about to leave when he saw an angel standing to the right of the altar of incense. He was terrified and fell down before the magnificent being that was in white robes and girded about with a golden belt. Terrified he had committed some offense against the Lord, Zacharias prepared to die.

Gabriel looked down upon the old priest. He didn't intend to frighten the man but he knew that humans generally were affected this way when a spirit appeared to them. His mission was of supreme importance and he began to speak to the priest in reassuring terms.

"Hear me, Zacharias," said Gabriel. "The Lord has heard your prayers!"

Zacharias looked up once more, now realizing he was in the presence of one of God's holy angels.

"Your prayer has been heard. Just as this incense is lifted to the Lord, so the prayers you have prayed have been received by the Most High God. Hear me! Your wife Elizabeth shall have a son! And you shall call him John."

"A son?" Zacharias managed.

"He will be the cause of great joy in Israel," Gabriel continued. "He shall be great in the sight of the Lord. He will drink neither wine nor strong drink. And he shall be filled with the Holy Spirit even in his mother's womb!"

"A son," repeated Zacharias.

"And he shall be the cause of many in Israel turning back to the Lord. He will go about in the spirit and power of Elijah. He will turn the hearts of the fathers back to their children, and the disobedient back to those who are filled with wisdom."

Gabriel paused for a moment to allow Zacharias to drink all of this in. The old man by now had managed to stand, albeit in a humble posture.

"And he shall make ready a people who are prepared for the Lord!"

Upon this pronouncement, Gabriel could feel a rumbling in Heaven. This was the beginning of the greatest prophecy ever given—it was the opening of a new phase of this long and bloody war with darkness. Gabriel awaited Zacharias' reply.

By now Zacharias had collected himself. Was this a dream? They had prayed all their lives for a son. Was his wife to give birth now, in her old age? Perhaps this was a deceiving spirit or the excitement of serving in the Temple on this special day. Doubt began to creep in.

"Forgive me," said Zacharias meekly. "But how shall I know what you have said is true? We have wanted a son for many years. But we are both old now and my wife remains barren. Elizabeth is…"

"I am Gabriel. I stand in the presence of the Most High God!"

Gabriel was a bit annoyed at Zacharias' doubt. Why can't humans simply realize God can do anything He desires?

"Gabriel?" Zacharias repeated.

"And I have been sent by the Lord to tell you these marvelous things that must surely be." As Gabriel spoke he clearly heard the Spirit of God speak into his mind the next pronouncement: "And hear me! Because you did not believe these words I have spoken, you shall not be able to speak until these things take place—for surely they will happen at the appointed time!"

Suddenly, Gabriel was gone.

Zacharias took a minute to recover from the vision, then hurried out of the Temple to join the other priests waiting for him in the Court of Israel. It was the custom that whoever ministered the incense would also pray a benediction when he emerged from the sanctuary. The priests wondered what had taken him so long in the burning of the incense. Zacharias fell at the feet of the first priest he saw and started to tell him of the wonderful thing that had just happened. But instead of sound there was only a silence.

The priest looked at Zacharias strangely. This frustrated Zacharias, who began making all sorts of wild motions, pulling on his robe and pointing back at the Holy Place. His face was pale. The man thought Zacharias had indeed lost his mind.

The poor man looked to some of the others for help. The priest, still in the grip of Zacharias, pulled away from him in horror. Would no one come to his aid? Zacharias remained on the ground, surrounded by the curious priests who stared and muttered among themselves while he continued to gesture wildly. He sank to his knees in despair. Finally, one of the priests, named Eli, approached him soothingly.

"What is it Zacharias?" he asked. "What has happened? What did you see?" Then Eli looked at the old man's face and asked, "Did the Lord speak to you?"

Others crowded around the old man who by now was on his feet gesturing toward the Temple but unable to speak the words. The men concluded he had indeed had a vision of some sort. After a few moments he gave up, frustrated. He decided to quietly complete the remaining week of his duties in silence; then he would take the news to the one person who was sure to understand—Elizabeth.

Chronicles of the Host

Elizabeth's Joy

And so it was that just as Gabriel had prophesied, Elizabeth, the wife of Zacharias, conceived. For five months she kept herself in seclusion, perhaps to keep her reproach of so many years hidden until it was evident God had so blessed her.

As for Gabriel, his ministry continued in the matter of this great event. Our opponent was convinced for a season that Elizabeth would bear the Seed, and she was under constant watch. She was, of course, well protected by the Host, and nothing the enemy brought against her came to fruition. As for Zacharias, he continued in silence, counting the days until his wife's delivery.

*Six months after Elizabeth had conceived, the angel Gabriel
was sent to Nazareth, in Galilee, to a maiden who was
betrothed to a man named Joseph. The virgin's name was
Mary. The attention of the Host shifted dramatically to this
young woman. The attention of Lucifer also shifted...*

"Greetings, O highly favored one!"

Mary dropped the lamp, which broke at her feet.

Standing before her was an angel of the Lord. She had often
heard stories of visiting angels—even dreaming of them on occasion.
But she never thought she would actually see one. Angels visited holy
men and kings—not ordinary people! After a few seconds of studying
the figure that stood in front of her in her little home, she began to
question not only why he had come, but what he had just said.

"Highly favored?" she whispered.

Gabriel spoke to her in a soothing voice full of compassion and
joy. He wanted her to understand completely what he was about to
tell her. He continued.

"Mary, do not be afraid—you are indeed highly favored of the
Lord!"

She remained silent.

"You are to give birth to a Son and shall call his name Jesus,"
Gabriel said. "He will be great and will be known as the Son of the
Most High! He will be given the throne of David and shall rule over
the house of Jacob forever. His Kingdom shall see no end!"

Mary was staggered. A baby? She had never been married or even
been with a man before. She was engaged to be married! How could this
be? Overcoming her fear of the situation, she spoke to Gabriel.

"But how can this be? I am a virgin."

"It will not be by man that you shall conceive but by the power
of God," answered Gabriel. "The Holy Spirit of the Most High shall
create in your womb this coming Son—this Son of God."

"But…"

"Listen! Your cousin Elizabeth, who has been barren, is also going to have a child."

"Elizabeth?" Mary responded, a rush of joy beginning to supplant her fear.

"She is already in her sixth month," said Gabriel. "You see? Nothing is impossible for the Lord!"

Mary considered everything that had been spoken to her. It was impossible to drink it all in at once, and yet she knew in her heart it must be true. If this was of the Lord, then she was indeed highly favored. She looked up at Gabriel.

"I am the Lord's servant," she said. "May everything you have said about me and Elizabeth come true."

Gabriel smiled at her and could not help but contrast her willingness to believe with Zacharias' disbelief. He vanished as quickly as he had appeared. Mary was left with her thoughts. She was to carry the Son of the Most High? But why? What was the Lord doing? What did Elizabeth have to do with it all? Most of all—what was Joseph going to think?

She decided that she must go and see Elizabeth at once.

Lucifer's leadership was meeting to discuss the recent appearances of Gabriel concerning the birth of the One who would be called Jesus. Lucifer had reconvened many of the Council members that had been with him in the days before the rebellion, before the Council of Worship had become the Council of War.

The chatter around the table was a mixture of reminiscing over the old times in Heaven to the new threat posed by Gabriel's intrusions. Many of these angels had not spoken to or seen each other since their expulsion from Heaven. It was quite a different arrangement around the table now—stripped of their offices and former prestige, they vied for whatever bits of power Lucifer tossed their way. The memories of this group were both bitter and sweet.

Lucifer strode in and the room became quiet immediately. They met in an abandoned temple on Crete, in deference to Pellecus, whose principality over the Graeco-Roman world was now a brightly shining star. The temple was a Minoan structure dedicated to a long-forgotten sea goddess. The great civilization at Knossos, which once flourished here, had been destroyed in a violent earthquake. All that remained were pitiful ruins and relics of a glorious past.

"Not exactly the same surroundings as when we met in Heaven," said Lucifer, noting the ruined temple. "But an appropriate setting to be sure."

The angels looked at each other knowingly.

Lucifer stood at the end of the long bronze table that had once served as a Minoan priest's place of offering. He eyed each angel individually: Rugio, Vel, Nathan and Prian, his warrior commanders; Fineo, Drachon, Sar and Rega, former angels of worship; and Tinius, Pellecus, Lenaes and Kara, angels of wisdom, now turned angels of deception. Lucifer smiled faintly.

"Brothers, it is good to have you back again as in the beginning," he said. "We represent the future of this planet and the strategy of this present war. Of course we will have to do without Sangius, who betrayed us. But all in all we are united and represent the most powerful and resourceful angels in our realm."

Lucifer gestured at their meeting place.

"I called this place fitting because it was once a place of greatness and glory. You are well acquainted with the former priests of this land who performed all manner of sorcery and conjuring." He paused for a moment. "But the glory of their day faded and they have become dust awaiting judgment at the end of the age."

Lucifer ran his fingers along the ornately carved altar. He was brooding and melancholy. Finally he began speaking, looking more at the altar than at the angels staring back at him.

"Like these once-proud Minoans, who have come and gone, we are on the threshold of a faded glory. We have fought and fought and fought. We have seen the destruction of countless humans and over-thrown many nations. We have planted our lies deep into the hearts of men who seek the glory of the Most High in things He created for their amusement. And yet the war goes badly for us. The Child who was foretold has now been conceived by His mother. The Seed has been delivered."

The group, whose mood was becoming increasingly desperate, looked to Lucifer for some note of hope. Lucifer smiled and continued, "I have no answer for you."

The angels remained silent for a few moments. Finally, Tinius stood to speak.

"My lord, are you saying the war is lost?"

"Did I say that, Tinius?"

"No, lord," stammered Tinius, whose doubtful mind often played into Lucifer's harsh disposition. "I'm not doubting your ability to lead us…"

"I said I have no answer for you…at this time."

He produced a scroll.

"When waging war it is wise to learn as much as you can about your enemy. In the case of our enemy, He has given us much intelligence with which we might surmise our next move."

He began unrolling the scroll before them.

"The prophet Isaiah, among others, has given us ample infor-mation on what we are to expect from this…this 'Son of the Most High who is to be called Jesus,' as Gabriel put it. We have discussed some of this before. But more recent prophecies bring new light to this reference. I often wonder at the wisdom of the Most High who seems bent on giving it all away."

He took the scroll and began to read:

"For unto us a Child is born, unto us a Son is given,
and the government shall be upon His shoulders;
and His name shall be called Wonderful, Counselor,

The Mighty God, The Everlasting Father,
The Prince of Peace.
Of the increase of His government there will be no end,
Upon the throne of David, and upon his Kingdom,
To order it and to establish it with judgment and
With justice from henceforth even forever."

"The throne of David," muttered Kara. "The same old dream. When will these people ever give up on that dreary idea?"

Pellecus scoffed at Kara's ignorance.

"Why should they give up on the idea when the prophet Isaiah and others fan it for them?" he asked. "More importantly, why should they give up on the throne of David being established again when the Lord Himself places such hope before them?"

"David's throne was destroyed," grunted Rugio, whose bitter memory of Goliath's defeat still gnawed at him. "He is dust now."

"David is dust," agreed Lucifer. "But his legacy survives. Don't you see what this means? It is exactly as we feared. There shall be born in the derelict house of Judah the One who will regain the throne of David and establish it forever. Who could do this but the Lord of Hosts? And who but the Lord would be bold enough to foretell it?"

"But there are so many prophecies being bantered about these days," Kara said scornfully. "This nation thrives on them. What is another prophecy more or less?"

Lucifer looked at Kara.

"I would agree with you, Kara," he began. "This is certainly a people from whom prophets spring forth constantly. This is different. The circumstances of His birth, the description of His form, even the mentioning of the city in which He shall be born—these and many other prophecies are too detailed not to have the Lord's sanction."

He looked dramatically at the council as he continued.

"And remember Jesus was not the only one who was prophesied over."

"John," muttered Kara.

"Exactly," said Lucifer. "Recall that Zacharias, upon the news of the coming birth of John, was told his son would be the herald of the Messiah, that he would preach repentance to all the people and pave the way for the coming King."

"Then this John must die as well," said Rugio.

"Patience, Rugio," said Lucifer. "The one thing we can count on in this land gripped by unscrupulous people like Herod, is that there will be many who will receive neither Jesus nor His prophet. When the right moment arrives, we can count—as always—on those who believe they understand the Most High best, to do their worst."

Rugio nodded in agreement, looking at his warrior aides.

"As for Jesus, He represents another problem," Lucifer continued.

"How then is He to be treated?" asked Rugio. "The woman is under constant guard by the strongest warriors among the Host."

"Then this is really it," said Tinius, grimly. The others looked at him. "I mean, the girl Mary and all. She truly carries the Seed of Eve. After all this waiting it is finally happening."

"Yes," snapped Lucifer. "Such a subtle plan. So marvelous and yet so simple. The Seed of Eve emerges from a virgin womb, retakes the throne of David and establishes the Lord's Kingdom on earth. It is nothing short of a brilliant invasion. Quiet, subtle, but brilliant!"

"Through Mary," grumbled Tinius, still in disbelief.

"Yes," said Lucifer, barely able to contain his growing contempt for the girl. "Recall also that the prophet spoke of a virgin giving birth. Mary is betrothed and has never known a man. Gabriel made it quite clear that she was to conceive—and she did."

"But how?" asked Kara. "If indeed she is a virgin, how then can she conceive? Humans are marvelous creatures, but when it comes to reproducing themselves they are as carnal as any other beast."

"By the Holy Spirit of the Lord," said Pellecus. "He created life in her womb. The same Spirit that gives life to every woman has given extraordinary life to Mary."

"And thus we must take extraordinary measures to deal with the situation," said Lucifer. "Through measures just as thoughtful and subtle as those which we are facing."

"How shall we attack her?" asked Rugio, ready to strike.

Lucifer smiled at his warrior chief.

"I suggest we begin our attack elsewhere," he said. "Mary will never be swerved from her conviction. She is convinced God has indeed favored her, which of course He has." He smiled. "But Joseph presents an interesting possibility. The innocent, unsuspecting betrothed. Who knows what might enter into the mind of a suspicious lover? We have seen it all too often among humans. There is nothing so fierce as the jealousy and rage of one who has been the victim of unfaithful behavior. Should he expose her, she would be stoned according to their bloody law. And the Child would die with her."

He looked at Kara.

"I believe Berenius is suited to this task."

"I will see to it at once," said Kara, who vanished.

Lucifer laughed.

"I had always believed one day we would carry the war back to Heaven." His eyes became vacant for a moment. "Instead, the Lord is carrying the war to us."

Chapter 3

"My soul magnifies the Lord."

Joseph was busy with the accounts from his business. One of the best and busiest carpenters in Nazareth, Joseph was taking advantage of a rare lull in his work to balance his financial affairs. He was doing very well—and this was important for a man about to be married.

He thought of Mary, and how beautiful she looked when they were betrothed. He could hardly wait until the day of their wedding. The place that he was preparing for her was going to make her very happy. He continued working a while longer, hoping Mary was enjoying her visit with her elderly cousin, Elizabeth. He began to pray for her.

"Lord God, grant Mary a safe journey from her cousin's house and bring her back to me. And thank you O Lord, for giving me such a wonderful wife!"

"And a faithful wife, too," entered a thought.

Yes indeed, Mary would not only be a beautiful wife and bear him many sons, but she would be a faithful wife as well.

"A woman who can be trusted…"

Joseph wondered why he was thinking such things, but again, yes, Mary was indeed a trustworthy woman.

"So beautiful a woman must be very desirable to many men…"

Joseph thought for a moment of how often he had seen other men looking at her and admiring her beauty. Yes, she was quite pretty.

"Of course she would never be unfaithful to her betrothed…"

Joseph was finding himself becoming increasingly agitated. His mind was running wild at a fever pitch and he wasn't sure why. Finally he responded, "Mary will always be true to me!"

He stormed away from the yard.

"Well done, Berenius," said Kara. "But not too much, too soon. We must ease him along in this until the thoughts become his own."

Berenius nodded in agreement as they watched Joseph disappear down the street.

The home in the hill country in which Elizabeth and Zacharias lived had become a place of quiet joy. It was joyful because Elizabeth was in her sixth month of pregnancy. It was quiet because Zacharias still could not speak! The elderly couple had become quite adept at communicating, and Elizabeth understood the vision that her husband had seen in the Temple. She knew her son would not be her own—that he was dedicated to the Lord. Such an honor!

"Eat," she said, as she sat a bowl of stew in front of Zacharias.

Zacharias looked up from the table and nodded a gruff thank you.

"The baby is becoming more and more active," she said. "I can feel him kicking like he wants to—"

"Elizabeth!"

She stopped and looked toward the door of their little home.

"Mary?" she said. "Mary!"

Elizabeth rushed to the door and hugged her cousin whom she had not seen for some time. "Child, what brings you here?"

Mary looked into her cousin Elizabeth's eyes and allowed her gaze to shift downward.

"Then it's true," she said. "Just as the angel said!"

Elizabeth was suddenly overcome with the Spirit of the Lord. Zacharias stood and watched as his wife began to prophesy.

"Blessed are you among women, Mary!" She reached out and touched her cousin's abdomen. "And blessed is the fruit of your womb!"

Mary was shocked to realize Elizabeth knew that she was indeed pregnant. Elizabeth sat down with a puzzled look on her face.

"But Mary, why are you here? Why should the mother of my Lord honor me so?"

"What do you mean, Elizabeth?" asked Mary. She walked over and put her hand on her cousin's shoulder. Elizabeth reached down and cradled her tummy.

"When you called my name the child inside of me leapt with joy. Blessed are you because you have believed the things told to you by the angel. Imagine, Mary, we have both been blessed of the Lord!"

"My soul magnifies the Lord!" Mary rejoiced.

She began crying out in a joyous hymn of praise to the Lord. Elizabeth and Zacharias watched as Mary sang a beautiful psalm to God. "Henceforth all generations shall call me blessed," she said. "He has done great things for me, and Holy is His Name!"

"Thus Mary became a part of the greatest event our Lord has ever wrought on earth," continued Gabriel. "Mary was to give birth to the Son of God!"

The angels sat in quiet contemplation of the marvelous story of God's unfolding grace. God Himself born of a woman! It was astounding to think about—and yet it had happened. But to what end? Why would God enter the world under such humble circumstances when surely He might have chosen a more glorious route?

Anticipating their questions, Crispin stepped back into the conversation. "Now, we cannot fully comprehend why the Lord is doing this. It makes sense if the Seed of the woman must be human yet the task He is to perform against the serpent is superhuman, then it follows that the combination of the two is both logical and lethal."

"The Most High cloaked in humanity," added Michael. "A fragile Child who will one day…overcome the shame of Eden."

"But how?" asked Vargas, a worship angel. "Why must the Lord go through all of this rather than simply vanquish Lucifer once and for all?"

"Why indeed?" asked Crispin. "Recall that Lucifer managed to deceive humanity in the garden. Now a human form shall make things right. God in the flesh to be sure…but still in the flesh." He winked at the students. "This will be a lesson to Lucifer in humility as well as justice."

"Will it be a spectacular battle?" asked an eager warrior angel. "Like when Michael batted him out of Heaven?"

Crispin looked at the angel. "I know you warriors are longing for a showdown—something dramatic. What form the final battle will take is not for angels to know. But I'm sure the conflict will be brutal and in the end, bloody."

"Lord Gabriel," inquired another. "What about Joseph? You delivered the news to him as well, didn't you?"

Gabriel walked over to the side of the room where the question had been posed. He nodded his head.

"Yes and no," he said. "I did indeed speak with Joseph one evening. But the news had already been broken to him about Mary. And the enemy was desperately trying to use it to his advantage."

"Then he knows?" asked Kara.

"Yes," said Berenius. "A friend of his who lives in the same town as Mary's cousin Elizabeth told him." He chuckled. "She couldn't wait to tell him the news—stupid woman! She thought she was being helpful."

"Well-meaning humans are some of our best weapons, Berenius," said Kara. "They often do more damage in a moment than we can manage in a year!" He looked again at Joseph, who was preparing for bed. "He doesn't appear upset though."

"He hasn't had time to really think it through," grinned Berenius. "I am about to give him something to think about."

Berenius walked over to the mat where Joseph was lying. The man was wide-eyed, his head resting on his arms. Sleep would be difficult tonight. He deeply loved Mary and wanted more than anything to marry her.

"A baby!" he groaned aloud.

To be pregnant before the marriage was one thing. But such a story! Angels and God and a Savior—this was all a bit fantastic. If only she had told him the truth—at least he could forgive her. Berenius approached Joseph, knelt next to him and began speaking into his mind.

"A baby...some other man's baby...how could she...?"

Another man? Would she really? But there was no other explanation. Unless of course the angel story was true. Angels are real. But still...

"She must be lying...she is trying to cover her sin against you...and her sin against the law..."

If she was lying she deserved death—at least according to the law. It would serve justice wouldn't it? His eyes filled with sad, angry tears.

"Mary, I love you!" he shouted aloud.

"Of course you love her...but she must never have truly loved you...she took your love and mocked you with another man...ANOTHER MAN!"

"Another man," Joseph whispered. "Another man."

"She deserves death..."

"The law requires it," Joseph mumbled. "Yet perhaps I can handle this discreetly. Perhaps if I put her away privately..."

Berenius looked up at Kara.

"The fool still believes he is in love with her," Kara said. "Demand her life. The law requires it!"

Before Berenius could turn back to Joseph a blinding light pierced the room. Joseph was unaware of the new presence, but Kara and Berenius jumped away from Joseph with a shriek. It was Gabriel.

"Out of here!" he demanded of the two deceiving angels.

"The Child will die one way or another," snorted Kara. "By Joseph's hand or by ours He will die!"

"OUT!"

Kara vanished.

"We are not finished here, archangel," said Berenius.

He then vanished as well.

Gabriel watched for a moment longer. Once he was certain Kara and Berenius were gone, he turned toward Joseph. The man was now crying quietly. Gabriel placed his hands on Joseph and soon a peace descended upon the room that, even in his fretful state, coaxed him to sleep.

"Don't worry Joseph," Gabriel said soothingly. "The Lord is with you."

He then placed his hands gently upon Joseph's head. Joseph remained asleep as Gabriel began to speak to him. Joseph suddenly found himself dreaming an angel of the Lord stood before him.

"Joseph, son of David, you must not be afraid to take Mary as your wife."

Joseph saw himself in the dream, sitting up in his bed and listening to the angel. An inexplicable peace and reassurance began to flood his troubled heart.

"Listen! The Child she is carrying is a work of the Holy Spirit of God. He is no ordinary Child. You shall call Him Jesus, because He will be the salvation of His people and will save them from their sins."

"Their sins…" Joseph repeated in his sleep.

"This is a work of the Lord foretold by Isaiah, when he said that a virgin should conceive and bring forth a Son whose name would be Immanuel, 'God with us.' So don't be afraid to take Mary as your wife!"

Joseph awoke with a start. He looked about the room—all was quiet and dark. But something had changed—he suddenly knew that everything was in the Lord's hands and under His direction. It didn't matter now—for God was with him in this. Jesus? A Savior of Israel? He suddenly loved Mary even more deeply than he ever had! He didn't understand what was happening, but he knew the Lord's hand was upon his beloved—and he could live with that.

Chronicles of the Host
The Births

Just as was foretold and has been recorded in the previous volume of the Chronicles of the Host, as well as the Kingdom Chronicles, the child John was born to Elizabeth and Zacharias. We watched with excitement and joy as Zacharias, finally able to speak, proclaimed the boy must be named John. And then, filled with the Spirit of God, he prophesied the ministry that John would one day take up—to usher in the ministry of the Lamb of God!

The Host did indeed gather around Bethlehem when Jesus was born to Mary. Such a glorious night was never before seen on earth! The shepherds worshiped and the great star filled the night sky and God became Man!

We could never suspect what was to take place in this special One's life, and would never have guessed the greatness of this gift to the world. Only Simeon, a prophet who had awaited the Messiah at the Temple, spoke words indicating a tragic destiny attached to this Child. After praying over the Boy upon His presentation at the Temple, Simeon told Mary that a sword would pierce her heart...indeed we did not know the same sword would pierce the heart of the Father as well...

Gabriel and Michael walked alongside Crispin after the class broke up. They had enjoyed being back with their old teacher who had taught them so well. As they walked along they recounted the discussion from the class, taking note of the angels' curiosity regarding the freedom of humans to rebel against a God who so dearly loved them.

"I don't think angels have good memories," snorted Crispin as they walked along the great street that led away from the Academy and toward the Grand Square. Several angels noticed Michael and Gabriel as they passed by, nodding to them courteously. "These in Heaven who are about to be assigned to earth—they are all too eager to complain about the willful rebellion of men and forget it was one of their own who began it all in the first place!"

They came to a place where a garden opened up to the Pavilion of Worship to the Most High, a great domed structure angels frequented in times of praise and worship to the holiness of the Lord. Several groups of angels were moving in and out of the building. Crispin settled down on a large rock near a beautiful grotto. Gabriel and Michael joined him.

"At least they were eager to learn," offered Gabriel. "They were certainly interested in the Mary and Joseph visitations."

"They are always interested in the dramatic," said Crispin. "I'm afraid some of our angels simply want the big battles—the final bout with the dragon—that sort of thing. They don't appreciate that most of the ministry of angels on earth is done in secret."

"They'll have their battles," said Michael, thinking ahead to the day when they must once more face Lucifer. "Now that the Child has been born, they will do whatever they can to destroy Him."

"Foolishness," said Crispin. "To think they actually believe they can defeat the Lord's plan. Being human, though, I suppose there is the appearance of vulnerability."

Gabriel and Michael looked at each other.

"You mean the Christ could be killed?" asked Michael. "His life might be taken away from Him?"

"Yes," said Crispin. "The Christ could die."

"How can God die?" Gabriel asked. "It makes no sense."

"You forget this is God in human form," said Crispin. "Thus, like any human, He could die. However, I see no real chance of that happening. I know Lucifer would like to see the Child destroyed. But why should the One who has come to save the world need to die?"

The Antonia was Herod's fortress overlooking the Temple complex. Named in honor of his friend Mark Antony, the Antonia, with its impressive towers, served as a visible reminder that law and order would prevail in a city fraught with religious fervor. Its proximity to the most sacred site in Jerusalem was not an accident. Herod's rule might be cruel, but it was tidy.

He had decided to receive his guests at the Hasmonean Palace, a short distance away. It was a grand palace and fitting for royal politics. The three guests had been invited to the royal baths and were now in their quarters awaiting the audience. "Show them some of our Judean hospitality," Herod had ordered.

Herod paced the floor, looking over a model of the city that had been a gift to him by his favorite architect. He stared at the scale replica of the various palaces and buildings he had erected and smiled to himself at his accomplishment. But far and above any other structure was the Temple—it was to dominate the city and would be Herod's monument to himself which would outlast even Rome.

He summoned his aide.

"Order my conveyance to the Hasmonean," he said. "We shall entertain our guests and satisfy our curiosity."

"Yes, O king," said the aide, bowing his head.

"And be sure all of my counselors are in attendance," he added. "These men are magi. It might do well for some of our own sages to see what real wisdom looks like."

The aide gave a knowing smile.

"It will be so ordered."

1 AD

"Poor Herod," said Kara. "He is a study in human depravity."

Lucifer nodded his head in agreement as they watched Herod enter his sedan chair. He had apparently ordered his guard doubled, a result of the earlier incident near the Temple site. Now he looked splendid in his royal robes, worn when receiving important visitors.

"Human fear motivates all sorts of unruly behavior," agreed Pellecus. "It works to our greatest advantage."

"Herod certainly has worked out well," admitted Kara. "We have been able to orchestrate his fears in the most marvelous ways. And I must admit, Pellecus, the Roman strategy has been grand. Your study of the Roman mind has been impressive."

"The Romans are useful tools," said Pellecus. "Easily led either through devotion to their gods or love of self. The Romans desire power. All I did was guide a few of the more ambitious families in Rome—they did the rest themselves."

"Herod's compliance was a gift as well," said Kara. "His paranoia has been challenging as well as amusing. To think the ruling family of the people of God is steeped in such political mischief and murder. Having his sons killed was one thing. But he was madly in love with Miriamne—so much so he became insanely jealous. I think her death was the most amusing of all."

"Murderous politics and religious fervor," mused Pellecus. "A powerful and intoxicating stimulus among men." Pellecus assumed his lecturing posture. "That these creatures are incurably religious cannot be denied, for indeed, wherever humans have managed to create some semblance of society, they have also managed some sem-blance of religion. Stone gods, wood gods, gods of the sea and gods of the forest, male gods and female gods, gods that demand bloody homage and gods that require simple ceremony—all of these and many more have been wrought in the minds and hearts of willing men. And when they become the religion of state it places an entire nation at our disposal!"

"Yes," said Lucifer, "as long as that nation continues to drift from the truth. But we have congratulated ourselves enough for now. True, Kara, Herod has been quite a trophy for us—at least in keeping the people subjected to his authority. But he will be dead soon. And there will be another king…always another."

"And we will manage him as well," said Kara. "Herod is only one of many. I think we have become quite adept at bringing humans along."

"Humans are one thing," snapped Lucifer. "But you are forget-ting that there is now One born among these men whose humanity cloaks something far deadlier."

"Ah, the Son of Joseph and Mary," said Kara "Little Jesus."

"The Son of the Most High!" retorted Lucifer. "In your eager-ness to play with Rome and Jerusalem, you seem to have forgotten our supreme enemy now lives within the very kingdom you and Pel-lecus so proudly manage."

"He's a Child who shows no signs of heavenly virtue," said Kara. "I have had Him watched since the day He was born. He acts like a normal, human baby boy."

"That's because He is a human," said Lucifer.

Pellecus, who had already understood Lucifer's thinking in the matter of Jesus, began to speak.

"Don't you see?" Pellecus asked. "The Seed of Eve comes to avenge her. Of course He is a normal enough Boy—for now. But He will grow up one day. Kara, you were there the night He was born. Thousands of the Host were gathered around Him. The prophet said Bethlehem was to be the place. The nightmare has occurred. Jesus is the One we have been looking to destroy all these years. And destroy Him we must."

"This is the brilliance of the Lord," said Lucifer. "The Son of God cloaked in the robes of humanity. When He becomes an adult He shall become our greatest threat." He made a wry smile and added, "Provided He lives to adulthood."

As they were speaking, Rugio appeared and took Lucifer aside. The other two angels watched as Lucifer's face brightened upon the words being told him by his chief warrior. He said "Well done, Rugio" and looked at Kara and Pellecus.

"It seems that Rugio's spies have discerned something interesting about the guests Herod intends to interview," Lucifer said. "Something that might justify your correct assertion that the Child must die."

"Really, lord?" said Pellecus. "And what do these wise men from the east bring to us that we could not discern ourselves?"

Lucifer smiled.

"They have been following that star," he said, looking up at the evening sky where the star hung over the city. "The star that has persisted these many months since the Child's birth; the star that has been a grim reminder, a death knell to lovers of freedom and the sure sign of an unfolding prophecy ushering in the era of the Christ."

Kara and Pellecus joined him as they all looked up at the early evening sky where the star shone over the region. All of them shuddered at the thought of the Lord's words in Eden beginning to manifest: The Seed of the woman would one day crush the head of the serpent.

"But take heart, brothers," Lucifer added, as the magi were being introduced to Herod. "The star, perhaps, shines in different ways."

My prince?" inquired Pellecus.

"One prophecy fulfilled, Pellecus," remarked Lucifer. "The Child has been born and this star has gloriously proclaimed His birth to men who have sought to worship Him. Now perhaps this same star will reveal something menacing to others who would be interested in the birth of a King." He glanced toward Herod. "Particularly another king!"

"Welcome to my kingdom," said Herod with a sweep of his hand in a magnanimous gesture. "I hope you have been well attended to?"

The magi stood uneasily before Herod. His reception hall was a mixture of Roman splendor and traditional Greek décor with a few Hebrew motifs thrown in. The couriers who fawned upon the old king stood to his left suspiciously eyeing the visitors. A scribe was writing down every word that was spoken.

"Yes, my lord," spoke Caspar. "We have been very well attended. Many thanks for your gracious hospitality."

"How very gratifying," said Herod. "Please sit and refresh yourselves."

Attendants brought in three sumptuous chairs, plumed with peacock feathers and gold braid. The three guests sat down.

"Wine perhaps?" asked Herod. "It's a Babylonian variety. Quite refreshing."

"Thank you, no, majesty" said Melchior. "Our business will take us from your hospitality tonight."

"Oh?" said Herod, as he took a goblet from a steward. "Such a shame. And what is your business with me? What is it that I might be able to help you with?"

"Something wonderful, my king," began Caspar. His face lit up as he began recounting the tale that had bound the three magi together for so long.

"We are all from the east, King Herod. All of us are skilled in the arts of divination and astrology. We are conjurers and seers, and have often served our own sovereigns in these regards. We realize these practices are abhorrent to Jews, but in our country it is a way we communicate with our gods and prophecy the future."

"Yes, I know all about you," said Herod. "My guards questioned your servants. You are quite renowned in your own country. But your mission is still a mystery. What brings you to Jerusalem?"

Caspar stood to speak.

"The star, majesty."

"The star?" asked Herod, amused.

Laughter echoed through the room..

"Yes, O king. The star that recently appeared in your sky."

"Oh that one," said Herod. "It seems this particular star has brought in all sorts of interesting people from many places: oracles and prophets and a seer from the desert..." He reached for another goblet of wine. "And of course a few frauds who were whipped and driven out of the city. That star has been a great source of trouble to me. But my own sages assure me it is beginning to wane. Isn't that right, Archelaus?"

Herod's son and heir answered as if startled from a dream.

"Why yes, father," he said. "That is their belief."

"So you see, gentlemen, the star that brought so many to Jerusalem—looking for everything from great treasure to great destinies—will soon disappear." Herod smiled. "It always amazes me how people run to this or that sign in the heaven. My own wise men believe it to be a harbinger of good will for my kingdom—the beginning of a glorious new season for the throne of Judea. I hope they are right."

He looked in the direction of the star as if he could see it through the palace wall. He seemed to sink back in a moment of private reverie.

"It is indeed a beckoning star that has caused dreamers as well as drifters to go looking for something larger than themselves. Somewhat like my father—a dreamer who found practical politics much more convincing than stars in the sky. He never trusted seers..."

Herod suddenly had a suspicious look in his eye.

"Pray tell me what is it the star had you searching for?"

"A King, sire," said Melchior.

Herod laughed and indicated himself.

"You have found him! The star was correct in bringing you here!"

The room burst out in laughter.

"We seek a very special King, majesty," said Caspar. "Not of this world."

"Oh?" replied Herod coldly. "Indeed? A King not of this world..."

He looked at his advisors who merely shrugged.

"Someone marvelous, your majesty," said Caspar, convinced Herod would share his joy. "We are searching for the One long foretold in your own faith. We are seeking the King of the Jews! The star was only a sign to us. It was a starting point. But your Lord spoke to us that this King was to be born around the time of the star's appearance. Surely your own priests have realized the star's significance?" He paused and added with a sense of one who has uncovered a great secret. "A King has been born in Judea!"

Herod could hardly control himself. He snapped an order for more wine. The terrified steward brought him another goblet. Herod drank, warily eying the magi who were awaiting his response.

"A King of the Jews?" he finally said. "In my kingdom?"

"Yes, sire," said Caspar. "But let Balthasar tell you. He was the one to whom the meaning became clear."

"Yes, please do," said Herod. "But first allow me to convene my own holy men. They will be interested in this I am sure. And as you have pointed out, they certainly could not have missed the significance of this incredible sign in the heavens."

He ordered his aide to summon all of the scribes and chief priests. The aide bowed and left. Within a short time he returned, and with him were several of the higher- ranking priests of the land, including Matthias, the chief priest who had just completed evening prayers at the Temple.

They all listened as Balthasar recounted how their journeys began independently of each other. All of them had been stirred by the strange new star in the east. And all had researched the ancient texts, but could find no record of any previous appearance by this particular star.

"But one evening, as I was reading the texts from the holy pages of other lands, I came across the writings of your own prophets. As I read I heard a voice directing me to Jerusalem where a new King had been born. I immediately knew this new King was the One whose coming was foretold by your own prophets. This was the King of Kings—the Messiah! That was when the significance of the star became clear to me."

Several men in the room muttered the word 'Messiah' with astonishment. Herod looked at his own holy men who were either complete fools for missing such an event or wise enough to realize that these magi were in error.

"And so, majesty, we came to your city to ask you where we might find the One born King of the Jews so we might worship Him."

Herod rose with a pensive look on his face. He paced distractedly, drinking in all of these words. The magi watched as he drew near his priests. Finally, he turned back to them and spoke.

"My lords, I would be honored to help you out in this wonderful mission," he said. "But I only ask that you wait in your rooms while I confer with my council. This is, after all, a matter of sacred as well as national interest and I shall seek an audience with my high priest. We shall then see you off as quickly as possible so you might fulfill your holy task."

The magi were escorted back to their rooms leaving Herod alone with his council in the reception hall. Once all of the servants had also departed, he turned to the high priest and demanded of him what this was all about.

"Is this star a sign or not?" he asked. "Are these magi to be trusted? Tell me, high priest—where is the Christ to be born?"

The high priest deferred to one of the scribes, who walked before Herod and declared, "When the Christ is born we should look for Him in Bethlehem, O king, in Judea. It is so written by the prophet."

The high priest looked at the other priests with a puzzled expression. He made a motion and priests huddled together to discuss the particular scriptures that related to the Messiah's birth.

"Bethlehem?" Herod said. "The Messiah is to be born in Bethlehem?"

He laughed at the thought of such an insignificant town being the birthplace of Messiah. Suddenly one of the priests began to quote the prophet:

"And thou Bethlehem, in the land of Judah, art not the least among the princes of Judah; for out of thee shall come a Governor, that shall rule my people Israel."

"Bethlehem," Herod repeated. "David's city. It might just be…"

"I must caution your majesty that this is perhaps not Messiah," said Matthias. "While there have undoubtedly been many male children born in Bethlehem since the star's appearing over these last months, it does not mean this is the Christ."

The priests watched as Herod sat down on his throne.

"Of course we might send to Bethlehem, my king," offered another priest. "We might inquire as to any newly born boys in the region…"

"Get out, all of you," Herod snapped. "It took men from another land to recognize that the Messiah might have been born just a few miles from here. Go and study some more—all of you!" He then added, "You, high priest—you shall remain."

The priests left the room. Herod called his aide in and had him send for the wise men. Perhaps he might gather more information from them. Within minutes the three men reappeared. Herod stood to greet them with an animated expression.

"Wonderful news, my friends," he said, stepping down from his throne. "The young King is to be found in Bethlehem!"

"Bethlehem…the house of bread," said Caspar. "How fitting!"

"Yes," said Herod, quelling his anger. "But before you leave, you must tell me how long you have been on this quest?"

"Sire, we have been inquiring of this for nearly two years—when the star first appeared. But we only recently understood the meaning of it all and began our journey."

Interesting," mused Herod. "So the Child might be up to two years of age?"

"I suppose so," agreed Melchior. "But one never knows until one sees the Child."

"Yes, well be off with you and have a wonderful and blessed journey!"

"Thank you sire," said Melchior.

The three magi thanked the king for his hospitality and his information. They bade him farewell and turned to leave.

"Also..."

"Yes majesty?" answered Caspar. "Was there something else?"

"A king's time is never his own or I would accompany you," said Herod. "For I, too, wish to come and worship the new King of the Jews." He sighed. "But urgent business holds me here in Jerusalem." He then looked up as if inspired. "Unless..."

"Yes?" inquired Caspar, warily.

"Unless when you have found Him you might send word to me. That way I can come and worship the Child myself at a more opportune time."

"Of course, King Herod," said Melchior. "We shall be delighted to send word to you when we have found the King. Your heart must be overjoyed that the true King of Israel has been born."

"Indeed," said Herod. "There is only one King over Israel."

Chapter 4

"Herod has been quite useful to us."

Demas was a spirit of control who had been assigned to Herod. He had thrown in with Lucifer at the last moment of the insurrection in Heaven when he discovered he fell out with some of the other angels at the Academy. He had become a skilled and discreet seducer of humans, and was able to inflame their ambitious natures. He was therefore also influential with Matthias, whose position as high priest was less pious than political.

Now the spirit was following Herod and the high priest into a private room where the two went into conference. They sat at an informal lounge area where Herod put his feet up on a pillow. He sipped his wine.

"Well?" demanded Herod. "I didn't give you this position so I could be made a fool in front of visiting dignitaries."

"Nor do I enjoy being made a fool of in front of my priests," said Matthias."

Herod smirked at his hand-picked holy man.

"The Lord appointed Aaron," said Herod. "But I selected you. He kept Aaron."

Matthias understood the subtle threat. Herod continued.

"I must know. Is this the Christ? I have lived with that fable all my life...a coming King. It's every ruler's nightmare—especially in a nation of religious misfits."

"Sire, I cannot answer you," Matthias said. "If these men truly heard from the Lord, then who can say? But why should the Lord speak to these men who worship pagan gods and not to his own high priest? This matter is of such importance."

"Perhaps pagans can hear him better," said Herod, who was playing with a flower he had pulled from a vase. "Still, I cannot risk the chance that they are right. I want someone to follow the magi to Bethlehem. Find the house where they enter and discover whether or not the Child lives."

"It will be done," said Matthias. "But in any case, majesty, when these holy men report to you from Bethlehem you'll have your answer. Then you can go and worship this new born King."

"And so I shall," said Herod smiling. "I will worship in my own way."

Demas grinned at the turn of events. He could sense the anger and desperate fear rising inside Herod. This would bode well for Lucifer's desire to see something done about the Christ. He left immediately to find him.

Lucifer, Pellecus and Kara listened with great interest to Demas' report. It appeared that finally Herod would discover the where-abouts of the Child. Then is would be only a matter of time before he sought to kill Him. They congratulated Demas on his work.

"For now we shall keep close watch on the family," Lucifer answered. "The only humans who were clever enough to recognize His presence thus far are the shepherds who were with Him on the night of His birth, and Simeon and Anna, who prophesied over Him at the Temple."

"And these magi," said Pellecus. "They are even now with Herod."

"Yes, well, I think you'll find by introducing Herod into the equation the solution may find itself."

"Herod is right about one thing," said Pellecus, as they strolled about a new level of the Temple recently completed. "His own priests were unable to discern the times. To think they missed the very One they have been waiting for! This marvelous Temple will be wasted on them."

"The Jews have been missing the Most High for years," sneered Lucifer. "Their holy men have become corrupt religionists like every other human who dons a priestly robe. The sacrifices are a mockery. They have been so bent on their own traditions they no longer know what genuine faith looks like!"

One of Kara's spies suddenly appeared in the room and stood nearby waiting to be addressed. The angel, Rhedi, was one of thousands in Kara's network. He looked to Kara, who in turn nodded approval for the angel to approach the trio.

"Well?" asked Kara. "Report."

"The magi are nearing the home of Mary and Joseph," said Rhedi. "The star ever draws them."

"Excellent!" said Demas, in a rare outburst. The others looked at him with contempt for speaking. "Herod's spy should also be nearing the house as well. This means his agents will not be far behind!"

Lucifer looked at Pellecus and Kara with a hopeful expression.

"I do have other news," said Rhedi.

Demas did not like the manner in which Rhedi spoke these words and looked at him.

"It seems Herod's spy was misdirected by three of Gabriel's angels posing as the magi," he added. "They took the man around the other way and led him into an alley. They then vanished before his eyes. The poor man almost died of fright and is at this moment on his way back to his hometown. Rather than face Herod with such news, he has deserted him."

Demas looked at Rhedi bitterly, and then to the others. He was quite unnerved at what Lucifer's reaction would be.

"This is astonishing," Demas finally blurted out.

"I suggest, Kara, that some of your angels need more training and discipline," said Lucifer. "Particularly when it comes to boasting of one's alleged assistance. Not only are they indiscreet but they are undependable as well."

Kara, embarrassed and outraged, agreed. "I will see to it that the offenders are disciplined," he said menacingly. Demas skulked away and vanished.

"At any rate the magi are arriving," said Pellecus. "They are still to report to Herod. He will then act."

"True," said Lucifer. "Herod has always been quite useful to us." He looked at Rhedi. "Perhaps this angel will become Herod's new shadow."

Rhedi looked up excitedly.

"You are to return to the Hasmonean and continue enflaming Herod's already tormented mind," said Kara. "Fuel his passion for discovering this Child. And fuel his fears. He is ever frightened of pretenders."

Rhedi almost shouted, "As you command!" and vanished.

As they came to an open area, Lucifer looked up into the night sky toward the star hanging over Bethlehem. A single shaft of light now extended from the star; a ray of brilliance penetrated Bethlehem.

"He points the way for them," said Kara bitterly. "He points the way to the Son."

"The light of the Lord upon His Son," said Pellecus. "A dangerous thing to expose one's Son when so many would take his life. Thrusting him into a darkened world—turning his back on him, so to speak."

Lucifer turned to the others.

"Make no mistake, Pellecus," he said. "This will never be. The day the Father turns His back on the Son is the day the Son will die."

"The Lord be praised!"

The shaft of light seen by the magi looked like a silvery-white thread of silk streaming from the star overhead. They had followed this beam ever since leaving the gates of Jerusalem when it began to appear. All three of the magi were astonished at the light, and hurried to reach the Child who had been the object of their devotion for nearly two years. The light had settled on a small house, much like the others in Bethlehem. One of the magi asked a man whose house this was.

"That is the home of Joseph the carpenter," the man answered.

"He did not see it," mused Melchior. "He did not see the light."

"Perhaps the light of God can only be seen by those who seek it out," said Balthasar, as he dismounted. "Shall we enter?"

The three magi had replaced their dusty traveling clothes with the luxurious robes they had brought with them to wear when they were presented to the Child. They also carried with them the gifts they had kept with them all these months. This was a sacred moment for them as they approached Joseph's front door. The light from the star immediately vanished as they stepped in the doorway.

Caspar knocked on the door. They thought they heard the sound of a small child crying within. He was about to knock once more when the door opened. From inside the dimly lit house Joseph appeared in the doorway. He held a small oil lamp in his hand.

"Yes?" he asked, surprised to see such splendid-looking men standing before him. "Are you from the palace?" he asked nervously.

"No, no," said Melchior, stepping up from the dark street. "I am Melchior. This is Caspar and Balthasar."

"We have been seeking you a long time," said Caspar. "Or rather, your Son."

Upon those words Joseph felt immediate relief. Considering the circumstances of Jesus' birth and the promises made to him and Mary by the angel Gabriel, it didn't surprise him that strangers should come seeking the Child. He had resigned himself that they would probably experience such strange happenings as long as Jesus was in their home.

"Who is at the door, Joseph?" a voice inquired.

"Visitors," said Joseph, opening the door for them to enter. "From far off. They are here to see our Son."

The three men entered the room. There they saw Mary holding a healthy, little dark-haired Boy of about a year or so. Tears filled the eyes of Caspar as he saw the Child for the first time. He fell to his knees, as did the other two. Joseph looked outside to make sure there were no others, and then shut the door.

After a moment or two Joseph spoke to break the spell.

"You came from…?

"It doesn't matter," said Melchior. "What matters is where this Child came from. We will not stay long. But we were required of your God to come and pay homage and to bring these gifts."

Upon these words, they presented to Joseph gifts of gold, frankincense, and myrrh—all costly and luxurious gifts.

"Please accept these humble offerings," Balthasar said. "And allow us only a moment's worship."

The men began praying in their native tongue, calling upon the God of Joseph and Mary and thanking Him for allowing them to have finally set eyes upon the King of the Jews. Shortly after, they stood to leave.

"I would offer you a place to stay, but as you see there is no room here," said Joseph. "Perhaps in the back…"

"Thank you, no," said Caspar. "We have already paid for our lodging here in Bethlehem. Then we shall return to Jerusalem."

"Jerusalem?" both Mary and Joseph repeated. "To Herod?"

"Why yes," replied Caspar. "He seemed quite anxious that we report to him."

"It seems a streak of devotion seized his heart and he, too, desires to come and worship the Child," added Melchior. "This Child invites worship, it seems. Even in the most unlikely quarters."

After the men left, Joseph looked at Mary with apprehension. Herod! Dealing with kingly visitors was one thing—but dealing with the unpredictable king of Judea was another. Mary knew in her heart the Lord would not permit Herod or any other person to touch their Son, and was content to leave it all in the Lord's hands.

Chronicles of the Host
Warning Dream

Mary was quite right. For no sooner had the magi settled into a deep sleep than the Lord appeared to them in a dream warning them not to return to Herod. Instead, they bypassed Jerusalem, spotted only as they slipped past Herod's well-watched frontiers. When Herod realized the magi were not going to return, he was beside himself. The enemy, under Kara's direct command, fanned Herod's fury telling him what a fool he had been and assuring him the Child would one day rise up and take the throne away from Herod's house...

Nobody dared speak a word. The messenger from the frontier had said it all. He remained on the ground where he had fallen after Herod struck him upon hearing the report that the magi had departed Judean territory.

"Get out!" he ordered. "And take this fool to the Antonia to be held until I decide what is to be done with him!"

A couple of Herod's personal guards picked up the trembling messenger and escorted him out of the room. The other members of Herod's council hastily exited the room as well. Herod was quite alone. Or was he?

Rhedi stood by ready to foment in Herod something that would earn him favor with Kara, and ultimately Lucifer. The angel had assumed the horrid appearance of a human with a rat-like face, grinning as he approached Herod. The old king was bent over a table looking at a map of Judea, unaware of the angel's presence or mission. He peered over the map for a moment or two longer and violently swept it off the table.

"I should have all the frontier guards killed," he raged aloud.

"And yet the Child lives..." Rhedi spoke softly.

"The Child lives," Herod thought to himself. "Somewhere in Bethlehem."

"If He is allowed to grow into adulthood, He will take the throne from your children. The name of Herod will forever be forgotten..."

"I owe it to my father to do something," Herod mumbled. He began crying tears of anger and shame. "Father I am sorry! All the work you did, all the groveling before these Roman dogs." He became furious. "These petty Jews! Always looking for their Messiah. How do we know this is not some trick of Satan? How do I know these magi were not demons disguised as humans to dupe me?"

"And yet the Child lives such a short distance away...a brief journey..."

Herod began thinking about how close Bethlehem was—how close the Child was to Jerusalem. Such a short distance—such a horrible threat. Surely his spy would have returned by now had he something to report.

"Bethlehem is so small...nobody would know...nobody would care..."

Rhedi stepped back to enjoy his work. This time his words had hit deep. Herod contemplated the bloody possibility. How many children could this be? Merely a handful of them, at most. It could be done quickly and quietly—even this very night...Rhedi approached Herod for a final thrust.

"Just the children born since the star's appearance..."

Enough!" he shouted to himself.

One of his aides came running in.

"You sent for me, sire?" he asked timidly.

"No, fool!" A pause. "Wait! Yes. Bring Zereth to me. Now!"

The servant left quickly and within a few minutes returned with Zereth, the commander of Herod's personal guard. Zereth was Herod's most trusted servant, and was adept at performing unpleasant, secretive tasks. He was particularly skilled in the art of assassination. Herod looked at his trusted killer.

"I have something for you," he whispered. "Utmost secrecy. Only your most trustworthy soldiers who know how to do as they are told and remain quiet afterwards. And of course a great reward will be involved."

"I am yours to command, my king," said Zereth, patting his sword.

"Excellent," said Herod. He walked to the window facing south. Already the star that had been over the land for these past many months was beginning to fade. He turned back to Zereth.

"It seems I have a problem in Bethlehem."

"Joseph!"

"Joseph!"

Joseph wasn't sure if he was dreaming or not as he found himself confronted by another angel. This one seemed different from Gabriel—somehow commanding even greater authority. Joseph listened as the angel began speaking to him.

"I am the Angel of the Lord," he said. "You must listen. Take your family and go down to Egypt. Herod's soldiers are coming to kill the Child. Go now!"

"Egypt! But how long are we to stay in Egypt?" he asked, looking around the house and mentally packing.

"You will remain in Egypt until I bring you word," the angel answered. "Herod will not rest until the Child is dead. Go!"

Joseph suddenly awoke. There was nobody in the room. His wife and Son remained asleep. Was it real? Suddenly he felt a sense of urgency overwhelm him as visions of his family slaughtered began playing before his mind. He awakened his wife and began making preparations for Egypt.

Chronicles of the Host

Egyptian Escape

And so it was that Joseph, having been warned by the angel, took his family to Egypt where they were able to live comfortably on the gifts given to them by the magi. For his part, Herod was content that the killing of the children in Bethlehem had ended his problem. But peace eluded the suspicious man. In one of his final acts of brutality he even had Zereth and all the soldiers involved in the Bethlehem massacre killed under suspicion of conspiring to assassinate him. Herod himself finally died, and his son Archelaus, a known brute, took his place as king.

Upon Herod's death, the angel appeared once more to Joseph and beckoned him back to Bethlehem. But because Archelaus was on the throne, the angel instructed Joseph to settle in Nazareth so that the prophecy about Jesus being called a Nazarene might be fulfilled.

12 A.D.

"Have you seen my Son?"

Mary held her hand out her hand as she looked about her frantically. "He's about this tall."

She ran to the next woman.

"Have you seen a Boy of twelve? His name is Jesus."

The woman shrugged her shoulders and indicated that she had seen no one. The group of pilgrims was returning from the annual trip to Jerusalem for the Passover. As the men traveled separately from the women, Joseph and Mary each thought their Son was with the other parent. When it was evident that the Boy was not among the women and children, Mary raced ahead to the group of men.

Joseph was surprised to see Mary hurrying to the men's camp. He immediately realized something was the matter.

"Is Jesus with you?" she panted, looking among the boys playing noisily nearby. "Please say He is…"

Joseph's eyes told the story and Mary began crying. Joseph told the others Jesus was missing and that he and Mary were returning to Jerusalem to see if He might be somewhere behind—perhaps with another group. They prayed as they left the camp that God would help them to find their Son.

"He is an amazing Boy," mused Serus. "He is engaging those priests as if He were one of them!"

Crispin and Serus stood in one of the outer courts watching the young Jesus discussing matters of faith with the doctors of religion at the Temple. The priests were both amused and astonished that this young Nazarene should be so skilled in theology. Serus had been watching over Jesus ever since he had become separated from his parents, lingering behind in the house of the Lord—a place that felt strangely familiar.

"Of course He engages them," said Crispin. "Remember, Serus, though He is a Boy, He is also the Son of God." He snickered as the priests continued their questioning. "They are discussing Creation with the Creator!"

"Surely they realize there is something remarkable about the Lad," said Serus. "How many boys entertain such thoughts?"

"Or grown men, for that matter," said Crispin. "Again, Serus, we angels must remember that Jesus is both God and Man—a splendid blending of humanity and the Divine into a single person. And yet the

Boy has acquired His knowledge through study and discipline and grown in favor with both God and men."

Serus looked at the Child, who was now looking less the scholar and more the tired little Boy. Such a sweeping and profound thought: God Himself invested as a human. From the prophecy in Eden, to the promise through Abraham; from the pleadings of the prophets to that dramatic night in Bethlehem—somehow a wonderful plan known only to the Lord was unfolding and the Host were the astonished witnesses of it. And yet the question loomed unanswered and nagging…

"To what end?" asked Serus vacantly.

Crispin looked at the angel who had once been an enemy and was now an adept fighter for righteousness.

"To what end?" repeated Crispin.

"I mean, why must God become a human?"

"I suppose," answered Crispin, "because as God He cannot fully do what He must do. Remarkable thought. At least that is what I tell the students at the Academy. Short of that we don't really know."

Serus was not satisfied. He decided to press the scholarly angel.

"But why?" he continued. "Why must the Most High do all of this? Why doesn't He simply finish off Lucifer and his followers and be done with it?"

"Now that is the question," said Crispin, as the two watched Mary and Joseph enter the court and collect their Son. Jesus disappeared with his parents leaving the priests in their discussion. The angels followed Joseph and Mary out of the courtyard. After leaving the Temple area they asked their Son why He had not returned with them.

"Mother, father, why were you searching for Me?" Jesus asked. "This is where you'll find Me…in My Father's house. I have to be in My Father's house."

Serus watched the parents as Joseph gave Mary a knowing look. They set the Boy upon His donkey and led Him out of the city.

"I have to be in my Father's house," repeated Crispin. "Incredible! Somewhere in that phrase is the answer to your question, Serus. But how it shall unfold is beyond the speculation of mere angels."

CHAPTER 5

"I baptize only with water."

"He must be in His Father's house?" said Kara with an attitude of disdain. "He was in His Father's house until He came to earth. Better He should have stayed there!"

The angels laughed at Kara's remark.

"Obviously His coming to the Temple is intended to start some enormously important task for the Father," returned Tinius.

"Or perhaps to finish one," said Lucifer, who had just entered the Council with Pellecus and Rugio.

The Council immediately came to order. Lucifer seemed peculiarly jovial for one who was being increasingly pressured to act in the matter of the young Jesus. He nodded to the assembled group that he was ready for the reports. One by one the angels stressed their loyalty to their chief, and pledged that, come what may, they had confidence their lord would deal with Jesus decisively.

"Thank you all for your confidence," he finally said. "But as our young Opponent demonstrated earlier at the Temple, this conflict is becoming less and less carnal and more and more philosophical." He smiled at the group of angels.

"Meaning...?" inquired Kara.

"Meaning this battle will be won or lost in the mind. It has become a contest of wits, now, and is therefore decidedly in our favor."

"How so, my lord?" asked Rugio, who favored an all-out bloody conflict rather than what he considered the niceties of a more cerebral war. "You always said it was men who would decide the war in the end."

"And so they shall, Rugio," said Lucifer. "We have shed much blood on this accursed world. We have the blood of millions on our hands. And yet the contest is still in play. I tell you, brothers, this war will indeed be fought in the minds of men—not on their battlefields."

Kara, who had become something of a loyal opposition leader ever since the birth at Bethlehem, stood to question Lucifer on behalf of others who were less bold, or perhaps less wise. Though he would never oppose Lucifer outright, he felt it his duty as a former elder in the Kingdom to propose debate whenever it seemed prudent.

"My prince, we are all indebted to your leadership," Kara began. "It has taken us far. And true, the ordinary human mind is quite manageable. Our experience with humans since Eden has borne that out. But this Jesus is not an ordinary human. He possesses a superior mind—the mind of God. If it becomes a war of the mind, then we are in grave peril."

A few affirming grunts arose from the Council. Kara. Emboldened by this and relishing the attention, he continued.

"It therefore seems to me the ordinary strategies we have employed will not suffice…"

As Kara spoke, Lucifer sat silent and listened. Pellecus could only smirk at Kara's pompous show. Kara ignored the antagonism and continued forcefully.

"This is no David, who succumbed to Bathsheba in the passion of lust. This is no Solomon who corrupted his wisdom in carnal pursuits. This is no Samson who squandered the Spirit in prideful disregard. This is the Son of God! And we must deal with Him lest we all perish!"

Some of the Council cheered Kara with hearty agreements, but were quickly subdued under Rugio's glaring eyes. For his part,

Lucifer stood as if in deep thought, as if he had been challenged in a point he had not yet considered. Kara sat down with the others awaiting the response.

"Wonderful summation of your opinion, Kara," said Lucifer. "It brings to mind those glorious days when you were one of the twenty-four elders." His smile quickly vanished. "But those days are long over. This is not Heaven and you are no longer an elder. Stop pretending to be one."

Kara sheepishly nodded in compliance. Pellecus beamed.

"As to your point, I have of course considered that Jesus is indeed no ordinary human. And yet He is still mortal. He must be! And if He is mortal then He is subject to mortal weaknesses."

"But He is God," Tinius complained. "He is not human. He was created by the Spirit of God."

"In a human womb," said Pellecus, whose scholarship held great weight with the Council. "He is both God and Man. Somehow the Most High is calculating that the human side will not tarnish the divine." Pellecus gave a hint of a smile and added, "Of course, that was the idea in Eden, too."

A few heads nodded.

"You see, the Lord's plan from the beginning was to embrace these human creatures," Pellecus continued. "That is where we missed it, I'm afraid. We saw A'dam as merely another beast to inhabit the world—the Lord created him to govern the world in His name. Indeed, He gave the man His own image. He turned everything over to this creature. And still the human propensity to corrupt itself overcame the image of God placed inside of it and rebellion resulted."

"Yes, yes," said Kara. "We know all of this. We helped place the propensity within him, don't you remember? But what is your point?"

"The point," said Lucifer, "is that humans have passed that same propensity down through time—all the way through so that every human uses the freedom God has given him in the most hideous ways."

He stood now, an imposing figure dominating the room.

"I propose that Jesus, being human, will have the same propensities—the same potential failings. Right now He is a Child. But give Him a few more years. Let Him grow up in the company of His parents. Let them instill in Him those primitive Hebrew morals. Allow Him to astound the doctrinaires and fascinate the local rabbis like some freakish prodigy.

"In the end He will grow into a Man—a Man who is tempted like any other. That is when we shall appeal to His human nature. I propose when the time is right we bribe Him with all that is in our disposal, that we tickle the human side of Him, offering Him the world if we must!"

"And suppose He refuses your generous offer?" Kara purred. "Suppose the Son of God will not take a bribe?"

Lucifer looked at Kara with darkened eyes.

"Then the stakes become much higher."

Chronicles of the Host

Jesus and John

True to his vow, Lucifer and the others stayed fairly away from the boy Jesus as He grew up in Nazareth. The angels assigned to His young life observed a natural inclination for things of His father, becoming a carpenter like him. Favored by both God and man, Jesus grew in wisdom and stature, awaiting the day of fulfillment in the world.

In a few short years, John, the cousin of Jesus, came to the Jordan River, baptizing men to repentance. This was during the reign of the debauched Emperor Tiberias, who abused his power for the sake of perverse pleasure. And so John, like a prophet of old, demanded the people change their wicked ways and return to the Lord. The religious leaders, many of whom were jealous of his audience, shunned or scorned him, but John carried on as a stalwart minister of the Most High, preaching repentance and baptizing the penitent.

And then on that incredible day, Jesus came to Jordan to be baptized by John! It was the beginning of the Liberation! John baptized Jesus, and the Lord Himself spoke from Heaven, sending His Spirit down in the form of a dove to put His seal upon it all! How could we have known then that such a glorious beginning at a river's edge would end so tragically on a bloody hill outside of Jerusalem?

30 A.D.

"Quite a stir our young evangelist is causing," said Kara, as they observed John baptizing a woman in the Jordan. Along the shores there were many others who were either waiting to be baptized, or who had already been baptized by John. "As if the water can wash away the crimes of humanity," he sneered.

Kara was among a group of angels who had been assigned to keep watch on John's activities. Now that Jesus had been presented, it was obvious there would be a shift in priority. John still represented a threat as long as he continued to encourage repentance among the people. But the larger threat was his willingness to decrease among the people and allow Jesus to increase.

"It's so indecent of him," barked Tinius. "Most men would become jealous of their successor. But this John is bent on handing authority over to Him—even willingly!"

"It is astounding," agreed Pellecus, who with Rugio and Berenius made up the group who would lead the effort for the destruction of both Jesus and John. "John is unfortunately a rarity among humans—a man of true albeit ridiculous conviction."

"We'll see how conviction measures up against persecution," said Kara, looking at the group of ever-present priests and Pharisees who had been sent by the Temple.

"True, Kara," said Lucifer, who had joined the group after placing Rugio and a complement of angels to watch Jesus. The others looked back upon Lucifer, who was gazing at the arriving holy men. "The priests of this land represent possibly the greatest weapon we can manage against the Most High—the religious fervency of selfish men."

A shout of praise went up from the crowd as another person was baptized. Lucifer looked at John with scorn, and then scanned over to the priests. An angel, one of Kara's most competent agents, stood among them.

"I see Berenius is keeping our sanctified friends interested," he said.

"Yes," said Kara. "Berenius has become quite accomplished at…shall we say… stirring the pot a bit." He smiled. "He will definitely keep things quite interesting."

"However it is done, we must destroy both these men," said Tinius, who was eager to see John dispatched. He was fearful of these native religious movements that inspired men to seek the Living God. "The crowds have been increasing."

"Don't worry my nervous friend," said Lucifer. "We will eliminate both of these threats—beginning with John. Perhaps when Jesus sees His vaunted herald brought down He will realize His efforts are futile."

"As you said, my prince, the key will be finding humans willing to destroy them for us," said Pellecus. "And in that regard the religious authorities in this rotten nation will become useful accomplices…as always."

"Agreed," said Lucifer, looking once more at the priests. "For now we'll content ourselves with watching from a distance to allow the poison to set in. Observe."

Lucifer gave a signal to Berenius, who nodded and moved over to the leader of the group of priests standing nearby.

"Just a little something I arranged with Berenius," said Lucifer, as Kara and the others watched, perplexed. Kara felt a tinge of hurt that Lucifer had conspired with Berenius without his consultation.

Berenius began to speak into the mind of Zairus, a delegate from the Sanhedrin. The man looked at the others and then moved closer to the river bank. John looked at the man, splendid in his black priestly garb, who obviously was about to address him.

"You there, Baptist!" he shouted. "My name is Zairus. I have been sent, along with this delegation, to inquire as to your purposes here. What might I report?"

John looked up at the man who addressed him. The crowd had fallen quiet and only the sound of the river could be heard. One of Zairus' fellow priests, Aziah, joined him on the side of the river.

"Do you think you are Elijah or something?" Aziah asked with a sarcastic tone. "That is what some have said." He indicated the throng mingling on the river bank. "Who are you to be baptizing these poor people and telling them to repent?"

John looked at the men.

"I am simply a voice crying in the wilderness and saying to the world, 'Make straight the way of the Lord!' I speak the very words Isaiah did."

"I see. So you are the prophet!" exclaimed Zairus, hoping to obtain some sort of ridiculous confession from John that he might trap him.

"I am not the prophet, nor Elijah."

Zairus spoke loudly so that all could hear him.

"Then why are you baptizing?" Zairus asked. "Why are you telling these people they must repent, as if you had the authority of an Elijah or a prophet?"

"I baptize only with water, Zairus," said John, motioning for the next person to come and be baptized. "But there is One coming Whom you do not know. He will come after me and is preferred before me. And He will baptize with the Holy Spirit and with fire!"

He baptized a young man, who walked back, soaked, to his family on the shore. There was no shout of joy among the crowd this time. John looked back at Zairus and pointed to the priests. "You come here to judge my ministry, you who claim the priesthood. You are a generation of vipers! You think because you have Abraham all is well. I tell you that if God so chose He could make sons of Abraham out of the rocks that are around here!"

Zairus looked at Aziah.

"Need we hear more?" he whispered. "The man is a religious maniac."

Zairus nodded to John and walked away. The priests followed him, leaving the area. John called out after them.

"You must bring forth true fruits of repentance if you truly wish to escape the coming wrath of the Lord!"

Berenius looked back at Lucifer and Kara. They nodded to him to continue and he followed the men back to their escort.

"As I said, these priests will prove our greatest weapon," said Lucifer. "The very people that the Most High has set apart shall in the end bring about the destruction of John the baptizer. Let John have his moment. In the end it is Jesus with whom we must contend. Recall that John has already agreed that he must decrease while the Christ increases. Perhaps we can help him in his descent."

"And Jesus?" asked Kara delicately.

"Leave Jesus to me," smiled Lucifer.

"Here He comes now."

The two angels watched as the lone figure sat under a scant amount of shade provided by a rocky outcrop. The reddish desert in southern Judea was desolate and uninviting, and even the slightest bit of shelter was better than none. He looked tired, hungry and dirty. He also looked resolute, and began to pray.

"Can we help Him now?" asked Bakka, an aide to Serus who was assigned personally to minister to Jesus.

Gabriel looked at the angel.

"Not yet," he answered. "His time is not yet. He has fasted 40 days in this desert—we shall be able to serve Him soon enough. But not yet."

Bakka was puzzled. Why could he not bring refreshment to his Master? Why must they watch Him in the withering heat of day and the cold nights without comforting Him? He looked at the archangel in confusion.

"I don't understand."

"Perhaps I can help you, Bakka," answered a voice.

"Well," said Gabriel, looking at Lucifer, who appeared as a desert holy man in the Edomite fashion. "I was wondering when you would come."

"Thank you, Gabriel," he said "It has been quite a while since we last spoke. I believe it was at Bethlehem."

"What are you doing here," snorted Bakka.

"Didn't you tell him?" asked Lucifer in mock astonishment. "I'm surprised. The war must be going better for me than I realized if Heaven is withholding such basic information."

"Tell me what?" asked Bakka, looking at Gabriel.

Before Gabriel could answer Lucifer continued.

"Why, my right of accusation, of course," Lucifer said. "Surely the Academy has taught you such things?" He gave Gabriel a smirk. "The Academy has certainly fallen on hard times since we vacated the Kingdom. Pellecus will be delighted."

Bakka was still waiting for an answer.

"As prince of this world I have the right to tempt and bring accusation of every human," Lucifer said proudly. "This includes Jesus."

"You would tempt your Lord?" asked Bakka, horrified at such a thing.

"How innocent is the Host," Lucifer said. "I don't intend to tempt Jesus the God, you silly angel. I intend to tempt Jesus the Man. I am something of an authority in that regard."

"And we are to allow this?" asked Bakka defensively. He looked to Gabriel for some show of support. "Surely not!"

"It is his right," said Gabriel. "He has a measure of authority on this fallen planet. But it is both short in limit and short in life." He turned to Lucifer. "It is the Spirit of the Lord who leads Him to be tempted. Get on with it, Lucifer!"

Lucifer bowed his head low.

"As you command, archangel," he said, looking over at Jesus, who was still in prayer. "And when this exhausted, hungry Man Jesus succumbs to what I offer, the war will be finally decided."

"Try with all your might, Lucifer," scoffed Bakka. "Jesus might be a human but He is still full of the Lord's Spirit and full of the Lord's Word!"

"True, Bakka," mused Lucifer smiling at Gabriel "The Lord's Spirit and I have long parted company. But I am quite acquainted with His Word."

"Quite a wilderness, hmm?"

Jesus looked up at the stranger.

"A most desolate place," the stranger continued. "Makes one wonder why the Lord ever created such a place."

Jesus ignored the man.

"I see by Your clothes You are a Jew," the man went on. "A fine people, the Jews. It's such a pity they have lost their way…"

No response.

"Of course, the God they worship seems to have cast them somewhat adrift," said the man, walking in front of Jesus, who was still seated on a flat rock. "Such a promising start, too. But all gods, it seems, end up disappointing…"

Jesus looked at the man.

"So You are the Son of God?" the man asked. He snickered. "Forgive me, Jesus, but You look so...so ordinary. Not quite what one would expect of the Son of God."

Jesus looked down and began drawing in the sand with His finger.

"Is that what they told You? That You are the Son of God? It's amazing what religious excitement can bring on." He laughed out loud. "Just look what it has done to that poor baptizer named John. The man is absolutely insane!"

The man sidled down beside Jesus and sat next to Him.

"He fancied himself to be the fore-runner of..." The man jumped back as if caught off guard. "Why...of You! Can You imagine the Most High sending a fanatic like that to introduce His Son to the world?"

Jesus looked at the man once more.

"Do You really believe these things, Jesus? Or is it possible that Your mother's love and Your father's zeal caused them to force these things upon Your mind? What with John's father serving in the Temple and all. I hear he even had a fit upon him for a while that took his speech away. Perhaps he had a devil..."

"What do you want, Morning Star?" asked Jesus.

Lucifer's Edomite character immediately changed into the form of Lucifer, splendid in a white tunic and archangel's golden belt. Lucifer spoke soothingly.

"I am merely trying to help You through this delusion," he said. "Holy men come cheaply in this part of the world. Even sons of the divine are common. Tiberias himself claims heritage through the gods. The last thing this poor nation needs is another prophet. And so I must ask why You persist in this tragic drama?"

Jesus remained silent.

"I suppose You will continue this delusion, therefore I shall assist You in dispelling it," said Lucifer standing up.

"It isn't that I don't believe You, Jesus," reasoned Lucifer. "And I realize if the Lord indeed wanted to use a Man such as Yourself—

even an ordinary Jew—He could do so. But I am no ordinary creature, and require proof."

He smiled at Jesus.

"I would imagine, after all these years of Your mother feeding You these stories, You have often wondered Yourself. You have, haven't you?"

Jesus ignored him.

"I understand You have been out here forty days," he continued. "Forty days with no water or food. Not an entirely gracious entrance into the world for a Son of the Most High, hmm? Nevertheless the fast is over, Jesus. I congratulate You. This is a great feat for a man or a God. And now let us break the fast and put the matter to a test so that once and for all You shall know who You really are…"

He looked around leisurely, and then, with a slight gesture, caused a small stack of rocks to pile up before Jesus' feet. "Something I have learned since being consigned to this wretched world," he said with false modesty. "This should do nicely."

He waved his hand casually at the rocks.

"Jesus, if You are truly the Son of God, then command these stones to become bread. A reasonable, if not practical, test. You must be hungry."

Jesus looked at Lucifer.

"My Father has said that man shall not live by bread alone, but by every word that comes from His mouth."

The rocks remained cold and hard.

"Well stated," admitted Lucifer. "That is indeed what the Scriptures say. You are a credit to Your faith. However, come with me, Jesus; I wish to show You something."

Jesus suddenly found Himself on the roof of the still unfinished Temple in Jerusalem, with Lucifer standing beside Him. They stood looking far down below into the city, the Antonia Fortress nearby.

"This is the Temple built for Your Father," Lucifer said. "It is of course not as magnificent as the one built by Solomon, but it is nevertheless a great house and will help me make my point."

He took Jesus by the arm and escorted Him to the very edge.

"Like You, I am a student of the Scriptures," Lucifer said. "I know You hold great stock in the Holy Writ—they are Your life, so to speak. I recall a verse that goes like this: 'He will command His angels concerning You, and they shall lift You up in their hands, so that You won't even strike Your foot against a stone.' If You truly believe this, and if You are truly the Son of God, then throw Yourself from here. The angels will surely protect You."

Jesus looked down into the courtyard. Lucifer stood close to Him.

"How easy it would be…what a glorious way to allow the Lord's Word to prove itself…what a sure way to demonstrate Your trust in the Most High and to convince these religious fools You are indeed who You claim to be…"

Jesus stepped back and looked at Lucifer.

"The Word also says we should not put the Lord to the test!"

Jesus suddenly felt a cool breeze as He found himself standing with Lucifer upon a high mountain top. They were at a vantage overlooking a great valley in which many great cities were spread out before them. Lucifer stood in front of Jesus, indicating the greatness of the world which was before His eyes.

"Look at it Jesus," he said. "All of this and much more belongs to me. You are a Jew—the Son of a poor carpenter. There is nothing extraordinary about You. You look like any other Jew in this forsaken and forgotten province of Rome. You shall never amount to anything other than that which Your father has left You—a few simple skills in carpentry and a devotion to Your Lord."

He walked over to Jesus, almost pleading.

"Keep those if You like. Keep Your faith and Your father's trade. But I am offering You much more! I am offering You this world. It has been mine since Eden and it shall be Yours if You will only bow Your knee to me and worship me! That is all I ask! That is all I wanted in Heaven! It is all I require on earth."

"AWAY FROM ME, SATAN!"

Upon those words Lucifer was thrown back and fell to the ground. He managed to get on his knees as Jesus spoke again.

"It is written that you shall worship only the Lord your God…and you shall serve only Him!"

Lucifer stood, his anger rising within him as several holy angels began descending upon Jesus to minister to Him. He looked up as they began surrounding Him.

He scoffed at them.

"Very well, Jesus," he said finally. "Let these weak-willed slaves tend to You here and now. But this is not yet over!"

He vanished as hundreds more angels settled in and around Jesus. Serus arrived with Gabriel. They had watched their Lord overcome the great temptation set before Him by a very cunning enemy.

"I saw one man fall in Eden and start this war," said Gabriel, as they watched Jesus eat food provided by the angels. "I praise God I have not see another fall and finish it."

"Was there ever a doubt?" asked Serus. "I mean, Jesus is the Son of God. How could He fall prey to something as common as temptation?"

"Because He must prove Himself," came the familiar voice of Crispin, who was leading a group of students to earth to witness the ministry of Jesus, which was about to unfold in earnest. "For whatever reason it was important to the Lord that Jesus overcome the temptation of Lucifer. Sort of makes Eden not quite so painful."

"But I wonder what the ultimate goal of Jesus will be?" asked Serus. " What is His strategy? He just met the enemy. Why didn't He simply humble him?"

Crispin winked at Serus.

"I believe He just did!"

CHAPTER 6

"The Lord has zeal for his Father's house."

"Behold the Lamb of God!"

John watched as Jesus, recently returned from his contest with Lucifer in the wilderness, approached the area where he was baptizing. The people around John began drifting toward Jesus, gawking, whispering and silently contemplating just who this Man was John had singled out.

"He is the Lamb of God!" repeated John. "He has come to take away the sins of the world!"

Jesus acknowledged His cousin John, whose wild appearance had created such a stir in the region that even some representatives from the Sanhedrin had come to see this holy man. Some of these same priests now looked upon Jesus, waiting to see if He, too, might begin baptizing in the Jordan or preaching repentance. Upon hearing John declare that this Man, this Jesus, had come to take away the sins of the people, the priests looked at each other with puzzled expressions. They began to mutter among themselves.

There was another who heard John's declaration of Jesus. His name was Andrew. Watching Jesus move among the people, he thought of the weeks leading up to this moment. It was beginning to somehow make sense. John's ministry was already well known, and his preaching had initiated a popular and personal search for faith. Andrew had been touched by the baptist's fiery call to return to the Lord and become one of his disciples.

But now John was declaring this other Man—this Jesus of Nazareth—to be the very Man for whom he had been sent. He even said he had seen the Holy Spirit fall upon this Man! And now John was abdicating in favor of the Nazarene. Andrew thought about following along with the crowds and finding out more about Jesus. He chased after them until he caught up with Jesus.

"Master!"

Jesus turned and saw Andrew coming toward Him. Andrew was of medium height and build, and wore the clothes of a common laborer. But his eyes shone with remarkable intensity—as if he were sizing up Jesus even as he neared Him. With him was another of John's disciples.

"Master!" repeated Andrew.

Jesus stood and looked at the two men.

"Master, where are You staying?"

"Come with Me and find out," said Jesus, who turned again and began walking.

Andrew looked at the other man who shrugged with a "now what?" expression. Andrew looked once more at Jesus, who was walking away.

"Let's go with Him," he decided.

The day spent with Jesus at the place where He was staying was the most amazing day of Andrew's life. Jesus spoke to them of wonderful, simple truths. He gave them vision for a coming world which would see the Lord vindicated and Israel consoled. Most of all, Jesus spoke of hope—something Andrew had only recently begun to rediscover under John's teaching. He thought about staying longer with Jesus—but then decided to go and tell his brother Simon about the Man.

Simon was a large man—much larger than most of his fellow Jews, certainly bigger than his brother Andrew. He was older and bore the obvious marks of a laborer. His hands were massive and well-worn, and looked as if they could easily crush a man's skull—and yet Simon's eyes were clear and strangely compassionate.

Simon snorted a bit.

"What does He mean come and see?" he whispered to his brother. "Why should we come and see? Seems to me this is an ordinary enough Fellow. We have a catch to make!"

Andrew pleaded with his brother.

"Simon, listen to me," he said with intensity. "I cannot explain it to you. But I believe this Man is the Messiah!"

Simon dropped the net he was folding and looked at his brother quizzically. He walked over to Andrew and sniffed his breath to make sure he hadn't been drinking some wine.

"Stop it," said Andrew. "I'm not drunk. I'm telling you the truth!"

Simon shook his head in disbelief and left the net to follow Andrew. The two continued talking about the younger brother's insistence that Jesus was indeed the Messiah. Finally Simon had enough of it. He would see to this Jesus nonsense and make sure He stopped filling his younger brother's head with ridiculous ideas. He might even have a word with John's disciples.

"You think this Jesus is the Messiah...*the* Messiah?" Simon finally asked as they walked along.

"That is what John said," Andrew responded. "There He is!"

He pointed to Jesus, who was drinking from a well near the house where He was staying. Jesus looked up as the two men approached.

"See here," said Simon, not even allowing Andrew to introduce him. "My brother tells me You are some sort of Holy Man. That's well and good. But don't be going around calling Yourself the Messiah." He winked at Jesus. "The last 'Messiah' we had was killed by the Romans in a skirmish north of here. His whole group was murdered by Pilate's cutthroats. I don't want my brother to get caught up in any of that."

Jesus looked at Simon and half-smiled.

"Your name is Simon, isn't it?" He asked. "The son of Jonah."

Simon was astonished.

"Why, yes," he admitted, looking at his smirking brother who shrugged as if to indicate he had not divulged the information. "Andrew must have mentioned it to you."

"From now on you shall be called Peter, the rock."

Simon, now called Peter, was dumbfounded. He could only nod his head and blurt out a meager 'thank you, Sir.' He looked at Andrew and motioned for them to leave.

"We best be getting back to our nets," he muttered. "Come on Andrew. We have a great deal of fishing to do yet."

"Yes, you do," Jesus said, as they left Him.

Michael and several other warriors followed Jesus into the house in Cana. Although He had only been in Cana for three days, He had taken on two followers, Philip and Nathaniel, who accompanied Him to the wedding. Philip was from Bethsaida, the town of Andrew and Peter. Nathaniel had been called when Jesus had passed through and spotted him under a tree.

Serus wasn't particularly impressed with either Philp or Nathaniel. But he understood that all men were deficient, and if the Lord felt He needed men around Him, then these were just as good as any other. He had questioned Michael about it all.

"These are not things for you or me to decide," Michael cautioned.

The archangel never pretended to understand everything the Lord did, but he had learned to trust Him. 'Whatever the Lord does is right' was one of his favorite maxims. And Serus knew this to be true. Still, it boggled him that the Lord should gather mere men around Him to begin organizing the Liberation.

"Of course He must use men," Crispin said.

The wisdom angel was in the company of Michael and the other warriors at Cana to study the early ministry of Jesus and record the events for the Kingdom Chronicles. He loved Serus, and wanted the angel to understand that the Lord's ways were neither the ways of men nor of angels.

They entered the house and walked through to a courtyard in the back where a couple of tables had been pushed together to form a large banquet setting. Jesus was greeted by the people and introduced around by His mother. Nathaniel and Philip also greeted the people. When they were all seated a servant brought refreshment to everyone and the celebration began.

"Humans are simple creatures really," Crispin observed, listening to the joyful noise of fellowship. "A bit of wine, some food, good company and they are as content as any creature."

"They certainly are easily contented," said Serus.

Michael looked at Crispin upon Serus' words and smiled.

"What do you mean, Serus,?" Michael asked.

"Look at them," he said. "I know they are made in the image of the Most High but…"

A burst of laughter filled the area as the host told a story about a member of the wedding party. Serus shook his head.

"I don't understand your attitude," said Crispin. "Since when does the indifference of humans become so problematic for you? Humans have been indifferent toward the Lord since after Eden. What makes this occasion any different?"

"Here they all sit with the Lord of the Universe," continued Serus. "They are happily eating and drinking and making merry. They don't even know Who is seated in their midst!"

"Is that what concerns you?" said Michael. "As I recall there were two humans who were in the Lord's very Presence in an ideal setting…"

"Yes, and they settled for much less as well," said Serus.

"As did your former master in Heaven," noted Crispin. "Lucifer was one of the most privileged creatures in Heaven. He, too, settled for something far inferior in the presence of the Most High."

"Then the plan is doomed," said Serus resignedly. "It seems any creature with a free will eventually choose poorly."

The wedding party was now in full swing with a live band of musicians playing in the courtyard. Jesus was engaging in lively conversation with the host. His mother was also enjoying herself. The angels watched the party for a moment.

"Not every creature with a free will turns on his Creator," said Crispin. "I have not. Nor has Michael, nor Gabriel. Nor has the remaining Host. Freedom does not necessitate an evil choice—it merely allows for it."

"So when will Jesus reveal Himself?" asked Serus. "Being consigned to using men in His quest, He must reveal Himself to them at some point."

As he spoke, one of the servants whispered something to the chief servant, who made a horrified expression. The bridegroom spoke something back to the servant, who went to the others to report their unfortunate circumstances. Their master had no more wine! Mary heard these things and whispered to Jesus that they had run out of wine and that He must do something about it.

"What have I to do with you in this matter?" He asked. "It's not yet time to begin such things."

Mary turned to the chief servant and told him to do whatever Jesus said. The angels watched as Jesus motioned the chief servant over to Him and told him to fill some water pots to the brim with fresh water. The man looked at Him strangely. But with Mary nodding he should comply, he shrugged and ordered the other servants to do just that. Mary motioned to the host all would be well.

After the pots were filled Jesus told the servant to draw from one of the pots and give it to the host. The host and the other guests watched the unusual drama unfolding. They had never been to such a feast! The host looked at Jesus and then tasted from the cup. It was wine. It was the sweetest wine he had ever tasted!

Crispin looked at Serus.

"In answer to your question, Serus, I would say Jesus has begun to reveal Himself today," he said. "At Cana."

Chronicles of the Host
First Days

Indeed at Cana, in Galilee, did the Host witness the first of many miracles Jesus would perform for men and women. It made sense to us that humans —being such limited creatures— would be drawn to such workings—and in fact they were. Following the event at Cana, these men close to Jesus, called His disciples, were convinced He was everything John had said. How better for the Son of Man to represent the mission He had come to complete than to demonstrate through such powers He was also the Son of God?

During a visit to the Temple in the Passover time, the zeal of the Lord overcame Jesus and He scattered the money-changing thieves who sat in the court. More profiteers than prophets, these men sat at counting tables exchanging Temple coins for the coins of the realm so pilgrims might purchase animals for sacrifice.

Because the Temple controlled the rate of exchange in commerce, they made a huge profit at the same time. But Jesus,

declaring the Temple to be His "Father's house" and a "house
of prayer" drove the counters out with a whip, and overturned
their tables, making quite a name for Himself both among those
who supported Him and those who deemed Him a threat…

30 A.D.

"Quite a show your Jesus put on at the Temple today," snickered Lucifer.

Gabriel looked at Lucifer, who was standing with several higher-ranking devils outside of the place in Jerusalem where Jesus was staying during the Passover. Several dozen warrior angels under Michael's command stood sentry in and around the house. Lucifer dared not enter, but instead exercised what he considered his right to roam as freely as he might. Several of the fallen angels who were with him laughed mockingly at his comment.

"The Lord has zeal for His Father's house," said Gabriel. "Something you never completely managed."

Lucifer peeked inside the window at Jesus, who was eating a light meal in the dimly lit room.

"Oh, I had zeal," said Lucifer. "But I also have a mind of my own. That is the difference between us, Gabriel. You exercise your mind on behalf of the Most High. I exercise mine in spite of Him. My zeal has lead to freedom—yours has imprisoned you and every other creature who remains the slave of the Most High."

As they spoke, a cloaked figure hurried down the street and rapped lightly on the door to the house. He was a man of some importance if his garb was any indication—in fact he bore the trappings of a member of the High Council of the Jews. But what was he doing here?

"Ah, Nicodemus," said Lucifer. "I know he has been troubled by Jesus of late. But to show up in person is quite astonishing."

Gabriel smiled a knowing smile.

"Yes, Nicodemus has been troubled by our Lord," admitted Gabriel. "However, I think you will be disappointed as to his appearance."

Lucifer cast a menacing glance at the angel who stood behind him, assuring him that Nicodemus would cause trouble for Jesus. He turned back to Gabriel.

"Indeed? Let us listen then, archangel. Perhaps one of us will become educated."

"Enter, Nicodemus," said Jesus, opening the door.

Nicodemus, a distinguished looking gentleman with a salt-and-pepper beard looked about him as if to make sure he was unseen and then entered the little house which belonged to a friend of Jesus. Jesus gestured toward food and drink, but the priest waved it off with a thank you. They sat down and for a few silent seconds looked at each other.

"Rabbi," Nicodemus began. "I represent some in the Council who know You are no ordinary Man."

Nicodemus stood to speak, as he was quite nervous.

"We have heard of the wedding in Cana. We saw Your action today in the Temple, and might I add I quite agree with You in that regard. We know You are a Man sent from God, for nobody could do the things You have been doing unless the Lord be with Him."

Jesus remained silent for a moment. Nicodemus looked at Him, not exactly sure what else he wanted to say, but needed to express some sort of confidence in this Man from Nazareth. He began to speak again when Jesus interrupted him.

"Nicodemus, you have said many things," Jesus answered. "But there is only one thing that matters. You must be born again."

Nicodemus was confused. What did He mean by this?

"Rabbi, how can a man be born again? Can a man enter into his mother's womb again after he has already been born?"

"Nicodemus, your heart is sincere in its search. But I must tell you that if you are to enter the Kingdom of Heaven, you must be born not only physically but of the Spirit."

Nicodemus sat down, perplexed and was framing a response in his mind when Jesus continued.

"Don't be amazed at what I have said," Jesus said. "The flesh gives birth to flesh, and the Spirit gives birth to spirit. That is why I have said you must be born again."

The old priest made motions as if he were trying to understand, but could not grasp what Jesus was saying.

"Nicodemus, just as the wind comes and goes and nobody can tell where it came from nor where it is headed, so it is with those who are born of the Spirit."

"But Rabbi, how can these things be?" he finally blurted out.

Jesus smiled at the old man.

"You are a teacher in Israel. And yet you do not understand the most basic truth of the kingdom? The Lord God loved this fallen world so much that He gave His only Son, so that whoever shall believe in Him will have eternal life."

He placed his hand on Nicodemus' shoulder.

"Nicodemus, whoever believes on the Son will be saved by the Father and he shall enter the Kingdom of Heaven! The Light has arrived, but darkness will not receive it."

He glanced at the window as he spoke, making eye contact with Lucifer who peered at Him through the opening. Lucifer stood his ground and glared back at Jesus.

"This is why condemnation has come into the world," He continued, looking at Lucifer. He pointed toward the blackness of the window. "Darkness hates the light. But whoever loves the light comes to the light. And this, Nicodemus, is what you must do if you are to enter the kingdom."

After Nicodemus departed, Lucifer watched angels ascending and descending upon the house. He snorted at the sheer number of angels encamped about Jesus.

"You must think I am very dangerous," said Lucifer sarcastically. "I would never touch the Lord's person…not now anyway."

"You will never be allowed that opportunity, Lucifer," said Gabriel, who had moved between Lucifer and the window. Lucifer smirked and stepped back. He looked toward Nicodemus.

"I won't need to touch him," he said. "As long as there are humans, the Lord will be quite accessible. Take this Nicodemus. Here is a complete fool who has apparently been taken in by Jesus and his nonsense world of miracles and rebirths. "

He began snickering.

"Can you imagine what the other Jews will say when he reports to them the things Jesus told him?" he asked, looking back at the angels who were with him. "Born again! Pellecus will have quite a time in that meeting, I'm sure."

"You're wrong, Lucifer," said Gabriel. "You're actually quite afraid of Nicodemus and others who are listening to Jesus. Didn't you hear? He just told Nicodemus how he might enter the Kingdom of Heaven. The way is clear."

"Not yet," said Lucifer. "The Lord cheapens Heaven by allowing entrance to any human fool with a bit of interest. But He also said it was a spiritual course. I suggest that humans will never enter the Kingdom because mere humans shall never overcome their fall at Eden. Humans have never understood spiritual matters."

Gabriel watched as Jesus extinguished the little lamp and the house darkened.

"You're right, Lucifer," said Gabriel. "Humans shall never overcome Eden. But then, perhaps it will not be a mere *human* who overcomes Eden."

"Light and dark...a new birth...eternal life..."

Lucifer repeated the words for Pellecus and Kara.

The three had met to discuss a new strategy conceived by Pellecus. It was his contention that as long as Jesus and John continued to work together unopposed, their influence would only continue to grow. Even now they were both baptizing at different spots in the Jordan. Such coordination was devastating.

"Of course you know what this means," said Pellecus.

Lucifer nodded. Kara merely looked deeply concerned.

"Light and dark. New birth. What exactly do these cryptic phrases mean?" asked Kara. "Are they a key to Jesus' destruction?"

"No, Kara," said Lucifer. "They are a key to our own destruction."

"And the deliverance of humanity, apparently," added Pellecus. "Although I must admit it is rather discouraging to realize that Heaven's doors are open to such creatures."

"How so?" asked Kara, toppling a bust of a Greek hero in the small temple in which they were speaking outside of Caesarea. "The Lord will never again allow corruption in Heaven. Not anymore..."

Lucifer and Pellecus looked at Kara, astonished at his stupidity.

"Nevertheless, I heard Jesus tell Nicodemus that he might be born into the Kingdom of God by the Spirit of God," said Lucifer, almost pleading with his voice as he tried to figure out the mysterious words of Jesus. "He cheapens Heaven with such grace. But I was certainly not going to let on to Gabriel that I was so alarmed at this business of a new birth."

"Still, the plan must somehow be worked through the Christ," reasoned Pellecus. "The key lies in destroying Him."

"And don't forget John," added Kara.

"True, Kara," said Lucifer. "John's preaching has legitimized Jesus—he has paved the way for his cousin. Perhaps it's time we split up this relationship."

"Precisely," said Pellecus, happy at last to bring the meeting back to its reason for having been called. "John and Jesus must be diminished. If we can discredit John, who introduced Jesus to the world, then perhaps Jesus' reputation will fall as well. Then we would be rid of both of them."

Lucifer thought for a moment. Looking over the sloping Greek countryside, he briefly remembered the days in Heaven when he enjoyed his authority and position as the Anointed Cherub. Now he was a fugitive trying desperately to win back a measure of the authority that had been lost to him.

"Agreed," he said finally. "Kara will take on the responsibility of John's destruction. Do what you must to bring discord within his ranks; cause strife between his disciples and the vermin Jesus is gathering around Him. In the end, destroy him."

Kara nodded.

"And you, Pellecus, will have the honor of stirring up those enemies of Jesus who have more lofty motivations," said Pellecus. "I mean, of course, the priests—the Pharisees and Sadducees and those aligned with the Herods. Fan the fear that is already in their rotten hearts concerning Jesus and bring them to a point of collusion."

He snickered.

"The fools will destroy the very One who was sent to help them."

"That is something humans are quite good at," said Kara.

"They have had a good teacher," said Pellecus.

Lucifer smiled.

CHAPTER 7

"I am Herod Antipas. I am king now!"

Gehazi, one of John's disciples, was seated on the riverbank resting. The sun felt particularly hot that day. Even while attending his master, John, in the water, it seemed as if his head was on fire. He shaded his eyes and looked to the sky as if expecting to see some clouds moving in. Instead he saw only the brightness of the burning sun.

"What I wouldn't give for a cloud the size of a man's hand right now," he said to Jadok, another disciple. The two men moved closer to the tree, taking advantage of what little shade it offered. Jadok, a younger man, who had left his father's trade as a baker to follow after John, laughed.

"Well, we have no Elijah here," he said, looking at John in the middle of the river. "But we do have quite a prophet."

"Yes, but with Elijah's spirit," said Gehazi. "Just one little cloud…"

The men laughed.

Unseen by either man, Kara appeared and took a seat nearby. With him was Berenius, who had come to assist in the mission to bring John down.

"There is One who has that Spirit upon Him," said Jadok.

"Jesus of Nazareth," said Gehazi. "The Lamb of God! Such exciting times."

Berenius moved in closer to Gehazi and whispered in his mind.

"Have you noticed that ever since Jesus arrived we are baptizing fewer and fewer people...?"

"The crowds are down these days," Gehazi said, squinting at the three or four people gathered at the riverside with some of the other disciples of John. "Seems like Jesus has taken them away."

Jadok looked about him.

"I haven't really thought about it," he said. "But I suppose you are right."

The two remained silent for a moment, until someone called out to Gehazi. He looked up and recognized Justus, a friend from Judea who was in the company of several others. They were traveling through the area and had heard of John's ministry at Jordan.

The interruption annoyed Kara, who decided to wait and see what might develop."Gehazi!" Justus called again. The two men embraced. "I thought I might find you here with John."

"Justus, my old friend," said Gehazi. "Take refreshment." He pointed to the others. "All of you."

The men sat down and ate and drank. John had completed his baptisms and was joining some of the other disciples down the river. They all watched him climb up the bank.

"Your master has made quite a name for himself," said Justus, wiping his mouth after taking a drink from a waterskin. "Just as mine is doing."

"Your master?"

"Yes," said Justus. "Jesus, the Nazarene. He baptized me two days ago a few miles up river."

Kara and Berenius looked at each other knowingly. Berenius then moved back over to Gehazi.

"I wonder how many Jesus is baptizing these days...?"

"How are the crowds with Jesus?" asked Gehazi. "As you can see it seems baptisms are no longer what the people are wanting."

Justus was puzzled.

"How many have you baptized today?" he asked.

Gehazi looked at Jadok.

"Not sure. Around six I think."

"Jesus and his disciples are baptizing many more than that every day," said Justus. "They are quite busy."

"Interesting that the man who introduced Jesus is now being forgotten by him and his disciples..."

"Er...does Jesus speak of John?" Gehazi asked, as if somewhat bored with the conversation.

"Not really," said Justus.

"Why should He concern Himself with John? He has become the greater Light..."

"We must be off, my friend," said Justus. "We must be in Jerusalem this evening. But tell your master if he wants to baptize more people, he should move closer to where Jesus is!"

Gehazi watched as the men mounted and began their homeward journey. Jadok looked at Gehazi, trying to figure out what he was thinking. Finally Gehazi turned to Jadok, obviously upset.

"Let's go speak with John," he said.

Kara smiled at Bernius.

"Yes," said Kara. "Let's go speak with John!"

"I told you a man can receive nothing unless it is given him from Heaven," John said. "Gehazi, you must understand. Jesus will increase even as I decrease. All of you must realize this."

The men sat around the fire, watching the flames dance in the evening coolness. Gehazi had brought the subject of Jesus' disciples baptizing many more than John's, and found comfort in the fact that he was not the only one who had observed this.

"But master," he said. "You are the one who baptized Him. You are the one who bore witness of Him. It seems somehow unfitting that you should now bow so low before Him. It seems unfitting…"

John stood up.

"Brothers," he began. "He that comes from above is already above all. Jesus is the Son who is loved by the Father. And eternal life will come from Him—not from me. He must therefore increase while I decrease. It must be."

Berenius looked disappointed at John's attitude. Most humans would have become petty and jealous. And yet John was staying true to his Lord. It didn't make sense. And it was proving difficult. Kara saw the anguish in Berenius' face.

"No matter," said Kara. "I didn't think to destroy him here at Jordan anyway."

Berenius looked up hopefully. Kara smiled at him.

"Just so, Berenius." Kara said. "One does not increase in popularity without also increasing in enemies. Our friend the Baptist has not only made a name for himself in the mud of Jordan but also in the mind of Herod."

He watched as John waded back into the water to continue baptizing.

"John is bent on decreasing," Kara continued. "Perhaps we can hasten that decline."

Herod Antipas was the son of Herod the Great. Like his brothers Archelaus and Philip, he was educated in Rome—partially because of his father's desire to school the boys in the culture of the world's great power; and partially to clear them out of the way of the murderous intrigue that always surrounded Herod. Naturally ingratiating, Antipas became a favorite of the Roman court. After his brother's short reign, he was eventually named tetrarch of Judea by none other than Augustus.

Politically astute and foxy by nature, Herod's chief aim was to govern with as little unrest as possible and so stave off any Roman intervention in Jewish affairs. In order to demonstrate his allegiance to the Romans and to show his influence in Judea, he established a new capital, which was named after the new emperor Tiberias.

In matters of religion, Herod Antipas tried to set an example of outward piety. He celebrated Passover with great passion and had managed to snuggle up to the leading Jews who occupied places of political and religious importance. His was a kingdom of compromise, however, and his hypocrisy was not lost on John the Baptist.

"How long will I endure this man's insults?" asked Herodias. "How long will you allow him to humiliate you in front of your subjects?"

She sneered.

"If your father Herod the Great were king... "

Herod violently flung his wine cup across the room and stopped up his ears as if to drown out a deafening noise.

"Do not invoke the name of my father the late king!" he screamed. Several guards looked into the chamber of the Hasmodean Palace where Herod and Herodias were staying in anticipation of the Passover. "I am Herod Antipas. I am king now!"

He looked up at his wife, who walked over to his side. She was lovely—but so, so demanding. Herod had first been married to Phasaelis, the daughter of an Arabian king. But taken in by the persuasive enticements of Herodias, he divorced Phasaelis.

Herodias had been the wife of Herod Antipas' half-brother, and when he married her, though a common scandal among royalty, John condemned it as sinful and had begun railing about it publicly. Seizing upon the rage of Herodias, Kara had seeded in her mind a plan to humiliate John once and for all.

Herod told the guards to mind their own business and they hastily disappeared from view. Herodias moved in to console her husband, whose frequent outbursts—like this one—played into her hands. She knew how to handle men—and Herod was something even less than that.

"My husband, I am only looking out for your best interests," she purred. "What do I care about this holy man? But you. You are king, are you not? Can you afford for this unlettered man of the wilderness to publicly mock you? And what about me? He has all but called me a harlot! Herod's whore!"

She waited to see what effects her words were having upon him. Herod sat down in an ornate chair that was a gift from the king of Parthia. She picked up his cup and poured more wine. He sipped it and looked up at her.

"You do love me, don't you my dear?" he pleaded.

"Of course my pet," she answered, stroking his hair. "I love you so much I cannot bear anyone insulting you. That's all. But I will drop the matter of John if you prefer…and if you are weary of opposing him…"

Kara and Berenius appeared behind Herod. They laughed aloud at this clownish king being manipulated by this very powerful woman. Kara looked at Herodias.

"Herodias is quite a potent women," he commented. "She is subtle and clever and cold. Herod is absolutely captivated by her."

"Herod is a fool," said Berenius. "But he is a political strategist. I'm not sure he will move against John."

Kara looked at Berenius, who stood to Herod's left.

"He'll be moved," said Kara. "He may be politically wise, but he is also proud. In the end we shall appeal to his pride—just as his wife is doing. As Lucifer has said many times, pride is our greatest asset in waging this war. It is human pride that forced the decision at Eden. Human pride will bring about John's destruction!"

Herod drank the cup of wine Herodias had given him. She continued to soothe his mood, stroking him and whispering affectionately in his ear.

"My sweet, you are my king and I only wish to see you lifted up," she said.

Kara motioned to Berenius and knelt down beside Herod opposite where Herodias was bent down. As she whispered in one ear, Kara spoke into the other.

"And yet how can a king be lifted up in a country where every holy man with a mission can accuse the king and his wife..."

Herod's eyes glazed over as he looked straight ahead. He shifted uncomfortably in his chair.

"You are king, Herod. And must act like one," Herodias continued. Herod nodded.

"But what she means is that you are not a real king as long as this dangerous man, who has the people's heart, is allowed to freely charge the king with adultery..."

"Herodias?" Herod finally asked.

"Yes, my love," cooed Herodias.

"I realize that this John is a nuisance," he said. "And he has offended us both. But do you think he might be dangerous...I mean truly dangerous?"

Herodias moved in front of Herod, kneeling on the floor. She looked into his eyes.

"Dearest, you are such a loving and generous man," she began. "You love everyone and desire to be loved. Your only fault is that you love your people as a good king should. But I believe your love for all of them has blinded you to the danger of some of them."

"And John?" he asked. "A nuisance or a threat?"

"Anyone who violates the peace of the king violates the peace of the kingdom," she said. "I believe he is a threat, my king."

Herod stood and walked over to the window that looked toward the Antonia Fortress. To its right the work of the Temple proceeded. He turned to Herodias.

"This Temple begun by my father shall be completed by me," he said. "This city, left to me by Herod the Great, shall be even greater after my reign. I have seen to the stability of this nation; I have placated the Romans; I have pacified the priests; I have brought order to the land. Am I not as great as my father?"

Herodias rushed to his side.

"Of course you are, my love," she said. "You are the greatest of kings!"

He turned back toward the Temple. Kara sidled up to him.

"And yet one man—a self-declared holy man—dares to insult you—to instigate among the people a discontent…possibly even an insurrection…"

"And yet John preaches," he muttered.

Herodias was taken aback.

"Yes, my king," she said. "He is still preaching his hatred for you."

Kara turned to Berenius.

"Well put," Kara said. "That one sunk deep. I can sense his rage."

"His hatred for you…"

Herod turned to the room and walked toward his chair. Kara followed him.

"Adultery…"

Herod sank down in his chair.

"What must the other nobles be thinking? What must the Romans be thinking?"

Herod was getting angrier by the moment. Herodias stood back, hoping her venom was finally hitting home.

"TREASON…"

Herod stood up and called for his guard.

"Bring me Aristas," he ordered. "At once!"

Herodias smiled to herself.

Aristas, the chief of Herod's security forces, came into the room. He bowed low.

"Majesty?" he inquired.

"I have a delicate matter of state that needs to be taken care of," Herod began. "I want John the Baptist arrested and brought to Antonia."

Aristas glanced at Herodias knowingly.

"It shall be done, majesty."

"He is not to be hurt. He is merely to be detained for further investigation."

"I will see to it," said Aristas.

Herodias fawned upon Herod after Aristas departed. She wiped his brow with a cool rag and poured more wine for him.

"Now that was a king in action!" she said. "That is why you shall go down as one of the greatest of kings!"

Herod closed his eyes, relishing a rare, decisive moment.

Kara snickered and looked at Berenius. "Inform Lucifer that John's detention has begun," he ordered. "We await his final order on the matter."

Berenius nodded at Kara.

"I am beginning to believe Israel is a nation of fools," he said.

Kara looked at the royal couple and agreed.

"Yes, Berenius. And Herod is king of fools," he sneered.

Chronicles of the Host

Galilee

The disposition of John was seen by Lucifer as a great victory and a step toward the elimination of Jesus as a threat. With John safely out of the way, it seemed only a matter of time before Jesus and His message of Kingdom would soon follow.

But Jesus continued teaching and preaching, establishing Himself in Galilee. The fame of Jesus began spreading throughout the land, for He was seen as a Man of authority and power, One filled with the wisdom and power of the Spirit of God.

At Cana, He healed the son of a nobleman, causing the people of that city to gloriously exclaim that two miracles had been wrought in their midst! But when He came to His own town, Nazareth, He knew that not everyone in Galilee was in agree-

ment with Him. For He had said a prophet has no honor among his own people...

The synagogue at Nazareth was abuzz with excitement—a new holy man was to read today. Many Jews, both old rabbis and young students, gathered to hear the words and reading of One of their own—Jesus of Nazareth. Much had been said about this Man—the Son of a carpenter. All eyes were upon Him as He entered the little building and was given a seat of honor.

Nazareth itself was a small town, crowded for its size and very strongly attached to its Jewish roots. Jesus grew up here and was educated in the very synagogue in which He was about to read. His grasp of Hebrew and Aramaic, His understanding of history, and His knowledge of the Scriptures was a credit to the rabbis and other mentors who had educated Jesus as a young Man. When He left them, He was regarded as One of their greatest pupils. Unknown to them, He now returned as their greatest Teacher. Outside the synagogue, Crispin and several other angels watched the activity of the Sabbath. Men streamed into the synagogue, eager to continue the custom of their fathers.

"Men and their religion," said Millas, a wisdom angel accompanying Crispin to the synagogue. "They do love it so."

"Little good it does them, I'm afraid," said Crispin, observing the pious men entering the building. "To be sure these men of Nazareth are simple and passionate. Good men for the most part. But we have seen that religion in and of itself leads nowhere. Perhaps this day our Lord will bring more light into their darkened hearts."

"Darkened hearts?" came a voice.

Crispin turned to see Pellecus standing with a group of his own students. He looked over the angels with him.

"I see you are still accumulating students," said Crispin.

"A good teacher never stops teaching, nor accumulating students," said Pellecus. "Had the Academy of the Host realized that I would still be there."

Crispin's angels looked around at one another. A group of warrior angels moved in around the synagogue as if to protect it. Pellecus laughed at their arrival.

"I forget how dangerous I am," he said. "I can assure you I have come only to witness the unveiling of Jesus of Nazareth. It should be interesting."

Crispin smirked.

"I'm sure Jesus will be interesting to you and your charges," he said. "Not to mention refreshing. The truth does that, you know."

"These are the core of my own Academy," said Pellecus, pointing out the angels who stood with him. Most of them were former angels of wisdom who had subsequently thrown in with Lucifer. "It shall rival the Academy of the Host, I assure you. And its doctrines will be forever remembered as great doctrines of truth."

"Doctrines of demons you mean," said Crispin. He shook his head. "I'm afraid, Pellecus, that for all of your philosophical juggling of Lucifer's attitude, in the end it is nothing but shameful pride. And pride is the wellspring of every doctrine originating apart from the Most High."

All eyes in the synagogue turned toward Jesus as He made His way to the front of the room. He picked up the prescribed book for the day. He took a moment and found the place in Isaiah from which He would read. The rabbis in the room closed their eyes to drink in the holy text as He began:

> *"The Spirit of the Lord is upon me,*
> *because He has anointed me to preach the gospel to the poor;*
> *He has sent me to heal the brokenhearted,*

to preach deliverance to the captives,
and recovering of sight to the blind,
to set at liberty them that are bruised,
to preach the acceptable year of the Lord."

Jesus set the scroll down and took His seat. The rabbis awaited the customary commentary from their former pupil. Jesus looked at them earnestly, then announced, "Today, this scripture of the prophet is fulfilled in your hearing."

The men looked about astonished. Some smiled at Jesus. Surely they had misheard...or perhaps he had misspoke. Others began to mutter among themselves that this was the son of Joseph the carpenter. Still others scowled at such insolence.

Outside among the angels, the declaration was just as dramatic as it was inside the synagogue. Pellecus smiled at the reaction of the humans. He looked back at his angels as if continuing one of his lectures.

"Once again the Lord is creating more problems than He is solving," he began. "Notice that here is the Son of God—the very One they seek—declaring Himself the fulfillment of this remarkable prophecy. And what are they doing?" He glanced over at Crispin. "They are seething—as humans are prone to do. The Messiah is before them and they cannot see Him. It's quite delicious."

"Jesus declared Himself because it was His time," said Crispin. "He isn't here to impress these humans. He is here to enlighten them."

"Well they are definitely enlightened," said Crispin. "In fact they are enraged!"

As Pellecus spoke, the voices in the synagogue became louder and louder. Pellecus smiled at Crispin, who had a look of concern on his face. The warrior angels advanced, in case Jesus should call upon them.

One of the venerable old rabbis moved to the front of the room and put up his hands to hush the many voices. He turned to speak to Jesus with great courtesy.

"Excuse our indignation, my Son," he began. "But it is just that we know You from this town. You are the son of Joseph and Mary. How could these Scriptures possibly apply to You?"

Several voices echoed in affirmation.

"No prophet is accepted in his own country," said Jesus. "Do you recall the story of Elias, the prophet? There was great famine in those days but he was sent only to the widow of Sidon. And then there was the time when Elisha healed only Naaman of his leprosy even though there were many in the land who were afflicted. So it is that I must go where I am sent."

The door burst open and the men of the synagogue took hold of Jesus, forcing Him out into the street. As He was being taken out, Jesus locked eyes with a man who was coming up the street toward Him. The man watched as Jesus disappeared into the growing crowd.

A painful memory seized the man as he recalled a similar situation when he was a little boy and his own father had been taken away from him in the streets by Herod's soldiers. He followed along behind the mob, curious as to the outcome.

"Mind Him there!" ordered one of the angels.

Crispin and the other holy angels quickly moved in among the cantankerous people, who had determined to throw Jesus down the steep hillside on the edge of town. Pellecus and his troop watched with great interest as the angels moved in, and Jesus suddenly walked out from among the throng as if they didn't even see Him!

"Well done, well done!" shouted Crispin to the warriors, whose swords had blinded the minds and eyes of the men to Jesus' escape. Some of the masses caught a glimpse of Jesus as He departed, but they continued with the crowd to see what would become of the blasphemer.

Pellecus watched as Jesus continued down the street. His disciples joined Him and they left the town. He looked at Crispin with an annoyed countenance.

"I was rather hoping they would tear Him limb from limb," snorted Pellecus. "But no bother. We will have our way with Him in the end. Lucifer has vowed that Jesus of Nazareth shall yet die. He bleeds like any other man."

"I can assure you, Pellecus," said Crispin, "If Jesus bleeds it will not be like any ordinary man."

"Bah! Away from this wretched place," said Pellecus, who vanished along with his students.

The remaining angels watched as the warriors moved out of town to join Jesus. Crispin turned back to look at the angels who remained with him. Sensing a question among them, he finally invited their curiosity.

"Good Crispin, why did these men behave so violently?"

"Because men are always threatened by that which is greater than themselves," he answered. "And some angels too, it seems."

"But this is the Man they have been waiting for," said another angel. "He told them so just now."

Crispin nodded.

"Yes," said Crispin. "Jesus is the Man for which the whole world has been looking. Unfortunately they don't have the eyes to find Him."

CHAPTER 8

"Jesus intends to do what the prophets could never accomplish."

"Keep an eye on Him," said one of the warriors following Jesus.

"I have Him," said the other.

The two angels assigned by Michael to stay with Jesus at all times had become particularly interested in one man since Jesus left Nazareth. It was the man who had been following Jesus ever since the altercation began—the one who had made eye contact with Him while He was being hustled away.

Jesus was walking along the road leading away from the city and the man was catching up to Him. One of the warriors was at the ready as he approached Jesus.

Just as he was about to call out, Jesus turned and looked at the man. He was about 34 and looked like an ordinary laborer. He also bore the marks of many fights on his body. Jesus locked eyes with him once more and the man trembled a bit.

"I...I saw You in the street," he began. "Back there."

"And I saw you," Jesus said.

They stood there in silence for a moment. The man acted as if he wanted to say something but could not find the right words for it. Finally, in a stumbling manner, he began speaking.

"I am not certain why I am here," he continued. "But I wanted You to know that when You looked at me I knew You were innocent. I have seen many men die—but they were always guilty...or deserved it. Except for one...many years ago."

Jesus remained silent as he continued.

"I was prepared to step in and help You!" he said with urgency. His eyes fell to the ground. "But...I only spill Roman blood. My father was killed by the Romans. Or at least he may as well have been. He was butchered by Antipas' father, the Herod called the Great. I say death to all who play the harlot with Rome."

As he spoke his mind burned with anger at the memory of his father being taken away while his mother pleaded mercy from Herod all those years ago. He looked hard at Jesus.

"I am not sorry for the men I have killed since then" he said. "I have dedicated my life to overthrowing this bloody tyrant and seeing my country free again. I seek a new kingdom for Israel."

Jesus motioned for the man to sit beside Him under a small tree near the road. The warriors moved in close just in case the man might try something.

"We are alike then. I, too, wish to see My people set free," said Jesus. "I, too, am looking for another Kingdom."

"Then You are a Zealot?" whispered the man. He laughed aloud. "Excuse me for laughing, but You don't look like the sort of Man who would spill the blood of others."

"I am zealous, Simon," answered Jesus. "But not like you. I have not come to spill the blood of others."

Simon was astonished that the man knew his name.

"Who are You?" he asked.

"Jesus of Nazareth." He laughed. "My home town has very little use for Me it seems."

"Nor does mine," Simon said, a far-away look in his eyes.

"One day you shall find your home, Simon."

He looked up toward the sky. "Someday we both shall discover that Kingdom for which we long."

Lucifer sat silently at the large marble table gracing one of Tiberias' rooms at his Capri palace. Before him and around the table stood the three angels in whom he confided most, and to whom he had given the greatest authority on earth.

Rugio, who was commander of all of the warriors and whose special delight was in the oppression of people through sickness and disease, sat opposite him. Next to Rugio was Kara, whose cunning and ability to gather information made him one of the most feared angels in Lucifer's domain. He specialized in encouraging occult behavior among humans. Finally there was Pellecus, the leader of Lucifer's philosophical wing whose plan it was to bring all the world under one humanistic, yet decidedly Luciferian religion. The three of them made up the leading angels who stood in opposition to the plans of the Most High on earth.

Lucifer glanced through a window of the Domus Augustus, the palace built by Augustus on the Palatine Hill overlooking Rome. In truth, Augustus, who had become the first true emperor of Rome, lived a very simple, almost Spartan lifestyle. The Domus Augustus was an incredibly beautiful place. Ornate and marbled, adorned with statuary and housing an enormous library, the Domus had become the center of imperial life.

Rome under Augustus had seen much construction and the emperor had personally overseen the erecting of such structures as the Senate House, the Temple of Apollo, the Temple of Jupiter, the Temple of Mars and other religious sites. He also oversaw an expansion of the Circus Maximus, the aqueducts which were falling into ruin, and many roads and bridges. Being something of a showman at heart, Augustus had instituted great gladiator shows and games that saw the participation of athletes from all over the empire. Augustus was a consolidator and his reign was seen as a time of universal peace, the Pax Romana.

"The Romans have certainly impressed the world," mused Lucifer as he turned back to his three aides. "They rule a filthy rabble with blood and carnage, and have forged an empire mightier than most. Jewish stubbornness and the Roman virtue of law and order will prove useful to us in Judea."

Lucifer sat at the enormous marbled table. Outside a great roar went up from the crowd at the Circus where Tiberias had recently convened a game. The others sat at the table awaiting further direction from their master. He looked at Kara and, without saying so, demanded a report from him.

"My lord, before I give my report on the enemy let me say that you are doing a magnificent work here in Rome with Tiberias," Kara began.

Rugio and Pellecus sneered at his pandering.

"You have managed to fan his debauchery so quickly," he added. "Augustus was so…so bent on modeling simple Roman morality. But Tiberias. Now there is a man who has managed to degrade himself and the empire by turning everything over to his trusted Sejanus while he lounges about at Capri. Excellent work, my prince!"

"My time in Rome will be short, Kara," said Lucifer. "True, it is expedient that the emperor remain numb to matters of state. Sejanus has a bitter hatred of the Jews. His appointment of Pilate over Judea is evidence enough of that. Pilate is concerned only with keeping his standing in imperial politics. Men are such fools."

He walked to a map of the empire that hung in the council room. Touching a point on the large hanging until it actually burned through he then commented in a halting, almost whispering voice, "But the real war is not in Rome—it is here in Jerusalem. Always Jerusalem."

"My prince, the enemy is gathering around Him certain men He is calling disciples," interjected Pellecus, trying to direct the conversation from the melancholy turn it was taking. "A rough lot of men.

Common fishermen, laborers, the dregs of society really. Not one noble in the bunch of them. Not one priest. Not even a Maccabbee."

"Ah, but they have among them a descendant of their greatest king," said Lucifer.

"Of course you mean King David," said Kara. "But which one of these men validates the others?"

Pellecus only shook his head at Kara's ignorance.

"He means Jesus," said Pellecus. "He is descended from David just as the prophecy foretold."

"But these others—these disciples He is gathering about Him—are rather ordinary," said Rugio. " Peter seems quite unotable. And his simple brother Andrew. The Lord pulled them right off their fishing boat. Not much of an army, if you ask my opinion."

Lucifer smiled and added, "Apart from the Zealot who has joined them I have no regard for them at all."

"Nevertheless they bear watching," said Pellecus with caution. "As we have often seen, the Most High seems to relish taking ordinary men and doing the spectacular with them."

Rugio grunted an affirmation.

"What Jesus wishes to do with these men He is gathering is not the issue," said Lucifer, becoming upset. "We must organize against the plan of the Most High. Jesus has come—the Seed of Eve has arrived. We must continue to deal with it or be destroyed."

"I for one have seen the threat all along," said Kara, who stood to promote himself. "And as is well known throughout our world, I have disposed of John, with the help of Berenius. He languishes even now at the Antonia prison."

Kara beamed with pride.

"And so my lord, I have been serving both you and the war's outcome quite capably, I believe."

"Sit down Kara," said Lucifer, not even looking at the angel who humbly sat back down amid the snickering of Pellecus and Rugio.

"True, John had to be put away," said Lucifer. "But in putting John away all we did was to increase the prominence of Jesus. Many of John's followers are now beginning to rush to Him. The crowds are beginning to follow him. He is gaining a name among the people." He looked at Rugio and added, "The common people."

Rugio nodded, understanding.

"So Jesus is recruiting commoners for His leadership because He is building an army of common people to rise up and..."

"Not an army, Rugio," corrected Lucifer. "A movement...a philosophy...a faith."

"Then Jesus intends to do what the prophets were never able to accomplish," said Pellecus. "He intends to regain the world by capturing the hearts of the people." He looked at Lucifer meekly. "And in doing so to vanquish its present authority."

Lucifer smiled.

"Have no fear, Pellecus. It is no secret the Seed has arrived to do me harm. But remember, my brothers, I shall not be the only spirit caught up in the wrath should the day ever come."

A spirit suddenly rushed into the room, bowing low and begging audience with Lucifer and the others. This was Jerob, one of Rugio's devils who had been assigned to the religious leadership in Judea. Lucifer looked at Rugio scornfully. Kara did likewise. Rugio walked over to the demon who had prostrated himself before the powerful fallen angels.

"Well?" growled Rugio, angry and humiliated that one of his own should interrupt this important council.

Jerob, who had been a wisdom angel in Heaven, kept his face toward the floor and began speaking. As he spoke his image became less and less human in form and took on the hideous ape-like appearance of most spirits of religion.

"Commander, I must report an incident involving Jesus," he began.

Rugio shot a concerned look at Lucifer and then looked back at Jerob. Lucifer remained impassive.

Yes?" asked Rugio. "What about it?"

"It was at Capernaum," Jerob began. "As you know, my lord, I have been the chief spirit of religion over that city for many human years. It has been my assigned task to fan into flames the rigid and selfish religion that the covenant with the Most High has become.

"Most recently I was in possession of a man who faithfully attends synagogue. He is married and has family. He is well-respected. And yet nobody was aware that this man had given himself over completely to his lust for religious intoxication. Thus he was quite useful to me in the religious community of Capernaum."

"Go on," said Rugio.

"Jesus came to Capernaum to teach in the synagogue." He turned to Lucifer. "He is working miracles there. And He teaches with an authority unknown to these fools. You must do something, my prince. Everywhere He goes there is opposition and trouble..."

"Silence!" said Rugio. "Do not speak to our lord in so impertinent a manner!"

"Let him speak," said Lucifer, glaring at Rugio. "Miracles? Teaching? Authority? Jesus is indeed beginning to trouble us. His opposition is growing. I'm gratified that even this idiotic warrior of yours can see that!" He turned back to Jerob. "Now what did Jesus do?"

"I immediately knew He had come into the synagogue," said Jerob. " I intended to lie quietly within the man to avoid being detected. But suddenly, He looked in my direction and I began to scream out through the man at Jesus!"

"Astounding!" said Kara. "And why did you do such a foolish thing?"

"I was compelled," said Jerob humbly. "This Jesus looked in my direction and I suddenly found myself wrestling with the man's will to be set free."

Jerob stood and explained the situation as if he was reliving the horrifying event in front of the angels. He looked pleadingly at Lucifer. "Faint as it was, the man's desire for liberty was emboldened by the presence of Jesus and I found myself shrieking at Jesus to leave me alone. And I was not alone in this matter. I was accompanied by several other devils."

"And what happened?" asked Pellecus anxiously. "How did you resist?"

"I thought to expose Him," said Jerob. "I was desperate and thought if I made Him look ridiculous before the others in the synagogue it would bring trouble upon Him because of the offense He caused at Nazareth. I screamed out that He was the 'Holy One of God.' I intended to mock Him and make others think I was one of His disciples so as to discredit Him."

"And...?" said Lucifer with a resigned demeanor.

"Most humiliating of all," Jerob said, his head down, "Instead of responding to my accusations, Jesus turned to me and said, 'Be quiet! And come out of him!'

"I fought the man as best I could. But now he desperately sought to be free. I threw him down in a savage fit, hoping to injure him and thus bring charges against Jesus—anything that might deliver me from this brutal power."

He looked up quietly.

"In the end it was to no avail. I found myself thrown out and the man was uninjured. I have come to report this incident and to beg you for more spirits—legions of them. We cannot oppose this Man. I implore you, my prince, before we are all cast out and made powerless. Do something about Jesus..."

"Enough!" growled Rugio. "Get back to Capernaum! Rally the demons there and await further instructions. In the meantime continue your work. Continue the sickness and the religious deception among the people. Go!"

Jerob nodded and vanished.

There was a brief silence in the room as they considered what they had just heard. Finally Kara rose to speak.

"He has the authority to cast us out of men?" he said incredulously.

"It seems if the human's will responds to the Lord there is still hope for him," said Pellecus. "Jerob fought not only Jesus but the will of the human as well. If they ever begin to figure out the authority Jesus brings them…"

"This would explain the need for these disciples," said Lucifer, as if thinking aloud. "I finally understand. Perhaps the more humans who are brought up with such dangerous knowledge, the greater the authority they shall exert over us. After all—there is much illness we cause. Jesus cannot be everywhere at once. Thus, the disciples will become the hands and feet of the Messiah."

"And what are we to do?" asked Kara nervously. "Wait for Jesus or one of His bloody followers to oppose us as well? To destroy us in turn?"

Lucifer turned to the group.

"No Kara. We shall do exactly what Jerob begged of us," he said, looking at the charred mark he had made on the map. "We shall do something about Jesus."

Pellecus looked at Kara and Rugio, shooting them a glance that spoke of his confidence in Lucifer to lead them.

"What do you propose we do?" he asked Lucifer.

"Jesus puts great store in gathering disciples around Him," Lucifer said, as he stood and walked back to the window overlooking the city. "Perhaps we need a disciple of our own."

Chronicles of the Host
Kingdom Come

Capernaum was only the beginning. The Host watched as Jesus continued to gather men about Him, and called on people everywhere to return to their Father in Heaven. We had known all along that the Most High loved men. But when Jesus began calling the Father their Father as well, we began to realize the special place God held in His heart for these creatures who had turned on Him.

As for Jesus, these were golden days—days of popular and miraculous ministry; days of refreshing and teaching; days of wonderful fellowship and powerful deliverance throughout Galilee. It was at this time He called another follower to His side...one whom we thought an odd choice: Matthew, the tax collector.

A rather unsavory character by nature, Matthew was a pariah among his own people and was looked upon as a water carrier for the Roman state. And yet Jesus called him! Matthew obeyed immediately when Jesus invited him to follow him, leaving his tax table behind him—along with some stupefied people who stood in line to pay their tax.

What a marvel! Who but Jesus could dare bring Matthew the tax collector and Simon the Zealot under the same tent? And who but the enemy would see this as an opportunity to accuse Him?

"And so these men actually tore through the roof of the poor fellow's house and lowered the man in on his pallet!"

The astonished group listened with rapt attention as Andrew recounted the extraordinary healing of a man riddled with palsy, that happened a few days earlier in Capernaum. Peter looked on as his brother spoke, enjoying the retelling.

"How is it, I wonder, that your Master eats and drinks with sinners and tax gatherers?" came a voice from the other side of the table.

Andrew looked up from his meal at the Pharisees who were seated around the room talking and eating. One of them, by the name of Zichri, was looking at Andrew.

Andrew smiled at the man.

"What was that?" he asked.

Peter looked up as well when he heard Andrew's voice. Zichri gestured toward Jesus at the end of the table seated next to Matthew, whose spectacular hospitality they were now enjoying. Around Jesus and Matthew were a number of known misfits of society, all engaged in lively conversation.

Behind the grouping of Pharisees who occupied one-third of the table at which everyone was reclining stood Pellecus and a number of religious spirits, including Jerob. They were busily engaged in fanning the passions of these holy men so that they might find an occasion to accuse Jesus.

Pellecus liked what he saw in the Pharisees. This group of priests saw themselves as the caretakers of the Law, as the treasurers of the Covenant. Yet, in their selfish zeal to be right, they had defrauded the very religion which they sought to promote. Jesus represented to them another menace—an interloper whose casual handling of the Lord's Word was becoming increasingly dangerous. Too many people were beginning to fall under His sway and this did not set well with them.

"How vain is man and his religion," said Pellecus. "Observe how just being in the presence of true righteousness sets these legalistic religionists in a smoldering anger. Jesus will have His hands full with these fools."

Jerob nodded in agreement.

"It is true, my lord," he said to Pellecus, as many demons moved in and among the Pharisees, stirring them to further anger. "I have learned that among men religion is quite useful. From the eastern oriental kingdoms to Rome, from the most backwards tribes in the jungles to the simple desert nomads, men and women are swept away by their religious whims—and there is no place where religion is as brooding, melancholy, and tense as in Jerusalem."

The man continued to chide Andrew.

"I said, why does your Master, who says He is a Holy Man, take fellowship with such people? Matthew is known to us, and therefore we tolerate him and attend his feasts.

He wagged a finger toward Jesus, who saw and heard what followed.

"But your Master consorts with such people all the time! I therefore put it to you that a truly righteous man who claims to be a teacher from God would never behave in such a manner!"

The Pharisees agreed with him, some of them pounding the table with the flat of their hands. The room fell silent as Jesus rose and walked over to the men who were confronting Andrew. Peter remained silent. Simon the Zealot prepared himself for a fight.

"Why do you question these men?" asked Jesus. "It is not as if you are seeking the truth. But to answer your question, I go where people need Me. When you are sick you go to a physician, don't you? I go to those who are sick of heart and spirit and body, not to those who have no need or use of Me. I haven't come to call those who are righteous, but I have come to call sinners to repentance."

The Pharisees looked about at each other and at Andrew's beaming "any more questions?" grin. They murmured among themselves, seething at Jesus' presumption to judge between the righteous and sinners. Pellecus delighted in what was unfolding. If he could continue to stir up the already charged minds of the Pharisees, they would eventually turn on Jesus completely.

"As I observed, human religion always finds a way to corrupt the truth," Pellecus said. He smirked at the priests. "Like the vicious wolves that they are, they will soon turn on the very One who was born to them."

As they spoke, Aleph, one of John the Baptist's disciples, stood to be recognized. Having been encouraged by the Pharisees' line of questioning, he now posed a question to Jesus. Pellecus found this quite amusing. He even winked at the large warriors who stood constant vigil at Jesus' side.

"Bad enough the priests are turning on Him," said Pellecus. "Now it's one of His cousin John's disciples!" He looked at the others and laughed. "If only Kara were here to enjoy this!"

Aleph looked around the room before he spoke. The Pharisees were nodding with encouraging gestures that he should go ahead. Finally he did.

"Master," Aleph began. "Why is it the disciples of my master John and even the disciples of the Pharisees fast often, and yet Your own followers do not?"

Pellecus couldn't help but snicker at the discomfort he could feel welling up within Jesus' disciples. The Pharisees also enjoyed what was to them a most agreeable moment. Jesus, ignoring the antagonistic eyes following Him, looked with compassion at Aleph and began speaking.

"Aleph, the friends of the Bridegroom will not stop eating while He is with them," He explained, indicating His disciples. "These are with Me, and as long as I am here they shall eat. But some day the Bridegroom shall leave them. Then they shall fast."

"Going somewhere, Lord?" sneered Pellecus. Several demons snickered.

Jesus glanced at Pellecus who stepped uncomfortably back into the shadows and then vanished from the room. His aides followed him.

"I am teaching you something new," Jesus continued. He held up a skin of wine which one of the merchants had brought in with him. "Look at this wine skin. Now nobody would pour new wine into an old skin, would they? If they did it would burst the old skin and ruin the wine!"

He handed the skin back to its owner, who grinned at having been part of Jesus' illustration. Jesus continued speaking.

"Instead, new wine is poured into a new skin and both are preserved." He glanced in the direction of the Pharisees, who were huddled in counsel. "The old ways will no longer suffice. I teach you something new that will grow sweet like old wine."

The Pharisees stood and excused themselves from the meal. As they departed they muttered and sneered at Jesus and His followers. Jesus by now was seated once more and was speaking with one of Matthew's friends. After they left, Matthew approached Jesus and sat next to Him.

"I'm afraid, my Lord, You have offended the Pharisees," he said cautiously. "You make a dangerous enemy in them."

Jesus swallowed the bread He was eating and looked toward the door that the priests had just exited. He then turned back to Matthew.

"Jesus' enemies are our enemies," Simon the Zealot said forcefully. "Be they Roman or Jew."

Jesus smiled at His eager disciple.

"It will not be by your sword that our enemies will be conquered, Simon," said Jesus, looking at the warrior angels standing beside Him. He glanced at the powerful-looking sword held by one of them. "It will be a sword of the Spirit by which nations shall fall. And that not of angels nor of men. But of the Lord Himself!"

CHAPTER 9

"He has just raised a dead boy at Nain!"

The water at the pool of Bethesda had been quiet for many months. Nearby, ranks of people with all sorts of maladies awaited their chance to be healed. It was said that an angel would stir the waters from time to time and the first one to get into the pool while the water was moving might be healed.

Serus, recently assigned to Jerusalem, stood near the pool looking at the sick and elderly who dared believe this might be the day an angel would visit the pool. He felt compassion for them—so many sick and so few chances to be made well. He looked at Gabriel, who had accompanied him to the pool.

"You are only to stir the water upon the Lord's command," Gabriel reminded.

Serus noted the sick humanity that surrounded the edges of the pool. Many of them were attended by demons of illness who had either caused or exacerbated the malady being suffered. They looked up at Serus and Gabriel casually, as if they knew they had a right to their dark assignment.

"There are so many of them," he said, singling out one in particular. "This one will not live a week if he is not healed."

He pointed to a man who was dying of a condition in his lungs. Gabriel shook his head in sad agreement as the man gasped for air.

"Lucifer certainly has mastered the art of disease," he said.

A snicker of laughter arose upon those words as several demons looked up from their assigned humans and began to mock the archangel. Serus glared back at them.

"One day you shall all be overcome!"

"Poor Serus," said a demon who was causing a tumor within the brain of an old man. He was massaging the tumor as he spoke, his scaly hands gripping the man's head and his cat-like features smiling a grim grin. "This is only the beginning of our destruction of humans. These only fear for their lives on earth. They have no idea what awaits them."

A chill hit Serus as he thought of the millions of men and women who had already gone before and were awaiting an impending judgment no angel really understood, but of which they were all aware.

"They had better stand in line," said Gabriel to the demon. "For you and your master shall be judged first!"

The demons howled and jeered, cursing the holy angels.

"Nevertheless, leave the waters alone," cried out another, who was slowly taking away the sight of a middle-aged woman. "You spoil our work here!"

Laughter again among the wicked spirits.

"Jesus!"

Every eye, both angel and human, looked toward the narrow street. A Man in simple clothing appeared, attended by several people. The demons began muttering, some of them vanishing, others simply burying themselves in their unwitting victims. Gabriel and Serus bowed low at the sight of their Lord.

"Looks as if we shall not need to stir the waters today," said Gabriel discreetly.

Jesus continued to walk through the area while the crowd made room for Him as best they could. He seemed about to pass through altogether, when He suddenly stopped and looked at a man. The man looked up in return.

He was in his thirties, although he looked much older. He had been afflicted with a debilitating disease from birth, and had been at the pool for many years, living off the mercy of others and hoping for a chance to be healed by the angelic waters. Jesus knelt down to the man.

"Would you like to be healed?" Jesus asked.

Several demons growled at this question. They could no longer be seen, but they were still in the proximity of their charges. Jesus ignored them.

"I...I would love nothing else," he began, hardly looking at Jesus. "But when the angel stirs the water I am never first to the pool. You see, some of these have friends who wait with them and help them into the pool." He finally looked at Jesus. "I have nobody..."

"Here," said Jesus. "Take My hand, rise up...and walk."

Gabriel and Serus watched as a bright haze filled the area around Jesus and the man. No human eye saw this. But the demons did and began shrieking loudly, cursing Jesus and begging Him to go away.

At first the man seemed to resist, but slowly he rose, first on his knees and within seconds found himself standing with Jesus. The astonished crowd began to praise the Most High, calling to Jesus to come and heal them as well. The demons could no longer stand the anointing which accompanied the healing and began vaulting out of the area, blaspheming as they went.

The man could not believe what had happened to him! He was walking! He began jumping up and down and didn't even notice as Jesus slipped away. Others crowded around him and rejoiced with him. Some wondered if perhaps an angel might yet visit the pool, and stationed themselves even closer to its edge.

Gabriel watched as the Lord departed, accompanied as usual by several large warrior angels. He nodded at them as they passed by.

Serus pointed at another angel who loomed nearby, brooding over the scene. It was Kara.

"I didn't see you Kara," said Gabriel. "Another demonstration of our Lord's greatness, hmm? One day the world will be filled with such events!"

Kara smugly looked up at Gabriel.

"Perhaps, archangel," he said. "And Jesus has certainly made some friends today of these mongrels."

He glanced at a group of Pharisees who had come to the pool to investigate the commotion. As they received the story they seemed increasingly agitated. "But it seems He makes as many enemies as He does followers!"

"What do you mean, Kara?" asked Serus.

"I mean, you stupid angel, that today is the Sabbath. A day sacred to the Jews, you know."

The Pharisees approached Jesus.

Kara grinned at Gabriel and Serus and added, "And your Lord Jesus has just broken His own law!"

"Rabbi!"

Jesus turned to see a group of Pharisees approaching Him in the narrow street. He could also see Kara and Berenius accompanying them, as well as a host of unclean angels. The Pharisees approached Him smiling.

"We have just heard, rabbi, how You healed a man!"

The crowd that had begun gathering gasped at the news, turning to each other for more information about the healing. Some around the pool were still crying out to Jesus to come and heal them as well. Jesus looked at Kara and then back at the spokesman for the priests.

"Indeed," said Jesus. "The Lord has healed a man."

"You realize of course this is Sabbath," said another priest.

"Yes," said Jesus. "I love to celebrate the Sabbath. Especially in Jerusalem."

"And yet You celebrate it by breaking it," said their leader, the man Zichri who had challenged Him in Matthew's house. "How odd."

"Not so odd," said Jesus, looking at the crowd gathering about Him. Andrew and Peter had by now caught up with Jesus and were pushing their way near Him. "My Father is always working. And so must I."

Jesus then turned away from the astonished priests and disappeared down the street. Berenius moved upon Zichri's mind, and began fanning a sting of hatred for Jesus. Zichri scowled at the others and brought them into a nearby house where they might speak.

"This Man goes too far," he said as the group assembled around a table in the house that belonged to one of the priests. "Something must be done."

"Perhaps we should tell the High Priest?" offered one.

"We need not soil the High Priest's hands in this," said Zichri. "At least not yet. But if this Man begins convincing people He is the Son of God Himself, then we shall all be swept away!"

"*The man must be put away somehow...*" Berenius spoke into Zichri's mind. Kara looked on delightedly.

"We must meet further on this," said Zichri. "And we need not involve the High Priest...at least not yet."

"*Not unless it comes to blood...*"

Zichri looked at the others, fearful they could know his thoughts.

"Should it require sterner measures," said Zichri, "we shall certainly bring in the High Priest. The weight of his office would prove important."

As the men went their separate ways Zichri could only wonder what made him think such a thing. And yet there was a single thought which had begun to slowly emerge, pounding away at both his conscience and his resolve. He dared not speak it before. But now he could hardly contain the word.

"Murder," he whispered to himself, shuddering as he did.

31 A.D.

"Twelve of them?"

"Yes, my prince," said Pellecus. "They are His disciples. He is organizing them to do works in the name of the Most High."

Lucifer paced the ornate receiving room that Herod the Great had built and which was now used infrequently by his son. Pellecus, Rugio and Kara watched as their master thought about the implications of such a thing.

"So that's it," he finally said.

The others looked at each other and then back to Lucifer.

"What droll irony. The very creatures we tripped up in Eden, He will now empower to contest us. Interesting."

"And humbling," said Pellecus. "Should it prove successful."

"I could bring in a troop of warriors to crush His movement before it takes hold," offered Rugio. "Perhaps we could begin attacking their families with sickness…"

Kara sneered.

"Your warriors have yet to be successful at anything that contests the Most High," he said. "What makes you believe you could touch one of His own?"

Rugio raged at Kara.

"You proud, foolish spirit!" he yelled. "How dare you accuse me? You are the one who has misread everything the Lord has managed through humans!"

Pellecus only smiled as the two angels began bickering and blaming for the past efforts to stop the Seed's progress. Lucifer allowed this to go on only for a moment. He glanced pointedly at Pellecus and then put a stop to it.

"Enough!" he shouted. "If we have learned anything from this war it is that we cannot possibly win if we are not united. Human history has even shown such a truth. Herod, once called the Great, is now dust. We are meeting in the room in which he once played host to the world."

He glared at Rugio and Kara.

"Understand this—our only hope of surviving in a world in which we can have some sort of satisfaction—some vestige of authority—is to remain bound together. There will be time to settle scores later."

Rugio nodded in agreement with Lucifer's assessment. Kara shot a prideful look at Rugio before heartily affirming Lucifer's wisdom.

"He certainly made quite a showing for Himself on the mount," said Kara. "A lot of nonsense about the meek and the mournful and the poor being blessed. Astonishing! How can He possibly capture a world if He is only interested in its most depraved citizens?"

"I believe it is brilliant," said Pellecus, as they all seated themselves at Herod's massive table which was overlaid with gold and stood near the reception throne. "The great King taking the world through its weakest members. Quite humbling really. That sermon indicates the sort of Kingdom Jesus is establishing—a Kingdom not born out of conquest but out of love and humility."

Lucifer noted the throne on which Herod had once received the kings of the East not so long ago. He snickered a bit.

"If only Herod had been able to kill the Child back then," he said with a morose tone. "It would all be over now."

"And now His following increases," said Kara. "They come to Him from all over. Even from the Decapolis! Our hold on the people is no match for His authority."

Rugio, whose warriors were largely in charge of oppressing the people, admitted it was true.

"Wherever Jesus goes, He casts out our angels," he complained. "Some of my greatest warriors—even legions of them—have been thrown aside as if they were nothing by His mere words!"

"My lord, if He gives this sort of authority to these twelve, we will be in a dangerous predicament," added Kara. "Something must be done!"

"And so the problem remains of how to handle these disciples to whom He is granting authority," observed Pellecus, who wanted to steer the conversation back to forming a strategy. "There are indeed twelve of them, as Kara noted."

"Yes," said Lucifer. "I told you once that the more knowledge of the Most High these humans gained, the more authority they would exert over us. As I see it there are two areas of attack that concern us. The first is John in prison." He looked at Kara and added only, "See to it!"

Kara nodded.

"I thought perhaps a living memorial of their one-time prophet might serve our cause," continued Lucifer. "Instead John's followers persist. With John dead his followers will all but vanish. The same will happen to the followers of Jesus."

"You are proposing that Jesus be thrown into prison?" asked Kara timidly.

"I am proposing we handle Jesus as we do His cousin."

"You mean…"

"Murder," said Lucifer coldly. "The trick of course is how to get to Jesus."

Kara began laughing.

"You are suggesting we kill the Son of God?" asked Kara, exasperated now. He looked at Rugio. "Our chief warrior has just said that even a legion of his best cannot hold Him. How can we expect to kill Him?"

"I am not suggesting we kill Jesus the Living God," said Lucifer slyly. "I am suggesting we kill Jesus the living Man."

At that moment an aide to Rugio appeared in the room, begging to be received. Lucifer motioned for the angel to approach. Rugio was uncomfortable at the prospect of another bad report.

"What is it, Olor," said Rugio.

"Jesus…He has…"

"Well?"

The angel stood up straight.

"Jesus has just raised a dead boy at Nain. A widow's son!"

The three looked sullenly at Lucifer.

"So now He not only heals the sick He is raising the dead as well," he said finally.

Lucifer stood from the table. "Now you see why it is expedient that Jesus die. Let Him heal the sick and raise the dead. But what shall His followers do when He is Himself a corpse? Raise Him up?"

They laughed.

"No, Jesus must die. Don't forget that while He is the Lord incarnate, He is also a human. He will bleed just like any other human. And He will die."

"And the twelve?" asked Pellecus.

"We need not be concerned with all twelve," said Lucifer.

Rugio looked at the others, then spoke up.

"How so, my prince? If He has granted them all a measure of His authority..."

"True, Rugio," said Lucifer. "He has given a dozen men authority to act in His name. Let them. Let Him keep them all...except perhaps for one."

The others looked at him with puzzled expressions.

"One?" repeated Pellecus. "What do you mean, my lord?"

"All it takes is one," said Lucifer, smiling at them.

The demons shrieked and threw the woman down, making her froth around the lips. Matthew and Thomas tried to hold her fast, but Jesus told them to step aside. With one more command from Jesus, the devils screamed an oath and left. The woman was still trembling, but her countenance had already begun to change—especially around the eyes. She looked up curiously at Jesus.

"Tend to her," said Jesus. He gazed at the crowd as they called upon Him to heal this person or deliver that one from an evil spirit. The Galilean countryside was swarming with people with all sorts of afflictions, hoping the Man of miracles might work a miracle for them. The disciples tried to maintain some order, but it was becoming increasingly difficult.

"Thank you, my Lord," said the woman, drinking the water offered to her by one of the disciples. "You have freed me and I will ever serve You."

Jesus looked down at her with compassion. As she stood, she dusted herself off. Suddenly she was ashamed. Her clothing gave her away as a local prostitute. She looked away from Him.

"What is your name?" Jesus asked her.

"I am Mary," she answered softly. "Called Magdalene. But do not look upon me Lord, for I am unworthy."

"You are now a free woman," said Jesus. "Now go and use your freedom to glorify your Father in Heaven."

"I will, my Lord," she said, as he walked off. "I will ever serve You."

"All seven of them!" exclaimed Serus excitedly. He started laughing. "Some warriors they have on their side! Rugio will certainly be out."

"Yes, Serus. Seven devils were ordered out of the girl as a commander orders a soldier," said Michael, who had come down to look after Jesus' second excursion into Galilee. "But don't be proud. It isn't the work of the Host but of the Most High."

"His popularity in Galilee is unquestioned," Serus said, looking at the smiling throng. "They love Him here."

They were following along the crowds, still amazed at how Jesus dealt with each person. Some He healed right away; others He sent along to be healed later. To still others He gave words of affirmation and wonderful teaching. All was going well.

As they passed by a group of Pharisees, Jesus looked at them. They nodded politely as He passed. He suddenly stopped and turned His head, having perceived their thoughts. Standing in their midst was Achsan, a devil sent by Kara to stir up the Jewish leaders in Galilee. Michael and Serus spotted Achsan as well, who looked back at them with a harsh countenance. His pig-like face seemed out of place among men whose religion forbade the use of pork. Out of place...and yet strangely appropriate.

"I know what you are thinking," said Jesus.

The crowds stood back from the Pharisees, hoping that they would exchange great wisdom with this Holy Man. Andrew and the other disciples stood cautiously aware of all that was happening, concerned that the crowds not press in too close to Jesus. There had already been numerous rumors of an impending attempt upon His life.

The Pharisees looked up. Achsan ducked down among them, hurrying into the mind of the leader of the group who sneered at Jesus.

"You were saying that I am casting out devils through the power of the chief devil," continued Jesus. "Through the name of Beelzebub. It is with good reason he is called the Lord of the Flies. But hear me! A house divided against itself cannot stand. Satan knows this. If therefore by Satan I am casting out his own devils, then by Satan I am dividing his own kingdom."

Achsan was becoming increasingly agitated. Kara would not be pleased if Jesus got the better of these Jews. He tried to encourage the priests to answer back. But before they could even manage a thought, Jesus spoke again. Michael, ever alert to any possible move by the enemy, signaled other holy angels to move in around Jesus.

"I am casting out demons by the Spirit of God!" continued Jesus. He pointed at the men. "And if you say I am casting out demons by Satan, or if you accuse Me of being in league with Satan, then you are committing blasphemy against the Holy Ghost—a sin that cannot be pardoned. You are a generation of vipers! All you speak is evil because out of the abundance of the heart the mouth speaks and corrupts you!"

One of the young priests stepped out of the group and approached Jesus.

"Then show us a sign!" he demanded. "That's all we seek. Give us a reason to believe You."

The others grunted in agreement, and even a few of the bystanders muttered among themselves that this was a reasonable request. The disciples remained alert to the crowd. Michael and Serus were alert to enemies of other sorts.

"Only an evil generation seeks a sign," said Jesus. "And yet the only sign given will be the same one that was given to Jonah when he spent three days and nights in the belly of the great fish. The generation to whom he preached will rise up in condemnation of this One because they repented at his teaching and there is One in this present generation who is greater than Jonah!"

The priests looked at each other, astonished at Jesus' remarks. Jesus looked directly at Achsan, who was trying to remain aloof.

"This is how it is," continued Jesus. "When an unclean spirit leaves a man he departs for a while and then decides that he will perhaps attempt to reoccupy the same man. And when he is allowed back in he finds the place clean and restored. But because he was allowed back in the man finds himself in a state seven times worse than when the spirit first left. This is how it is with all of you."

The men were astonished at Jesus' authority. In fact, they could not even answer him. Achsan had by now abandoned the effort lest Jesus speak directly to him again. For their part, Michael and Serus enjoyed Jesus' humbling of both men and angels.

"He is making complete fools of the priests," said Serus, watching the seething Pharisees. "They are dumbfounded!"

"Yes," said Michael, as they walked on past the priests, who were now accusing Jesus to anyone who might care to listen to them. "He is also making bitter enemies. I'm afraid our work shall become more urgent as this continues."

"I can assure you it will, archangel" came the voice of Achsan, who cursed the two angels and then vanished.

Kara watched John's slow demise in the cell in which Herod was keeping him. Too dangerous to set free and too popular to have executed, John represented a problem to the king. Nevertheless, for the sake of his wife and to placate her venom against the holy man, John was kept in custody. He would never tell her that, in comparison to some of the other prisoners in the Antonia, John lived in relative comfort.

Looking at John, however, one would not be able to see much comfort in his circumstances. Herod allowed John's disciples to attend to him occasionally, and they brought news to him of the outside world, particularly of the growing ministry of Jesus. In fact, John spoke of little else.

"Look at him Berenius," said Kara, standing near John. "Languishing in prison. A dreary end for one who came into the world so dramatically."

Berenius nodded in agreement, his grin casting an yellowish glow in the dark chamber seen only by Kara. He walked over to John and knelt down next to him. John's eyes were bleary and his body was becoming increasingly emaciated. For the past several days he had refused food.

"Is this how the Lord treats the forerunner of the Messiah?" asked Berenius mockingly. "I should be worried if I were Jesus!"

Kara nodded.

At that moment a heavy door could be heard opening and a small shaft of light pierced the room. Some words were exchanged from down a hallway followed by footsteps. It was one of John's disciples, bringing him news and nourishment. The man moved past Kara and Berenius, oblivious of their presence and began cleaning John's dirty face with a cloth he had brought with him.

The man talked of Jerusalem and John's family. He then began to speak of Jesus, telling John of His most recent excursion into Galilee. Ordinarily John was buoyed by the reports about Jesus. But this time he simply stared vacantly ahead. John finally turned his head toward the man.

"Justus," he said in a raspy voice.

"Yes, I am here."

"Tell me something, Justus. Is this Jesus…is this Jesus of Nazareth the One we have been looking for?"

Justus was surprised at the question.

"Is He what?" he could only manage.

"Is this the Christ?" John pleaded. "Or should we be looking for another?"

Kara looked at Berenius and nodded approvingly.

"He is giving way," he said looking at the man. "He is slowly breaking. He cannot believe the One whose sandals he was unfit to tie should abandon him."

Berenius smiled.

"I don't know what you mean," said Justus, confused at John's question and becoming concerned about his mental state.

"You must go to Him," said John. "You must ask Him if He is the One or if another is coming. You must go to Him today."

The man nodded and agreed he would. He carefully placed fruit and bread near John, then left to do his bidding. John bowed his head low, alternately praying and weeping.

"John is finished. That should put fear in the minds of the disciples, if nothing else," said Bernius.

"Finished, yes," admitted Kara. "But much too slowly. Lucifer has ordered him destroyed. And soon."

Berenius grinned a knowing grin.

"I do have a confession to make," he said.

"Go on," said Kara suspiciously.

"I have been seeding in the mind of Herodias against the day Lucifer orders John's death," Berenius said proudly.

"Really?" said Kara, interested in the involvement of Herod's wife who loathed John. "And…?"

"Herod's birthday celebration is coming up in a few weeks," said Berenius. "And Herodias is planning quite a surprise for her husband."

Kara nodded with satisfaction.

"I always liked surprises."

Chapter 10

"A farmer went out to sow his seed..."

"I have a story for you..."

The fisherman's boat from which Jesus spoke swayed gently in the water. The Sea of Galilee, well-fished by the disciples, was now host to the greatest Fisher of Men who ever lived. The crowd sat on the bank, enjoying the teaching of this remarkable Man whose healings and miracles were drawing people from all over. Young and old, men and woman, sick and well, rich and poor—all of them sat together as one taking in the teaching of this Galilean Holy Man.

"A farmer went out to sow his seed," Jesus continued.

He acted out the motions of a man throwing seed here and there as if He were planting. The people smiled in amusement.

"As he was scattering the seed, some fell along the path where he was walking, and the birds quickly came and ate it up. Some fell on places that were rocky, where it did not have much soil. It sprang up quickly, because the soil was very shallow. But when the sun came up, the plants were scorched, and they withered because they had no chance to root. Other seed fell among thorns and weeds, which grew up and choked the little plants and overwhelmed them."

He patted a young boy on the head and smiled at him.

"But...other seed fell on good soil, where it produced a crop—a hundred, sixty or thirty times what was sown. Now—he who has ears, let him hear."

The angels gathering in and around the crowd included Crispin, who loved to watch Jesus teach. In fact, he almost forgot himself, becoming one of the crowd rather than an angel on assignment. When he saw others of the Host scattered around the crowds, he nodded to them. Finally he saw Rufus, a fellow wisdom angel who taught at the Academy of the Host, escorting a group of angels who were observing Jesus.

"Such brilliance!" said Crispin, as Rufus drew near. Rufus could only nod with enthusiasm at the simplicity of Jesus' teaching which cut so deeply. The people were slow to disperse, watching for the next miracle, or talking among themselves about this recent teaching. Many of them did not quite understand the story of the farmer."

"He talks to them in these wonderful stories," said Rufus, as the disciples broke off from the crowd and followed Jesus. "These parables which illustrate the point of His lesson in ways even humans can grasp."

"Only those who have ears to hear," corrected Crispin. "Most of these are searching for a day's meal rather than a life's purpose and are thereby missing His point altogether. Even the disciples are having trouble with this one!"

They followed along to a more remote spot on a hillside near the great lake which Andrew and Peter knew so well. As they sat down, the disciples began asking Jesus to interpret the story for them. Jesus looked up at the men into whose lives He was pouring His own.

"You are given a great privilege," He began, breaking off a piece of bread and eating. "To you is given the mysteries of the Kingdom of God. I speak in parables so that in hearing them they may not understand."

"But what good is a parable that cannot be understood?" asked Thomas. "What good is a secret that has no meaning?"

"Thomas," Jesus answered. "Those who truly have ears to hear shall hear; those who truly seek to understand will gain understanding. The secret of the Kingdom is that there is no secret!"

The disciples looked at each other, nodding in agreement as if understanding, but most of them were still trying to figure out just what their Master meant. Crispin and Rufus, however, exchanged knowing glances.

"Think of it this way. The seed the farmer was sowing was the Word of God. Those along the path are like the ones who hear, and then the devil comes and takes away the Word from their hearts, so that they may not believe and be saved. Those on the rock are the ones who receive the Word with joy when they hear it, but because they have no root—remember the soil was shallow—they believe for a while, but in the time of testing they fall away. The seed that fell among thorns stands for those who hear, but as they go on their way they are choked by life's worries, riches and pleasures, and they do not mature.

"But the seed on good soil stands for those with a noble and good heart, who hear the Word, retain it, and by persevering produce a crop. Don't you understand?"

They remained silent, so He continued.

"Think of it this way: No one lights a lamp and hides it in a jar or puts it under a bed. Instead, he puts it on a stand, so that those who come in can see the light. That is what a light is for—to be seen by others. In the same way, there is nothing hidden that will not be disclosed, and nothing concealed that will not be known or brought out into the open. Nothing! Therefore, consider carefully how you listen when I say that you must have ears to hear. For whoever has, will be given more; and whoever does not have, even what he thinks he has will be taken from him."

After the men reflected for a few moments, John looked at the others and then spoke.

"That is why You say there are some who hear yet never hear," he said. "Understanding the Kingdom is not as much a matter of the mind as it is the heart!"

"Just so," said Jesus, "although the Kingdom's entrance is through the mind and the heart. It is through knowledge that one gains understanding. But one must first seek knowledge earnestly and with great passion."

Jesus looked around as if considering His next illustration and then He turned to the men and continued.

"The Kingdom of Heaven is like..." He paused and took a coin out of a small bag nearby. Holding up the coin He continued. "It is like treasure hidden in a field. When a man finds it, rather than tell everyone right away, he first hides it again, and then in his joy sells all he has and buys that field. Or, the Kingdom of Heaven is like a merchant looking for fine pearls. When he finds one of great value, he sells everything he has and buys it. Do you see? The Kingdom must first be secured by a man and then it becomes powerful in his life and something to be told!"

"Peter, you are a fisherman," He said, glancing at the brother of Andrew. "You know these waters well."

"Yes, too well," said Andrew, referring to the recent lack of catch. The men laughed aloud. Peter smiled at being the center of the story.

"Nevertheless, here is a story you will understand. The Kingdom of Heaven is like a net that was let down into the lake and caught all kinds of fish."

"Not like Peter's net then," chimed in Andrew.

They all laughed.

"No, this net was full," continued Jesus. "And so the fishermen pulled it up on the shore. Then they sat down and sorted the good fish in baskets, but threw the bad fish away. This is how it will be at the end of the age. The holy angels will come and separate the wicked from the righteous and throw them into a fiery furnace, where there will be weeping and gnashing of teeth. A horrible fate. Have you understood all these things?"

"Yes," they replied.

"This is why we have such conflict with the religious leaders in this land. You see, every teacher of the law who has been instructed about the Kingdom of Heaven is like the owner of a house who brings out of his storeroom new treasures as well as old. But they instruct from what they presume is the Kingdom—so they are like blind men who are only leading other blind men into the ditch."

As Jesus finished speaking, the crowds once more were pressing in, breaking into their private moment together. He ordered the men to prepare the launch so they might take off across the lake, escaping the crowds to preach the Kingdom elsewhere.

Crispin and Rufus watched as the little boat headed out across the great sea. The accompanying warriors stayed with the boat as always. The people continued watching the disciples' little boat as it headed into the middle of the lake.

"The people who live on the other side of Galilee are in for a wonderful surprise," said Crispin. "Quite an unexpected visit!"

Rufus nodded in agreement and ordered his angels back to Heaven with him. Crispin vanished with them. When they had left, two more angels appeared on the banks of the lake. They also watched the little boat.

"I would say there shall be another unexpected visit—upon the water," one of the angels said.

"See to it," said the other.

It was Rugio.

Above the little boat, which was about midway across the lake, the warrior angels who were with Jesus cast a weary eye. Above them, swirling like angry hornets were hundreds of demons. They seemed to be gathering in a great cloudy, dark mist. Above them was Rugio and his commander Nathan.

"They have spotted us," said Nathan. "The warriors with Jesus."

"Never mind them," said Rugio. "They cannot abandon their post to do battle. Besides we have them outnumbered." He smiled at the clouds beginning to broil around the dark morass of his warriors who were creating a violent disturbance above the lake.

"I sense fear among the fishermen," Rugio observed. "They, too, see this storm brewing. If there is one thing that paralyzes the Lord's ability to work among men it is fear. Let their fears take them to the bottom of the lake!"

On board the cramped little boat, the men were indeed watching the skies. Andrew looked at his brother, who was maintaining a steady hand on the rudder. Simon glanced back, shaking his head doubtfully. The others, particularly those who were not fishermen, also looked at the blackening sky. The winds began to rise.

They looked at Jesus who was asleep on the deck, leaning on one of the nets.

"Shall we awaken Him?" asked Thaddeus.

"Not yet," answered Simon, looking up at the sky's first flash of lightning. "Not just yet. But steady your oars, my friends. And steady your hearts."

"The storm is almost at the ready," reported Nathan. "Shall we commence?"

Rugio looked at the waves, which were beginning to rock the boat with greater and greater intensity. He gave the command and the hellish angels started swirling about faster and faster, creating a maelstrom within the air, bringing the storm to its greatest fury.

The boat began tipping violently. Sheets of rain blinded the men, droplets cutting into them like tiny needles. The waves lapped into the boat, splashing the men and causing some of them to panic. Rugio and Nathan enjoyed their handiwork, anticipating the drowning of the men.

"Even if Jesus should live this will deal a blow to the Kingdom," said Rugio. "What with John's upcoming termination, we shall soon see Jesus' Kingdom dreams vanish."

Aboard the boat, the men were rowing for land with all of their strength. But they were so turned around and being tossed about so violently they could scarcely make out where the land was, or if they were even going in a straight line. Finally, Simon gave the order to awaken Jesus.

"Master! Master!"

Jesus opened His eyes and saw the frightened faces of His disciples.

"Master we are going to die if You do not do something!"

Jesus stood up and looked at the men who were fighting the storm but whose tears had gotten the better of them. Jesus gazed into the sky as a lightning bolt exploded nearby.

"Why are you afraid?" he shouted. "Where is your faith?"

The men looked at each other. Simon was still barking orders.

"We are taking on too much water," he shouted. "Keep bailing!"

Jesus moved to the front of the boat which was dipping down into the sea and then rocking violently back He held on to the side, looked into the sky and spoke.

"PEACE!" He shouted into the sky.

Rugio and Nathan were knocked backwards upon the declaration of peace by Jesus. The devils who were spinning the storm into its greatest violence were suddenly flung into disorganization. Many, upon hearing the Lord's voice, shrieked in fear and began scattering.

"Hold that storm together!" ordered Rugio.

"BE STILL!" shouted Jesus.

When these words were spoken, all coordination fell apart and the demons scattered like a flock of frightened birds. The storm quickly subsided. Even Nathan was thrown back into the heavenlies for a moment at this great command. Only Rugio remained stubborn and defiant. He could not believe the carnage Jesus had made of his warriors with just a few simple words.

The men were exhausted as the surface of the lake calmed down. Jesus moved among them and sat back down. They could only whisper among themselves that even the winds and the sea obeyed this Man!

"Listen to their amazement," said Nathan. He then mocked them in Andrew's voice, "Even the winds and the waters obey Him!"

"Of course," said Rugio. "He created the winds and the waters."

"Then why did we even make this attempt?" Nathan asked scornfully. "All this did was build greater confidence among the disciples!"

"I was hoping to see some of these wretched humans destroyed," said Rugio.

"So how do we fight Him?" asked Nathan. "He cannot be attacked."

"Not from the outside, perhaps," agreed Rugio. "But I believe Lucifer is working on something from within."

Nathan wasn't sure what Rugio meant, but he understood this to be information to which he was not privy. They watched the boat as it finally turned toward a distant shore.

Rugio smirked. "Who is the prince over Gadara?"

"That is Lucien," said Nathan. "He is prince over the entire province of Peraea."

"Ah yes," said Rugio, recalling a bitter conflict he once had with Lucien because of his close alliance with Kara. "That proud and petty prince. I believe you should warn him of an immediate problem."

Nathan looked at Rugio with a puzzled expression.

"It looks as if they are bound for Gadara," Rugio said with delight. "Tell Lucien the Most High is coming to call."

Gadara was the capital of the Roman province of Peraea. It was on the summit of a mountain about six miles southeast of the Sea of Galilee. It was a rugged territory, and between the lake and the town was a deep ravine which was dotted with many tombs carved in the limestone cliffs.

The disciples did not frequent this region, preferring the more familiar towns to the northwest of the lake. Nevertheless, upon Jesus' command the boat made shore near Gadara and within minutes they were disembarking.

"I never liked this place," muttered Simon, as he and Andrew tied the boat up. "It's all the tombs. I hear the land is haunted by strange creatures."

The other disciples listened. They, too, had heard the strange tales about this country. They all felt as if they were being watched.

High above them on the summit stood Lucien who, along with Nathan and several of Lucien's angels, kept an eye on the party as it climbed ashore. Lucien conferred with his aides, trying to determine the best course of action.

"Rugio's orders are to hold this land," repeated Nathan. "Jesus' Kingdom must not gain a foothold here."

Lucien turned to Nathan.

"Tell your master Rugio that Gadara is not Capernaum," he said proudly. "There are not adoring crowds here to fawn upon Jesus. They will come and go with little to show for their efforts—just as happened in Chorazin and Bethsaida."

Lucien had mastered the art of engendering fear among humans. Years of legend had developed around the tombs which, when coupled with Lucien's loose control of his devils, promoted a sense of chaos and sheer horror among humans who might journey through that part of the land. He particularly prided himself on his ability to repulse even the most stalwart human through the shrieking spirits whose pig-like faces turned human blood to ice. He turned to Korah.

"Bring that fool out of the tombs," he said. "These men are tired and afraid. Perhaps a bit more fear will turn them away."

Korah nodded and vanished.

"And now, Nathan," said Lucien with disdain, "I will demonstrate how we handle disciples in Gadara!"

"What was that?" asked Thomas.

He scanned the hillside in the direction of the scream he heard. He saw nothing.

"There it is again," said another.

"Look there!" shouted Andrew.

Far away on the brim of a hill was the figure of a man. As he drew closer they saw he was completely naked. His loping, irregular stride added to the eeriness of the picture. Some of the disciples looked for possible weapons. Judas and Thomas climbed back into the boat. Jesus, however, simply watched the man.

The man, probably in his twenties, was badly scarred and bruised. Several open sores were bleeding, particularly on his arms and legs. He was drooling out of the corner of his mouth. On his legs and arms were what remained of shackles that the locals had used in an attempt to keep him secure and to stop his roaming around the countryside. But under the demons' influence, the man had actually broken the chains that bound him and was loosed to terrorize the region.

The most striking feature of this naked, dirty man was his eyes. They were like black coals with a slight reddish-tinged center. The man smelled like an animal, growling and grunting as he came.

Korah, the demon under Lucien who controlled the man, kept him running among the tombs, slipping on the sharp rocks and harassing the farmers nearby. Nobody wanted to come near the tombs anymore because of him. Ordinarily whenever he confronted some poor wretch who wandered into his domain, he would dispatch his victim quickly with a few simple screams and flails of the arms. The dangling shackles added to the scariness of the scene. This time was different.

The nearer Korah got to the man, the more agitated he became. As Jesus came into sight it was as if Korah was beginning to lose a measure of control of the man whose body he now inhabited. How could this be? The man had given himself over completely. Now the two were in a contest!

Korah managed to control the man's voice and in a guttural, but conflicted voice, he threw the man on the ground before Jesus and shouted, "What have I to do with you, Son of the Most High God?"

"Come out of him at once!" commanded Jesus.

The men around Jesus stared in wonder.

"I beg of you, Most High, do not torment me before my time!"

"Come out of him at once!" Jesus repeated.

"I beg you, Most High!"

"What is your name?" Jesus asked.

"We call ourselves Legion," Korah answered. "Because we are so many. We had permission to enter this house. Leave us alone!"

"You must leave him now," said Jesus again.

Korah was frantic. He could feel his hold on the man slipping away even as the man's mind was beginning to right itself. Then he spotted some swine on a hillside near the ravine.

"Son of God, I beg you to allow us to enter those swine rather than torment us," Korah begged.

Jesus looked at the swine.

"These people are filthy, Most High," Korah continued. "They violate the law by keeping these pigs. Send us into them that we might..."

"Go!" Jesus commanded. "Go into the swine!"

Suddenly the man convulsed violently, swinging his fists and almost hitting Andrew with the end of one of the chains dangling from his arms. He frothed and shook and fell to the ground. Then he was quiet.

The demons, in the meantime, headed straight into the swine. Upon their entrance the pigs went berserk and began stampeding, nearly running down their herdsman. The pigs headed straight for the cliffs and in an instant plunged over the side, while the devils inside shrieked with delight!

Jesus looked down at the man. His eyes were clear now—beautiful green eyes looking up at Jesus. He moved to cover his nakedness. Jesus ordered that clothes and food be given to the man.

When the local people arrived on the scene and saw the man in his right mind they were astonished. They also were seized with fear because of what had happened to the swine. Afraid Jesus might destroy their commerce, they begged the men to go away. And so Jesus and his disciples left Gadara, but not before He instructed the man who had been delivered to tell everyone what God had done for him.

Atop the summit, watching them as they left, Nathan stood with Korah. Grim and silent, he was glad they were leaving. But he also sensed he had lost a major portion of his authority in that land.

"So this is how you handle disciples in Gadara," Nathan could not help but say. "I will see to it that Rugio is given a full report!"

He vanished.

Korah turned to his aides, who were beginning to reassemble after leaving the drowning swine.

"Let Rugio report," he said sullenly. "I answer to Kara. But I shall be interested to see how they handle the disciples in Jerusalem."

Chronicles of the Host
Third Galilean Journey

By now the Lord's fame had spread throughout the land. He began a third ministry excursion into Galilee, including a second visit to His hometown of Nazareth. Once more, the people there rejected Him and He marveled at their unbelief.

Jesus went about the villages and cities of Galilee, preaching the Kingdom of God and healing the sick. He also began sending the disciples out by twos to minister in His name and authority. Thus did the Host assign angels to accompany the disciples as they set out to minister through the countryside.

He told them they were going out as "sheep among wolves" and that having Himself been accused of being in league with Beelzebub, the disciples could expect no less harassment. And so they went out and many were healed and delivered.

As for the Host, we quietly awaited the next move by the enemy. It was not long in coming, although it was unexpected. We had thought the enemy would strike at Jesus directly. Instead, he chose to attack Him through His cousin John...

Herod's birthday was proving to be one of his usual excessive triumphs. Exotic and imported foods and wines from all over the Roman world had been prepared. Lavish gifts and flowery congratulations poured in from various Roman governors and officials, as well as several senators. He had received numerous praises from foreign kings and diplomats as well. Herod loved birthdays and this one was no exception.

Next to him at the table, Herodias was sipping wine from the south of Gaul. It was an important gift from an important governor, and they enjoyed it in the governor's honor. She preferred the wine to the local vintages which were much too sweet for her taste—but then she had grown to hate all things Judean. She poured another cup of wine for her husband, as she had been doing the entire evening.

Watching the proceedings, Kara and Berenius were quite gratified. They had put into Herodias' heart an idea that would put an end to John the Baptizer once and for all.

"Keep filling his cup, my dear," purred Kara, as Herod sloppily grabbed the goblet and toasted with one of his military officers. "In a moment Berenius, it will be time for our drama to begin."

"So this is your plan to exterminate John?" came a voice. "To allow Herod to celebrate his ridiculous birthday?"

Kara turned to see Lucifer standing behind him.

"Humans enjoy celebrating the day of their miserable birth," shrugged Kara. "Berenius is about to give Herod quite a present."

"You've heard about the Gadarenes?" Lucifer asked.

"Yes, of course," said Kara. "I immediately stripped Lucien of that principality and gave it to Korah. At least Korah faced the Christ even if he was beaten by Him."

"In the meantime we have lost that region," snapped Lucifer. "The man who was delivered is busily telling the world about the Man Jesus and how He helped him. We must act quickly in this matter."

"Don't worry, my prince," assured Kara. "It begins tonight when we settle the books with John. Once he is gone, the whole rotten movement will begin falling apart from within."

Lucifer smiled. He was looking forward to John's death.

"And how do you know John will die?" he asked. "Why should Herod kill a man he fears?"

"Because the only thing greater than Herod's fear is Herod's pride," said Kara. "And Berenius is about to prove that point now."

CHAPTER 11

"I want the head of John the Baptizer."

Herodias looked across the banquet hall and nodded at the musicians, who began playing a tune that was strange to Herod. He turned to Herodias, his eyes becoming bleary from the wine.

"My lord, I have a special birthday surprise for you," she said.

Herod smiled at her and stood to announce that Herodias was about to present to him a special gift. When he sat down all the people toasted him and awaited the presentation.

"What is that music…Greek?" he muttered to Herodias.

"No, sire," she purred. "Something more exotic…something from Mesopotamia. A Babylonian dance. And performed by my daughter!"

Herod looked up, surprised to see Herodias' daughter enter the room in an exquisite Babylonian dress from the neo-empire days. He smiled and toasted her with his goblet. The girl danced through the hall, always keeping her eyes on the king. Herod watched her in stupefied satisfaction until the dance was finally over.

The room burst into applause for the wonderful dance and then the party guests were treated to a marvelous flaming dessert from

Egypt. Herod thanked the girl, who bowed before the king and then sat next to her mother.

Kara was watching as Berenius moved in between Herodias and the king. She hugged her daughter for her performance. The girl, about 15, was quite beautiful and many men in the room found her very attractive. She nodded to the guests who looked her way and were toasting or otherwise complimenting her.

Herodias looked at Herod with a sensual gaze. He looked back at her and smiled.

"What is it, my pet?" he asked her.

"My daughter wanted nothing more than to bless the king on his birthday," she said. "I do hope you were pleased, my love."

"Of course," Herod answered. "She was exceptional."

"She loves her great king," Herodias continued. "I wonder if perhaps the king should not grant her a gift as well. How noble that would be. Think of the stories these men of prestige would take back to their nations—of the magnificence and generosity of Herod the tetrarch!"

"A gift?" Herod asked.

"But what gift could Herod give that his great presence has not already satisfied?" she asked. "It could be no ordinary gift. What might a child want that a king could give her?"

Berenius moved in and began to whisper into Herod's mind.

"If the child was given the choice in the matter, you would look like both a great king and a great father to Herodias' daughter..."

"Perhaps we should let the child choose," offered Herod.

"But from what, my lord?" asked Herodias, glancing at her daughter next to her.

"What does it matter? What can a child wish for? Give her anything...grant her half your kingdom! The gesture will be noble and the child will choose something childish..."

"Hmm..." Herod considered aloud.

"And you shall have made the greatest gesture any king has ever made..."

Herod stood, somewhat shakily, and the crowd immediately became quiet. Herodias signaled the musicians to stop playing as well.

"In as much as my wife's daughter gave me such joy on my birthday," he began, I have decided to give her a gift in return." He wagged his finger. "But not just any gift! Oh no. I will give the daughter of Herodias anything she wants...even up to half my kingdom!"

Gasps filled the room as Herodias smiled to herself and then feigned a great shock as if overwhelmed by the gesture. She turned to Herod with great humility.

"Great king," she said. "You are making this offer before all of these great men? Such an important vow?"

Herod relished the moment.

"Of course, my wife," he answered. "I vow this before every person in this room! Up to half my kingdom!"

Herodias and her daughter whispered back and forth for a moment. Berenius, still in between the two looked over at Kara, beaming. The guests awaited the announcement.

"Well child, what shall it be?" Herod asked, filling his cup once more. "A palace? A stable of horses? A magnificent barge like Cleopatra once had?"

"No, sire" she said. "I want the head of John the Baptist."

Herod blinked vacantly a couple of times and set down his goblet.

"You want the head of John?"

He glared at Herodias, who only smiled back.

"Yes," she said. "I want it now. On a platter."

Herod began to stammer.

"This your doing," he said angrily to Herodias.

"Remember your vow," she said pointedly.

Herod looked about him. All eyes were upon him awaiting his decision. How could he possibly back down in front of all of these men—his royal peers and embassies from other nations. How could he back down in front of the Roman officials? Perhaps they would read such a thing as a sign of weakness. He looked at his chief aide and nodded. The aide bowed and left the room.

Lucifer, Kara and Berenius watched as the man took two guards with him and went down into the room where John was being held. John seemed to know what was to happen to him as they unshackled him.

"Is it time?" John asked weakly.

"Get on your knees," they ordered. "And look that way."

John began praying, grateful his imprisonment was over and thankful he had fulfilled his mission. He had ushered in the Messiah; now he could leave the world knowing Israel would one day be redeemed. He got down on both knees and held his head up, continuing to pray. He smiled even as the guard unsheathed his weapon. The sword came swiftly.

When it was over, the guards did as they were instructed and brought the head into the banquet hall. Herodias inspected the bloody basket and then nodded for the guards to take it away. She sat next to the king, who had determined to spend the next several days getting thoroughly drunk.

Standing next to John's body, Kara and Berenius congratulated each other. Lucifer joined the brief celebration as well, before turning to the next task.

"And now for Jesus," he said. "This should shake Him. With John out of the way, we must find a way to destroy Jesus. Your use of Herodias has further inspired my hope for finding someone close to Jesus who might be of use to us."

"But who?" asked Berenius. "I have been studying these men. They all seem solidly behind Him."

"Keep watching, Berenius," said Lucifer. "We must find a way in. It's difficult to be sure. The people love Him."

"Why shouldn't they?" sneered Kara. "He recently fed some five thosand of them with a few fragments of food. He is buying their loyalty."

"So I heard," said Lucifer. "But remember, Kara. Loyalty that can be bought easily can be sold just as easily. Perhaps we can buy it back."

"Do you really believe one of His own will betray Him?" asked Kara.

"I know something about men," said Lucifer. "I also know something about betrayal!"

Chronicles of the Host

Hard Words at Capernaum

Upon hearing of his cousin's death, Jesus returned to Galilee to the city of Capernaum, where His ministry seemed to have centered itself. Capernaum was located near the northwestern shore of the Sea of Galilee. It stood on the major road between Damascus in Syria, pointing southward throughout central Israel and beyond. The Host watched as many miracles occurred in or near the city, including numerous healings: Peter's mother-in-law, the centurion's servant, a paralyzed man and the casting out of demons. We also witnessed the miraculous feeding of the four thosand from only seven loaves of bread and a few fish!

And yet, it was also at Capernaum that the ministry of Jesus reached a critical point, as His teaching became less focused on the Kingdom of Heaven and more focused on His grim destiny—of blood and death—and many began falling away...

32 A.D.

"Capernaum again?" grumbled Thomas. "These people don't even like us!"

The disciples had recently come from Tiberias, where they had fed great numbers of people. Now those same people had followed them to Capernaum. It would be another long day for the disciples.

"Look at them," said Judas scornfully. "All they want is food."

"You are not a Galilean," said Andrew. "These people need hope."

"They may need hope," said Judas, who was tugging at his oar, "but it is bread they will get!"

Peter had heard enough. He joined the conversation and spoke to Judas.

"When Jesus broke the bread and fed all of those people with seven fish and two loaves of bread, He gave them more than food, Judas. He gave them hope. That was our task in Tiberias. And that shall be our task here in Capernaum."

Judas simply looked up at the big fisherman but didn't answer. Peter was too hot-blooded to engage in an intelligent dialogue. Besides, Judas had already determined that Jesus' popularity would soon see Him proclaimed King. He had already refused a crown once. He dare not continue to refuse. Once Jesus was made king, then perhaps He could attain a truly important position and be rid of the rest of them.

Many people flocked to Jesus after they disembarked. He spent the day healing and ministering as always. His disciples accompanied Him as well, teaching of the greatness of Jesus and telling the people He was a Man of God. That evening, as the group sat around a room that had been offered to them, Jesus began to speak.

"Tomorrow, it is time to begin a new teaching," He said.

The disciples looked at each other. Perhaps He was finally going to proclaim Himself King of this Kingdom He had been talking about for so long. Or perhaps there was some other wonderful revelation He would make.

"It will be a difficult teaching for many. Many will fall away because of it. But this must be so that the Son of Man might fulfill the purposes for which He has come."

That evening the disciples went to sleep wondering what the next day would bring. Judas was particularly interested, hoping that finally this popular movement would become an uprising that would sweep them all into authority with Jesus as their king!

"There they come," said Judas. "Just as I said"

The men scanned the lake and could see sails headed into Capernaum. Many had already arrived from Tiberias and elsewhere, having enjoyed Jesus' miraculous tour in their region. Jesus joined the men and saw the growing numbers of people. He led them to the synagogue. One of the men, a leader in the Tiberias community approached Jesus.

"Rabbi, when did You get here?" he asked.

Jesus looked at the man, all decked out in his official garb and answered, "I tell you the truth, you are looking for Me, because I have fed so many people with the loaves—that's all you are interested in."

He raised His voice so those around could hear.

"Do not work for food that spoils and only satisfies for a short time, but work for food that endures to eternal life, which the Son of Man will give you."

And so they all began to seat themselves in an open area in front of the synagogue. The disciples, as usual, seated themselves near their Master. Simon the Zealot, ever on guard, stationed himself on a bit of high ground to watch for any possible attempts on Jesus' life.

When they had settled down, the people began to ask him questions, as was the custom by now. "What work does God ask us to do?"

"That is a very important question," Jesus said. "The work of God is this: you must believe in the One He has sent." And then with great passion, "You must believe."

One of the men from Capernaum, who had been prompted by a local Pharisee, stood and asked, "But what miraculous sign will You give that we may see it and believe You? What will You do? Our forefathers ate the manna in the desert; as it is written: 'He gave them bread from Heaven to eat.'"

"Listen to me! It is not Moses who has given you the bread from Heaven. It was the Lord. But more importantly, My Father gives you the true bread from Heaven. This is the bread of God who comes down from heaven and gives life to the world."

Several Pharisees who were listening began to talk among themselves heatedly. The disciples near them kept an eye on them in case they might have any design on Jesus. Then another man came and asked Jesus: "Sir, from now on give us this bread."

"That what I am telling you! I am the Bread of Life," Jesus said. "He who comes to Me will never go hungry, and he who believes in Me will never be thirsty. But as I told you, you have seen Me and still you do not believe."

Clouds of holy angels had begun to arrive in large numbers around Capernaum—something important was stirring. Berenius and many unholy angels also were there to witness this critical moment.

"He is rather harsh today, isn't He?" Berenius remarked to his aide.

"Not really," said the aide. "He is always rebuking the people for their disbelief."

"Something different is happening today," said Berenius, surmising the gathering of the Host. "Something is stirring. Something out of the ordinary. We'd best keep our mind on the game—and on the disciples."

"All those the Father gives Me will come to Me," Jesus continued. "And whoever comes to Me I will never drive away—they shall be accepted." He stood and began pacing as He spoke. "Do you think I have come down from Heaven to speak My own words and to do My own will? No! I have come down from Heaven not to do My will but to do the will of Him who sent Me. And this is the will of Him who sent Me, that I shall lose none of all He has given me, but raise them up at the last day. Listen to Me—My Father's will is that everyone who looks to the Son and believes in Him shall have eternal life, and I will raise them up at the last day."

The Jews in the crowd could be heard decrying this teaching. They began to call out to the people, "Is this not Jesus, the Son of Joseph, whose father and mother we know? How can He now say, 'I came down from Heaven.' He is deluded!"

Jesus walked over to where the Jews had gathered. They stood with defiant stances, proud in the robes of their office.

"Stop grumbling among yourselves," Jesus said. "I assure you no one can come to Me unless the Father who sent Me draws him, and I will raise him up at the last day. Again I tell you all—I am the Bread of Life!"

He turned from the Jews and back to the crowd.

"Your forefathers ate manna in the desert, as the man mentioned a moment ago. Yet they died and were buried in the desert. But here is the bread that comes down from Heaven, which a man may eat and not die. Moses' bread was temporary. But I am the Living Bread that came down from Heaven. If anyone eats of this bread, he will live forever. This bread is My flesh, which I will give for the life of the world."

"What?" cried one of the Pharisees. "How can You dare to say such a thing?"

Then the Jews began to argue sharply among themselves, "How can this Man give us His flesh to eat? This is an abomination!"

"I'll tell you something more," continued Jesus, looking directly at the pharisees. "Unless you eat the flesh of the Son of Man and drink His blood, you have no life in you. Whoever eats My flesh and drinks My blood has eternal life, and I will raise him up at the last day. For My flesh is real food and My blood is real drink."

Many in the crowd looked at each other in confusion. Even some of the disciples were alarmed. One person from somewhere in the back shouted he was hungry right now. A few began to leave, deciding to come back later when He was ready to give them some real food. The Jews encouraged the departures.

"Whoever eats My flesh and drinks My blood remains in Me, and I in him," Jesus continued. "Just as the living Father sent Me and I live because of the Father, so the one who feeds on Me will live because of Me."

He turned back to the Jewish teachers and priests, who were still grouped near Him refuting Him even as He spoke: "This is the bread that came down from Heaven." He said to them. "Your forefathers ate manna and died, but he who feeds on this bread will live forever."

Later that evening, after the crowds had dispersed, the twelve disciples, as well as others who had decided to follow, had a moment to themselves. Still reeling from the day's teaching, they asked themselves exactly what it was Jesus was saying. Judas seemed particularly hard hit by it all. He was beginning to think perhaps Jesus was deluded. How could such a Man lead a Kingdom?

Aware that His disciples were grumbling about this, Jesus said to them, "Does this offend you? Here is an even harder teaching."

He stood and indicated the place where they were.

"This world, this flesh—it counts for nothing. Human kingdoms and power—it is all nothing. It is the Spirit that gives life. And the words I have spoken to you are spirit and they are life…"

He looked at the group.

"And still there are some of you who do not believe."

The men looked about, surprised at such a declaration. Those who knew they believed were particularly astonished. Those who had been doubtful were uneasy. Jesus had known from the beginning which of them did not believe and who would betray Him. "This is why I told you that no one can come to Me unless the Father has enabled him," He said.

As He spoke these words, several men stood to leave. Some left apologetically; others left defiantly; still others simply walked away. Many of His newer followers turned back and no longer followed Him. Jesus looked at the twelve who remained.

"Are you going to leave Me as well?" He asked the twelve.

The men were silent—ashamed at their thoughts. Then Peter spoke up and said, "Lord, to whom shall we go? You have the words of eternal life. We believe that You are the Holy One of God."

Jesus looked at the men.

"I chose all twelve of you," He said. "And all of you have remained with Me and did not depart with the others." Not looking at any one in particular He added, "And yet one of you is a devil!"

From a distance, Berenius had been listening. He turned to his aide.

"An interesting choice of words," he said. "Quite revealing."

He thought about it for a moment.

"One of the twelve is a devil. Send word to Lucifer. I will soon name the betrayer!"

"Who do men say that I am?" asked Jesus.

The question seemed to come out of nowhere as the disciples were following along on the road in Caesarea-Philippi. It hardly seemed to make a difference who other people thought Jesus was. And yet, this was the first time He had asked the disciples such a pointed question concerning Himself.

"My Lord?" asked Peter.

"I asked who people say that I, the Son of Man, am?"

The disciples looked at each other, not really knowing how to answer. Some people obviously scorned Jesus and thought He was a devil. Others were not sure. But this was not the answer for which Jesus searched. He was looking for something deeper—something inside the hearts and minds of the disciples.

"Well, some say You are perhaps John the Baptist, back from the dead," said one disciple.

"Others claim You are Elijah, the prophet," said another.

Jesus smiled lovingly at them—men with whom He had shared meals and ministry over the past two years.

"But what about all of you?" He pressed. "Who do you say I am?"

Nobody wanted to answer the question. It brought on a measure of discomfort—almost as if by answering the question truthfully one might expose one's weakness in faith. Then a voice came from the group.

"Why, you are the Christ. You are the Son of the Living God!"

It was Peter.

Jesus smiled at Peter proudly. He took him aside and held him up as an example to the others.

"Hear Me now! Flesh and blood did not reveal this to you, Peter. You did not figure this out on your own. This was given to you by the Father. But hear Me—I say no longer shall this man be called Simon by you, the unsteady one. Instead he shall be called Peter—the rock. Just as I called him the first day I met him! For upon this declaration—this rock—I shall build My church—and the very gates of hell itself shall not prevail against it!"

"And I tell you this, Peter," Jesus continued, "I am giving you the keys to the Kingdom so that whatever you bind on this planet shall be bound in Heaven; and whatever you turn loose on this planet shall also be turned loose in heaven."

Peter could hardly believe what he was hearing. All of his life he had lived with a reputation for being blunt, impetuous, headstrong, and simple. He was always the stumbler—the reckless one. And now he was declared by the Son of God Himself to be a rock—Peter!

It was something for which he had longed all his life but never realized it until now, listening to Jesus. His brothers understood this—particularly Andrew, who was now smiling at Peter and giving him a "well done" look.

"Where to, Lord?" asked Peter. "Where are we headed?"

"To glory, Peter," said Jesus, throwing an arm around him. "To glory."

Chronicles of the Host
Kingdom Progress

With two years of ministry now passed, Jesus' teaching continued taking on a more melancholy tone. The disciples continued following and ministering; healing continued and demons were cast out—but there seemed to be a new seriousness about their mission which had not existed in the early days.

It was about this time that Jesus began teaching something particularly hard for His followers to take—that He must die at the hands of men. To most of the disciples it was unthinkable and must not be. Was it possible for God to die? To one, however, the declaration destroyed the last bit of hope he held that Jesus' Kingdom might offer any true comfort. From that point on He would seek His comfort elsewhere...

CHAPTER 12

"Get behind me, Satan!"

"Well, Crispin," said Lucifer. "How very nice to see you again."

Kara laughed at the appearance of Crispin, who along with Alamar had accompanied Michael and several other angels to travel with Jesus. This was to be their last journey with Jesus before the next Passover, and they were all very alert that something dramatic was shifting in the life and ministry of their Lord. They had also come in response to the growing number of Lucifer's angels who had begun clamoring around Jesus and his disciples.

"Dear Crispin, when will you ever learn that Jesus does not need your most capable assistance?" Kara mocked.

"Dear Kara, when will you ever learn He does not fear any of your nonsense?" Crispin retorted.

"It seems your Man is destined not for greatness but for death," said Lucifer. "What does one do with a dead Lord?"

Michael looked over the group of angels, both holy and unholy, who now were with Jesus and His disciples on the road to Mount Tabor. As they walked, Jesus began speaking to them about what must shortly happen to Him

"Our Lord will not die," said Michael sternly. "He is speaking to them in parables again. It is you who has a grim destiny, Lucifer."

"Perhaps," said Lucifer. "But the way the Most High seems to operate, He always allows us room to contest Him. I'm sure He won't disappoint Him this time either."

Michael was about to answer when a commotion among the disciples broke out. Peter stormed away from the group. His brother Andrew followed along, trying to reason with him. But Peter would have none of it. After a moment or two he walked back over to the men.

"This should prove interesting," said Lucifer, who moved down among the group. Michael saw alarm beginning to grow among his angels but he held them back. He knew that Lucifer would never try something with the Most High outright.

"What is your dark master doing?" asked Crispin. "Fooling himself?"

"I rather suspect he is fooling Peter," said Kara.

"The 'rock'," added Berenius with contempt.

The men stepped aside and allowed Peter back in their midst. He moved up close to Jesus, shaking his head in disbelief over what he had just heard.

"It's true Peter," said Jesus. "You must understand this. All of you must."

The angels had moved in by now, wanting to make certain they too had correctly understood what Jesus had said. Lucifer remained behind Peter.

"We must begin a slow but certain trek to Jerusalem where the Son of Man will be delivered into the hands of the chief priest and the elders. I shall die there."

The holy angels shuddered at the statement. Crispin was perplexed. Even Michael was unnerved by such a declaration. As for Lucifer, he quickly hushed his howling angels so he could understand more of this mystery.

"But," continued Jesus, "on the third day the Son of Man shall be raised again."

He looked deeply into Peter's eyes. "Do you understand, Peter?"

Lucifer sized up the situation as a critical point in Jesus' ministry. If he could cast doubt on Him now—during this supreme declaration—then perhaps the whole rotten plan would come crashing down. He moved behind Peter and began to speak into his mind:

"Let these others watch him die. But you must not permit it. Perhaps the Man is over wrought…"

"Lord, this cannot be!" declared Peter. "How can You die when You have brought us so far? How can this possibly be part of the plan?"

Jesus looked through Peter directly into the face of Lucifer. The authority the angel felt being exerted over him was not unlike that which he had experienced when he was in Heaven serving at the Most High's throne. Only this time it was directed at him more pointedly.

"Get behind me Satan!" Jesus said.

Lucifer fell to the ground, cowering in a mass of light. Kara and Berenius buckled and fell where they stood, as well. The other devils scattered and disappeared. Only the holy angels remained standing at their posts.

"Satan, you are an offense to me! You are not mindful of the things of God, but would see My Father's plan undone by men."

Peter fell to the ground and asked Jesus forgiveness for having become an obstacle to Him. Lucifer managed to stand and, with a scowl at Michael, quickly vanished. Kara and Berenius followed him.

Jesus continued talking to all of them.

"Hear me now! If any of you would come after Me, he must deny himself and take up his cross daily and follow Me. For whoever wants to save his life will lose it, but whoever loses his life for Me will save it."

He picked up some loose dirt and let it sift through His fingers.

"What good is it for a man to gain the whole world, and yet lose or forfeit his very self? I tell you I am not jealous for My own life. If anyone is ashamed of Me and My words, then I will be ashamed of him when I come in My glory and in the glory of the Father and of the holy angels."

He looked the men over and felt a great sense of compassion. The twelve were silent as He said to them encouragingly, "I'm telling you the truth, some who are standing here will not taste death before they see the Kingdom of God."

"And so Lucifer is bested once more," said Alamar. "I have learned a great deal about the Lord's authority in this world."

Crispin, still shocked by what Jesus had said to His disciples, could only mutter to himself something about the Lord having to die. Michael walked over to him. The other angels closed ranks as well. The disciples had fallen silent.

"Why must He die?" asked Michael. "How can that possibly serve the interests of the Lord? Why must He die for the Lord?"

Crispin looked up at the angelic faces. He thought for a minute of everything leading up to this moment. He recounted to them how God had created A'dam and Eve to live in Eden; how they both fell and allowed the image of God inside them to become marred; how God sought through Abraham to create a new covenant that would one day see the world blessed; how God led this great nation through Egypt and into the land of promise; how Israel established itself and built the great temple to house God's very Presence; how the nation corrupted itself and God sent the prophets to warn of impending judgment; how the prophets spoke of One to come who would one day set them all free and establish a Kingdom which would last forever; how Jesus was born to a virgin as the prophet had said; and now how this same Jesus, the Son of the Living God, must die and be raised again. He finally summed it all up in answer to Michael.

"Michael, I would say in answer to your question that Jesus is not dying for the Lord as much as He is dying for men."

Mount Tabor jutted out of the Plain of Esdraelon, giving a marvelous view of Mount Carmel in the west and Mount Hermon to its north. The men who camped at its base were happy not to be doing any climbing, however. The disciples were weary of ministry and still alarmed at all the talk of death that had taken over their Master recently.

As they sat near a fire, some of them were chatting about the discussion. Thomas leaned in and whispered to Thaddeus and Bartholomew.

"I wonder if perhaps He has been traveling too hard," he said. "Judas thinks that maybe He is ill."

"Nonsense," said Thaddeus. "But I don't pretend to understand any of this."

"Here comes Peter," said Bartholomew. "Hush for now."

Peter moved over to the fire and warmed his hands. He looked at the men with whom he had shared his life for the last couple of years. He loved them all. As he contemplated what had befallen him since he and his brother had met Jesus, he watched Judas move in from the darkness and sit near the fire. Judas rarely spoke these days. He always seemed to be brooding about something.

"Peter."

Peter turned to see Jesus standing with James and John. He motioned for him to follow along with them. The others stayed in the camp and watched as Jesus and these three disappeared onto the mountain.

"There they go," said Judas. "Jesus and His favorites."

Andrew heard the comment and rebuked Judas.

"How dare you shame our Master like that!" .

Judas merely shrugged and curled up in his blanket.

Jesus led them to a spot where they were to pray. Peter and the others soon found themselves very sleepy. But Jesus continued steadfastly in prayer. Then, while He was praying, the appearance of His face changed, and His clothes became as bright as a flash of lightning, casting the whole mountainside in a silvery-white splendor.

Two figures, Moses and Elijah, appeared in glorious splendor as well, talking with Jesus. They spoke with Him about His coming death, which He was about to bring to fulfillment at Jerusalem.

Peter and his companions were still very sleepy, but when they became fully awake, they saw His glory and the two men standing with Him.

"Look at that," said Peter, slowly making his way toward them.

John fell to the ground in worship. James called Peter to come back. Just as Moses and Elijah were leaving Jesus, Peter, not really knowing what he should say, called out to Him, "Master, it is good for us to be here. Let us put up three shelters—one for You, one for Moses and one for Elijah."

While he was speaking, a cloud appeared and enveloped the men, and they were afraid as they entered the cloud. Peter looked about but could make out nobody in the fog. He called out to the others but he could hear nothing. Then, a voice came from the cloud, saying, *"This is My Son, whom I have chosen; listen to Him."*

When the voice had spoken, they found Jesus alone and no longer covered in the glorious white light. They could not believe what they had witnessed: Moses, Elijah and the Son of God—all in discussion! The Law, the Prophets and the King came together in advance of Jesus' final trip to Jerusalem. They agreed they should tell no one about their experience until it was proper to do so.

Another trio had watched the incident from a safe distance as well. These three demons—dispatched by Kara to maintain a vigil on Jesus and his movements—were shocked by what they had seen. They looked at each other in both disbelief and fear. But they made no such agreement to keep quiet about it. In fact, they hurried to their master to report on what had happened.

At Masada, the fortress-palace complex built by Herod the Great that overlooked the vast wilderness to the south of Judea, Lucifer met with his three supreme angels. It was fitting they meet in a place Herod had built in case of an insurrection, for as Lucifer put it, the strain of recent events was beginning to have a "closing in" feeling.

Masada was built atop an isolated rock cliff at the western end of the Judean desert, overlooking the Dead Sea. Dominating the low-lying landscape around it, the fortress was never used by Herod. Now it stood sentry over the southern Judean desert, waiting for a future time when it might be of some use to the Jews.

"How fitting that we meet in a fortress," said Lucifer, looking across the flat land below. "For we are indeed besieged."

Rugio watched silently as his master paced the wall that over looked the sheer drop looking toward the Dead Sea. He had never known Lucifer to seem so pessimistic. The report that they had brought concerning Jesus speaking with Moses and Elijah at Mount Tabor had upset him unlike any other disappointment in the long struggle that had begun in Eden.

Kara, ever trying to gain Lucifer's confidence, had offered the possibility that the specters they had seen were merely tricks of the Most High and held no real significance. Lucifer had brushed off Kara's remarks as his usual nonsense. Only Pellecus seemed to grasp the reality of the situation.

"It seems, my prince, that in conferring with the prophets He wanted to send a definite message," Pellecus said. "Why else should He bring them along?"

"Obviously Peter didn't get the point," sniffed Kara. "The Lord Himself had to tell him to be quiet."

Pellecus ignored Kara and continued.

"The question lies in the reason for the meeting," he said. "The answer must lie in who these persons were on earth and what they did while they were here."

Precisely," said Lucifer, turning from the desert panorama and looking back at the three angels. "When He rebuked me as I stood behind Peter, I could sense the intensity of His mission. No! Each of these represent a portion of the Most High's anointing on Israel. Moses of the Law; Elijah of the prophets; and Jesus the King."

"Prophets, priests, and kings," sneered Kara. "They were always Israel's downfall in the past. Perhaps they shall be again."

"Except for the fact the Most High is among them now," said Pellecus. "Try as we might to undo this situation, it looks as if they were in agreement to demonstrate a culmination of the Most High's plans. These three offices seem to validate whatever it is Jesus is doing."

Lucifer nodded his head in dismal agreement.

"And what are we to do about it?" asked Kara. "We cannot simply allow the Most High to do as He pleases in this."

"It *is* a bit difficult to keep Him from it, isn't it?" asked Rugio.

"I think we are doing all we can at present," said Lucifer. "Until an opportunity presents itself to discredit or destroy Jesus we will be in peril. Remember that whatever else happens, he has prophesied his own death."

"I have certainly held up my end of things," said Kara. "I have sent all manner of tempting possibilities His way." He shrugged. "But unlike most humans He has overcome them all."

"True," said Lucifer, thinking back to his own vain attempts at bringing Jesus down through temptation "Try as we might, tempting Him is not the answer. I learned that one in the wilderness."

Lucifer looked over the desolate plains below. Then he turned to the others.

"No! I am convinced the only way to get at Jesus is through the betrayal by someone He trusts. And I believe we are progressing in that area."

He looked at Kara as if waiting for a report.

"Yes, of course," said Kara, looking uncomfortably at the other two. "We believe we have found several possibilities among the twelve. Most of them are quite unaccomplished and rough men. Igno-rant. Poor. But of the twelve there are five who have been under our scrutiny as possibilities for betrayal.

"First there are the brothers, James and John. They are loyal to Jesus in many respects. But they seem quite volatile. Very tempera-mental. Their nickname the "Sons of Thunder" bears that out. Then there is Simon, now called Peter. Another hothead. Unsteady and abrupt. He might turn on Jesus if we can appeal to his impatient nature. Thomas is always asking questions and seems to be wondering about it all. And finally there is Judas. He is aloof and a loner. He scorns Jesus when He is not around and he sometimes robs from the common purse. I would say of all of them, Judas is the most promising."

"Interesting," said Lucifer. "I quite agree. Judas bears watching." He looked at the others.

"Very well. Then we shall watch for an opportunity to enter the heart of this man. In the meantime, we must continue inflaming the ignorant priesthood. In the end they will be the destroyers of Jesus. The Romans, as well, have no use for Him."

He made a sweeping gesture of Masada.

"Herod built this place as a fortress which in the end he never really needed. Oh, he used it a few times as a refuge, you may recall. But it never played the sort of role he imagined it might."

His head nodded slowly up and down as if agreeing with himself—trying to convince himself what he was about to say might possibly be true.

"So it must be with Jesus. In the end the priests shall have no need of Him. Mark me! Religious venom is the deadliest poison humans have ever invented."

He looked at the morning star which was rising above the east-ern horizon. The twilight was still a bit reddish at the crest where land meets sky. Lucifer strode to that side of the fortress and looked north-ward in the direction of Jerusalem.

"So that is where it shall end," he began. "Somewhere down there in the holy city."

He looked back at the others who were making their way cautiously toward him on the northwest point of the fortress.

"I lived in a holy city once. The holiest. I worshipped there, too. And angels sang at my choruses and the Presence of the Most High God was intoxicating. Every creature bowed at the throne of God. All of them!"

Lucifer stared at the morning star and continued speaking, as if he were speaking to Heaven itself.

"It was You to whom they bowed. But it was by my music that they worshiped. It was to You that they made their allegiance. But it was I who allowed them to think for themselves. It was Your law that bound them to servitude. But I have given them an opportunity for freedom. And now it comes to some sort of bloody end.

"I am prepared for the outcome. And I will see it through. But the cost to You, Most High, will be greater than anyone will ever understand. But why must it be? Why are we contesting over a rotten humanity which has no interest in You? These people have thrown You over. Their crimes against You are innumerable. They far outweigh any offense that an angel has brought! I accuse these people of being unworthy of Your attention and I further bring these charges:

"You created them to commune with You in Eden and were forced to expel them because of their disobedience; You made a covenant with them to become a great nation and they broke covenant; You introduced Law to them which they have not kept; You sent prophets to them to whom they would not listen. And now You come in Person and they still do not understand You?

"How long will You endure this shame, Most High? How long will You be the object of ridicule in all of Your creation? Hear me! Leave this miserable, rotten planet to me and I will train up these people so even if they do not respect Your mercy and grace they shall respect law and order."

He held his fist high toward Heaven.

"These people only understand blood, Most High. It is only by blood that they shall ever be conquered. It is only by blood that they will ever be subdued. How much more blood must be shed? How much more blood are You willing to dirty Your hands with in order to bring this war to a close?"

He looked at the others and smirked.

"I suspect there is a limit to the blood the Most High is willing to spill. And in the end, the blood will win the day. Mark me!"

Herod's Temple was the uncontested center of life in Israel. Jews from all over the world, and speaking all the languages of the Empire attended the Temple at least once in their lives, if possible. Elaborating on the Temple built in the days of Ezra, the Temple consisted of a series of common areas which were reached by climbing steps from one level to the next.

The first common area, called the Court of the Gentiles, was devoted to foreigners who had come to worship God. Herod had surrounded the court with colonnades so that foreigners could enter the complex and admire his building. Being non-Jewish, however, these visitors could not proceed any farther into the complex.

Heading east, one would come to the Court of the Women, which admitted only Jewish women. But they could go no farther into the complex itself.

Next came the Court of Israel, which was open to Jewish laymen, and was the last great court open to the public.

Finally came the innermost Court of the Priests, which excluded all lay people. In the eastern part of this court stood the great altar of burnt offering made according to the Law, of unwrought stone. West of this was the Temple containing the Most Holy Place. Between the Holy Place and the altar stood the laver of cleansing.

It was one thing for Jesus to promulgate His message in the countryside among the ignorant, but it was intolerable for Him to be teaching in proximity of the Most Holy Place on earth! The priests were grouped as usual, watching with disgust as people actually sat at the feet of this Man! They murmured and accused Him, always listening for an opening to accuse Him of heresy; always prepared to compare His doctrine to some facet of the Law He might have offended.

The crowds that gathered around Jesus always commanded the attention and anger of the Jews, but nowhere more than when He was teaching in one of the Temple's inner courts, as he was doing now in the Court of Israel. Kara and Pellecus stood in the middle of the priests, enjoying their fury.

"These priests are at a loss about Jesus," said Kara, noticing their icy stares.

"They are jealous," said Pellecus. "They command by fear and law, compelling people to listen. Jesus fills their heads with hope—something that religious law has never been able to do."

"Yes, well I prefer law," sniffed Kara. "It makes humans much more manageable."

"And disagreeable," added Pellecus.

"You would think there would be some sort of shame left in your cursed spirits," came the voice of Crispin.

Kara and Pellecus turned to see the affable teacher alighting nearby. With him was Alamar. They hailed him as if welcoming him to their own home.

"Welcome to the Temple," said Kara. "Built by a madman for madmen!"

He laughed.

"And mad angels, apparently." Crispin retorted, to Alamar's delight.

Pellecus came near to where his former colleague stood. One time legends in the angelic realm of instructors at the Academy of the

Host, Pellecus had fallen from favor when he began promoting Lucifer's mystical and independent brand of doctrine.

"Amazing what these humans can engineer," he commented. "Of course this is nothing like Solomon's Temple, but it is remarkable, isn't it?"

"I suspect there is enough of the image of God inside humans to do many remarkable things," answered Crispin guardedly.

"Of course," continued Pellecus, "these same humans with that same image inside them are capable of doing the most horrific things."

"True," agreed Crispin, watching a few more devils gathering in the court. "Humans have been taught well since their fall. Their horror springs from the heart of the most horrible of all."

"Come now, Crispin," boomed the voice of Lucifer. "Am I *really* that horrible?"

Pellecus and Kara laughed.

"Any creature who would have the impudence to turn on his Creator and then show up at His Temple is horrible indeed," answered Crispin.

Before Lucifer could answer, a burst of laughter came from the crowd around Jesus. He had just related a very funny illustration. Lucifer noticed as a priest came hurrying in and whispered frantically to the other priests. They in turn huddled and then scurried out of the court.

"They are up to something mischievous," surmised Crispin to Alamar, as if he forgot Lucifer was near.

"Priests are *always* up to something mischievous," said Lucifer. "Holding dear those things that are formal and devoid of spirit, keeping watch in the morality of others while they themselves step into heartless legalism or unchecked mysticism."

"Angels are known to work mischief as well," said Crispin.

As they spoke, several angels from both the holy and the unholy camps began gathering around the two. Crispin looked at them all.

"If you are waiting for some sort of dramatic confrontation, I'm afraid you are going to be disappointed," he said, causing an outburst of laughter among the host. "Besides, the Lord decided this battle a long time ago."

Lucifer glared at him and was about to answer when a stirring in the entrance to the court began. A mob of angry priests carried stones, as a young woman was hustled into the courtyard. The woman was thrown on the ground in front of Jesus. The people who had been listening to Him backed away and the priests, many of whom had been in the Temple minutes before, stood nearby fingering the large stones in their hands.

A devil rushed to Lucifer and told him what had happened. Lucifer beamed and gestured toward the woman on the ground.

"This will be an interesting dilemma, I suspect," said Lucifer to Crispin. "You are always promoting the righteousness of the Law that was introduced by the Most High, are you not?"

Crispin, looking for a verbal trap, agreed.

"I will always promote those things which are instituted by the Lord," he said firmly.

"Well, this woman was caught in the act of adultery," said Lucifer, almost drooling. "A definite breach of the Law which requires her life! Now as far as I am concerned whether or not she committed adultery is of no consequence."

He was now speaking over Crispin and directly to Jesus.

"But this is *Your* law, Jesus! You are the One who placed a death sentence upon this behavior. And now You may deal with it!"

CHAPTER 13

"I am the Light of the world."

Jesus glanced at Lucifer for just a second and then sat down and began to write upon the dirt with His finger. In the meantime, a spokesman for the priests emerged to accuse the woman of having been caught in the very act of adultery. The priests hoped they finally had Jesus in a theological corner which would expose Him as the fraud He must be. Jesus, however, only continued writing on the sand.

"Master," said the priest. "As you know, it was Moses who instructed us that this woman should be stoned to death. What do you say?"

"You speak the truth," said Jesus, looking at the girl who was trembling. "Moses did indeed instruct these things. And I see all of you are ready to carry out that part of the Law."

Lucifer was enjoying the predicament that he felt Jesus had been forced into. Kara and Pellecus exchanged comments as well. The other angels simply listened, preparing themselves that this girl must in fact die.

"I told you yesterday, in this very Temple, that you accuse Me of all manner of things. I told you that the things I teach are not Mine, but they are His that sent me. You speak of Moses and the Law. Did not Moses give you *all* of the Law? And yet you keep it only in part?"

He stood in front of one of the youngest priests and took His stone, holding it in the same manner as the others.

"Therefore we must do what the Law says," he continued. "But let the man here who is without sin in his life throw the first stone."

Lucifer's grin quickly turned sour as he saw the looks upon the faces of the priests. *What man can justify himself,* they were thinking.

Thud!

The eldest priest in attendance dropped his rock on the ground and walked away.

Thud! Thud!

More stones dropped as the men slinked away, from the oldest to the youngest, until finally the only people remaining were Jesus and the woman. She looked up at him, not knowing what to do.

"Where did they all go?" Jesus asked her. "Is there nobody here to charge you with this crime?"

She looked about and shook her head.

"No, my Lord."

"I do not charge you either," Jesus said. "Now leave here. But do not sin anymore."

The woman walked away, past the remaining Pharisees who had witnessed the entire episode. Jesus looked at them.

"I tell you—I am the Light of the world. Whoever follows Me and My teaching shall not be in darkness, but will have the light of life!"

Lucifer ordered Kara and Pellecus to begin enraging the Pharisees. The two angels slipped into the circle and made suggestions of various sorts, questioning Jesus' authority to make such statements and encouraging their desire to protect their traditions.

"This is as good a time and place as any to challenge Him directly," Lucifer said to the angels with him. "Let us see what these priests will do when their silly religion is being threatened! And go and fetch that stupid Zichri! He has hated Jesus ever since the time they spoke in the house of Matthew."

An angel immediately left to find Zichri, the priest.

As the priests spoke to Jesus, Kara and Pellecus spoke things into their minds:

"He has no credentials...no witness to His credibility..."

"The light of the world?" one of the Pharisees scoffed. "Here You are, appearing as Your own witness; therefore according to the Law, Your testimony is not valid."

Jesus answered, "You don't understand. Even if I testify on My own behalf, My testimony is valid, for I know where I came from and where I am going. But you and your kind have no idea where I come from or where I am going."

He began walking in front of the men, as an ever-increasing audience of visitors to the Temple listened to Him. "You judge by human standards; I pass judgment on no one. However, if I do judge, My decisions are right, because I am not alone. I stand with the Father, who sent Me."

"His Father! His Father! Who is His Father..." Kara purred.

"In your own Law it is written that the testimony of two men is valid. I am One who testifies for Myself; My other witness is the Father, who sent Me."

One of the Pharisees made a big show of looking around the grounds. "And just where is Your Father?"

The Pharisees laughed.

"You do not know Me or My Father," Jesus replied. "If you knew Me, you would know My Father also."

The crowds murmured, nodding their heads as if they understood and were sympathetic to the things He was saying. The priests took notice of this as Jesus continued speaking.

"Listen to me—all of you! I am going away, and you will look for Me, and you will die in your sin. Where I go, you cannot come."

"Only an insane man would speak such nonsense of going to a place where no other man can come."

Jesus continued, "All of you are from below; I am from above. You are of this world; I am not of this world. I told you that you would die in your sins; if you do not believe that I am the One I claim to be, you will indeed die in your sins."

"So clear it up," said a priest. "Just who are you?"

It was Zichri, out of breath from running. The devil had placed into his mind that Jesus was in the Temple. Zichri had interpreted it as a voice from the Lord and hurried over to defend the Law from this law-breaker.

"Who I have been claiming all along," Jesus replied, turning to Zichri. "I have much to say in judgment of you. But He who sent me is reliable, and what I have heard from Him, I tell the world."

They did not understand He was telling them about His Father.

"Who are you speaking of?" asked Zichri.

Jesus ignored him and continued.

"When you have lifted up the Son of Man, then you will know I am the One I claim to be and that I do nothing on My own but speak just what the Father has taught Me. The One who sent Me is with Me; He has not left Me alone, for I always do what pleases Him."

"Tell them, Jesus!" came an encouraging voice from the crowd. Many in fact were beginning to believe upon Jesus. The priests became enraged at this. There were even some priests who had begun to believe upon Him. To those He said:

"If you hold to My teaching, you are really My disciples. Then you will know the truth, and the truth will set you free."

"Words, words, words," sneered Zichri. "We are Abraham's descendants. Abraham! We are nobody's slaves. We are a free people. Even in the midst of pagan occupation we are a nation of free men under God's Law! How can You say we shall be set free?"

"Because," Jesus continued, "everyone who sins is a slave to sin. I know you are Abraham's descendants. Yet you are ready to kill Me, because you have no room for My word. I am telling you what I have seen in the Father's presence, but you do what you have heard from your father."

Lucifer's aura suddenly manifested as Jesus spoke these words. Kara and Pellecus backed a bit away from the purplish haze that was beginning to shine around him indicating his extreme anger.

"Abraham is our father," Zichri affirmed, to the approval of the priests. "I already told You that."

Jesus shook His head.

"If you were Abraham's children, then you would also do the things Abraham did. But instead, you are determined to kill Me, a Man who has told you the truth that I heard from God. Abraham did not do such things."

He looked straight at Lucifer and added, "You are doing the things your own father does."

"The only Father we have is God himself!" Zichri protested. The others gathered around Zichri now to support him. Many angels moved in to protect Jesus, should it come to that. The disciples were becoming increasingly tense as well.

Lucifer, still seething with anger, called out to his angels.

"This is exactly what was called for! I could not have planned it better myself!"

Jesus said to the agitated group of priests, "If God were your Father, you would love Me, for I came from God and now am here. I have not come on My own; but the Father sent Me."

He then pointed to the priests, but spoke through them and right into Lucifer's heart: "You belong to your father, the devil, and you want to carry out your father's desire. He was a murderer from the beginning, not holding to the truth, for there is no truth in him. When he lies, he speaks the language he best understands, for he is a liar and the father of lies!"

Zichri was muttering "Blasphemer!" under his breath.

A few of the priests began to pick up some of the stones which had been discarded earlier. The disciples moved in to protect Jesus and fight if necessary. Jesus simply continued speaking.

"And yet because I tell the truth, you do not believe Me! If you truly belonged to God you would listen to what God says. The reason you do not hear is that you do not belong to God!"

Zichri rallied the priests and began speaking loudly so all in the court would hear him.

"You are a Samaritan and demon-possessed, aren't you?!"

Jesus looked intently at Zichri and the others.

"I am not possessed by a demon," He said, "but I honor My Father and you dishonor Me. I am not seeking glory, but there is One who seeks it, and He is the Judge. And I tell you the truth, if anyone keeps My word, he will never see death."

Zichri looked at the others in stunned silence. That was it! He had crossed the line of reason. He really was possessed by a demon.

"Listen to me, Jesus," said Zichri, speaking now in a lecturing tone as a parent would speak to an unruly child. "I now realize You are demon-possessed. And here is why: Abraham, our father, died many years ago, as did the prophets. How can You say they never tasted death? It is even recorded they died and were buried with their fathers. But You say that if anyone keeps Your word, he will never taste death?"

Zichri was clearly playing to the crowd, as he dramatically asked Jesus, "Are You greater than our father Abraham? He died, and so did the prophets. Who do You think You are?"

Jesus was silent for a moment. He looked about Him at the faces of the priests and patrons, holy and unholy angels—all waiting for His response.

"Your father Abraham rejoiced at the thought of seeing My day. And I tell you that he saw it and was glad."

Zichri scoffed.

"You are not yet fifty years old, but You are telling us you have seen Abraham? What sort of nonsense is this?"

Lucifer glanced over at Kara and Pellecus.

"They certainly are not taking this well, are they?"

They smiled at him.

"I tell you the truth," Jesus continued, "before Abraham was, I AM."

The court was silent.

Zichri, realizing he had been played for a fool, looked to the ground where a stone lay. He picked it up and the others did likewise. It was time to deal with this blasphemer. The Host suddenly moved in around Jesus, forming a shield that would not allow the priests to find Him. Somehow, He vanished into the crowd!

"Find Him!" Lucifer ordered.

"Find Him!" Zichri ordered.

But Jesus simply walked out of the Temple under cover of the multitude of angels who hid Him. Lucifer could not believe He had slipped by once more. The commotion had attracted the attention of temple guards who were moving in to clear the area.

"Twice now the crowds were ready to rip Him to pieces," Kara complained. "And once again He merely walks out!"

"These fools cannot even find themselves," said Lucifer, looking at the priests dashing about here and there and asking people where Jesus had gone. Some looked behind the colonnades, others near the place where the offerings were received. But Jesus was nowhere to be found.

"Still, this sets a dangerous precedent that these priests must deal with," reasoned Lucifer. "In fact, I believe it is beginning already."

They strolled over to where Zichri stood, Berenius beside him, speaking into his mind the urgency of this situation. Immediately, Zichri called Aziah and another priest to his side. They moved over to where they could be alone—or so they thought.

"You see what this Man is doing?" Zichri fumed. "The people are beginning to be taken in by Him. Perhaps it is time we bring Caiaphas in on this."

"The High Priest?" Aziah asked. "He told us to deal with these sorts of…"

"This is no ordinary religious interloper," interrupted Zichri. "This Man poses a real threat to the nation. We must find a way to bring Him down. For the good of the nation, we must speak with Caiaphas!"

As they left, Lucifer turned to the others. By now he had calmed down to the point his aura had vanished. He summed it up for them.

"This bodes well for our cause," he said. "With the introduction of the High Priest, this takes the game to an entirely different level. These idiotic disciples will be completely out of their element. Caiaphas' intervention will also mean the involvement of Herod and possibly even Pilate."

"My lord," said Pellecus. "I realize the Jews hate this Man. But their hatred for the Romans and their disdain for the Herodians makes it a difficult proposition that they will form an alliance."

"On the contrary," interjected Lucifer. "The Herodians and the Pharisees shall be forced into this alliance by their common hatred and recognized threat of Jesus. They both know that should the peace be broken the Romans might put an end to it all."

He looked at them.

"A common enemy makes for uncommon alliances—even unholy ones. The Pharisees and the Herodians will put aside their hatred for each other because of the greater threat posed by Jesus. I would say that it looks as if the stakes have just gotten much higher in our little drama."

Chronicles of the Host
Galilee Farewell

True to Lucifer's sordid thinking, the Pharisees began having informal discussions with the Herodian Jews. The High Priest, Caiaphas, determined to remain aloof at this time, although he

did ask for regular updates on the Jesus problem. Lucifer con-
tinued fomenting hatred among the Jews while maintaining an
ever-increasing influence upon Judas Iscariot—asserting that
the combination of pressure from the outside and dissent from
within might prove a lethal combination.

As for Jesus, He bade a final farewell to the familiar country-
side and people of Galilee and began a course that would even-
tually take Him to His appointed destiny in Jerusalem. At the
time, of course, the Host assumed He was on his regular cir-
cuit of ministry, preaching from town to town, and making
His way to the Holy City in order to celebrate the Passover as
He was inclined to do. It wasn't until later we discovered that
the Passover He would soon be celebrating was His own...

The little city of Bethany lay on the southeastern slope of the
Mount of Olives, and was situated about two miles east of Jerusalem,
on the road to Jericho. The disciples were happy to see the lights of
the city and hoped the others who had gone on ahead to make
arrangements for food and shelter had been successful.

"I'm famished," complained Peter, whose hot, dirty feet were
aching. "I hope Bethany is more hospitable than its name suggests!"

Andrew ambled up beside him with mock concern. He put his
hand on his brother's shoulder and said, "Come now Peter. What better place for a man as miserable as yourself to visit than a city called
'house of misery'?"

As they spoke they could see James and John in the distance.
With them was a tall, middle-aged man. The man introduced himself
as Lazarus from Bethany. He went straight to Jesus and spoke.

"My sisters and I would be honored to have You and Your men
in our home," he said. "They are preparing Your dinner even now.
Come. Come all of you!"

"Thank you Lazarus," said Jesus. "And may the Lord bless your home."

"And your sisters' cooking!" Peter added, as they all laughed.

Martha and Mary welcomed Jesus and the others into their home. Lazarus was an important man in Bethany, and his house reflected this. But for all their importance, they were a humble family who lived quietly and enjoyed the company of others.

Mary was a natural hostess and loved to see to the comfort of her guests. She had the men sit and provided water and towels for them to wash their feet. Lazarus was also a wonderful host and a friend to everyone. The men warmed up to him quickly, and he particularly enjoyed the company of Jesus. Mary, the eldest sibling, was focused on the details of the dinner and after a brief introduction, scurried into the back of the house to prepare the meal.

The men gathered in the central room and sat about on large cushions and mats provided by Mary. She gazed at her brother with interest, as this was the first time since their father died that Lazarus had shown any real interest in conversations about the Lord. Lazarus was dumbstruck as Jesus spoke so naturally about a coming Kingdom and a Father who loved him very much.

Lazarus was asking all sorts of questions—things which he never discussed with his sisters. How deep her brother now seemed! As the conversation continued, it was as if Lazarus and Jesus had known each other for a very long time. Mary was pleased her brother was getting to know such an important Man.

"Mary!" came a call from the kitchen.

Mary tried to ignore her sister's summons. She knew she should help Martha out in the kitchen, yet something held her there at the feet of Jesus…listening to all He was saying.

"Mary, please come in here!"

Mary turned her head toward the kitchen, where she could hear her sister scuffling around. She started to get up, but the look in her brother's eyes as he listened to Jesus, and the wonderful words this Holy Man was speaking gripped her mind and spirit.

"There you are!"

Martha walked into the room, interrupting the discourse. Everyone looked up at the woman whose hospitality they were enjoying. She excused herself for the interruption, then spoke to Mary.

"Would you please come into the kitchen with me? Those figs are in need of some attention!"

Mary looked at Jesus apologetically and started to get up. He smiled at her and gave her an "it's OK" look and she sat back down. Martha was incredulous.

"Lord, You are welcome in this house," she said to Jesus. "And my brother is obviously enjoying your company. But why must You hold my sister in here when I need her in the kitchen and at the table?"

Jesus smiled at Martha and said, "Dear Martha. You are indeed quite a hostess and wanting to make sure everything is done just right. And I appreciate that. Yet there is really only one important happening in this house right now."

He looked down at Mary.

"Your sister has chosen something much more valuable—something that shall never be taken away from her."

Martha didn't quite understand, but she nodded her head and, looking at her brother one more time, excused herself. Lazarus got up.

"Hold on, Martha, I'll help you."

When they left the house of Martha and Mary the next day, the disciples thanked the women for their wonderful hospitality. Lazarus stood with Jesus. He had not only met the King of Kings—he felt he had made a friend in Jesus as well.

"Thank You for coming our way," he said. "I... I have been in want of a friend."

Jesus looked tenderly at the man.

"You are no longer in want of a friend," he said. "I shall always be your friend."

Lazarus hugged Jesus and bid Him a final farewell. He stood next to his sisters as the group left. Mary noticed a tear in his eye, as the three walked back into their house.

"How very interesting," said Berenius. He had been following Jesus ever since he departed from Galilee under Kara's orders. "Jesus has found a friend."

"What does that matter to us?" said Korah, whose disgrace at Gadara found him now an aide to Berenius. "We are to follow Jesus and look for any signs of vulnerability."

"You fool," said Berenius. "We just witnessed a vulnerability."

"What, Lazarus?" he asked.

"Friends make one vulnerable," said Berenius. "Friends require thought and emotion and responsibility. Not since the death of John has Jesus really felt close to another. Oh I know He has His disciples. But they are merely tools of the trade. No—this Lazarus is someone special to Him."

"Shall I tell Kara?" asked Gadara, desperate to get back in Kara's good stead.

"Not yet," said Berenius. "I suggest we first tell Rugio."

"Rugio?"

"Yes, Korah. Rugio is our commander of spirits of infirmity. I have a feeling that Lazarus will soon become ill."

He grinned at Korah who finally understood what was happening.

"Lazarus?"

"Just so," said Berenius. "Jesus will soon discover it isn't prudent for a Messiah to make friends!"

CHAPTER 14

"I saw Satan fall from heaven."

Jesus stood with His disciples as the seventy men assembled themselves. Flush with the fruits of a successful ministry in the surrounding countryside, the men were eager to share their experiences. Jesus had sent the seventy out in pairs to preach the gospel, heal the sick and deliver the oppressed. Now they had returned and awaited further instruction from their Master.

Nearby, Michael stood with several warriors. The sense of mounting danger with the seething hatred of the Jews, and growing opposition to the ministry of Jesus from the officials in the Temple had made Michael wearier than ever. He determined to escort Jesus personally through the remainder of His ministry.

With Michael was the archangel Gabriel, whose announcement to Zechariah about the birth of John the Baptist seemed so far away. The two archangels watched as the men, authorized, sent out by the Lord as "lambs among wolves" now exchanged stories on the miraculous power of God to heal the sick and send demons scattering. Opposite the archangels stood Lucifer and his aides. They had become increasingly obvious, especially since the death of John. Lucifer, like Michael, understood that the ministry of Jesus would soon reach a breaking point, and he wanted to be there when it happened. Michael noted Lucifer's presence.

"I sometimes wonder why the Lord tolerates such insolence," he mused, looking at the fallen angel who had taken so many holy angels with him.

"Jesus simply ignores him," said Gabriel. "But he is becoming increasingly bold. I have noticed he is becoming quite close to Judas now."

Michael looked at Judas, who at this moment was enjoying a laugh with a fellow Judean over some humorous mishap during an attempt to heal a woman. He seemed quite at home right now.

"Gabriel, will Judas betray?" asked Michael. "Or will he stay true?"

Gabriel shook his head.

"Who knows what the heart and mind of man might do?" he said. "That's what this war is all about. Of course Lucifer is a master at compelling creatures to switch sides in the heat of battle."

"Remember Serus," encouraged Michael. "He was with Lucifer until the last moment. But the Lord was able to preserve him. Perhaps this Judas will listen to his heart as well."

"I'm afraid that he already *is* listening to his heart," said Gabriel. "And that is what concerns me."

"Look at them," sneered Kara. "The two archangels come to watch over their Lord." He scoffed. "As if He needed watching over."

"But that's what archangels do, Kara," said Lucifer. "They watch things. The problem is that they watch and watch and watch…"

They laughed.

"Don't mistake Michael's absence of late as a sign of inactivity," cautioned Pellecus. "He is not one to remain idle."

"True, Pellecus," said Lucifer. "But he is recently interested in the day-to-day events surrounding Jesus, whereas in the past he watched from afar. I believe he knows the game is almost up."

Lucifer glanced in the direction of Rugio. "Of course there are always a few surprises in store."

Rugio nodded.

"The sickness is taking hold, my prince."

Kara and Pellecus caught each other's eye with the unsettled look of not having been a part of something important. Lucifer glanced at the two of them.

"Patience, my friends," he soothed. "Rugio is working on a little project I hope will present both a dilemma and a test for our Messiah-to-be."

Rugio remained impassive.

"It involves a dear friend of Jesus," he continued.

"A dear friend?" queried Kara. "Who does Jesus hold dear beside His disciples?"

Lucifer turned his head toward Jesus and said the word, "That simple brother of Mary in Bethany."

"Oh," said Kara casually. "Him."

They were speaking of Lazarus.

As the noise of the crowd began to subside, Jesus moved in among them. His disciples moved in with Him, looking for any sign of an assassin or any other enemy who might make an attempt upon their Rabbi. One man, a Galilean named Joshua, made himself heard above all the others who were coming near Jesus.

"Master!" he shouted. "We found that even the devils themselves were subject to the authority of Your name!"

Upon those words, Lucifer and the others looked sharply at Jesus. The crowd hushed itself to hear what response the Lord might give, for they, too, had experienced authority over demons in the name of Jesus. Taking a moment, Jesus looked first at the sky, then over at Lucifer, where he stood on the brow of the hill, overlooking the assembly. Lucifer remained stoic as Jesus spoke.

"I saw Satan fall from Heaven," he said. "He fell like lightning."

Lucifer's anger began rising within as the brow took on the purplish hue of his manifesting aura. Jesus turned back to the crowd.

"And indeed I have given you power to tread on such creatures—serpents and scorpions, all of them!" He looked into the eyes of Joshua, who had spoken a moment before. "I have given you all power over the enemy! Nothing shall harm you."

The crowd howled in delight at this prospect, creating an unnerving sensation among the demons gathered around the area. Jesus held His hands up to silence them.

"But," He continued, "don't think that this is the main thing. Far from it. Do not rejoice over the fact that devils are subject to you through the authority of My name. Rather, rejoice that your names shall be written in Heaven!"

As He left the area, He turned to Peter and the others, telling them, "The things you are hearing and seeing are the very things the prophets longed to hear and see. You are quite blessed!"

The woman pushed her way through the crowd. As people saw her they moved quickly to one side. Her infirmity had plagued her for 18 years, and she had spent her entire life's savings on doctors and cures—still she was crippled and marked as a woman who had brought this curse upon herself which made her an outcast of society.

The spirit of infirmity causing the disease had intended that the woman be dead by now. Drachus, the demon attaching himself to the woman nearly 20 years earlier, clearly wanted her dead. But she had fought and fought with a determination unlike most humans. Now she wanted to appear before this Holy Man who was moving through her region. Perhaps He might be able to help.

Drachus attempted to frighten her into staying home that day. He had thrown every doubt into her mind that he could muster; he even had inflamed the condition today to force her home. But on she walked, in pain and doubled over at her middle, seeking out the Man Jesus. Drachus continued speaking to her mind, even as she plodded on toward the commotion of the crowd ahead.

"This Man has no interest in you…"

"These people are tired of seeing you; tired of this sickness…"

"Why don't you go back home and pray? The Lord is more likely to answer the prayers of a woman seeking Him than one searching out some trickster…"

"Here she comes!" someone shouted. "Make way for the sinner!"

The people moved away from her quickly as she began catching up to the crowd had enveloped Jesus. She made a pitiful figure, repulsive to people, almost monstrous as she hobbled along doubled over in pain. To them, it was obvious she had committed some horrible sin that placed her in this predicament. She had long ago searched her heart to see what she might have done. But now she ignored their catcalls. As she neared Jesus, Drachus felt the uncomfortable sensation of the Lord's holiness as she got closer. He panicked.

"Get home now! Before you make a fool of yourself!"

The woman would have none of it. There! She caught a glimpse of the Man everyone was trying to reach. She had heard of the woman with the issue of blood whom Jesus had healed when she touched His garment! If only she might get to Him….even touch Him…even reach out and…

Before she could actually touch Him, Jesus turned to the woman. Their eyes met and the woman felt something she had not felt in a long time: hope. Drachus, on the other hand, felt paralyzed with fear.

Jesus reached out to her and laid hands upon her. He then spoke to her, saying. "Woman, your infirmity has been loosened. You are freed from this sickness!"

Upon those words, Drachus was compelled to leave and did so, silently giving up the woman he had plagued for so long. He vanished immediately in search of his next victim whom he intended to kill more quickly.

The woman began to straighten up. The crowd gasped with amazement as she stood straight for the first time in 18 years and began rejoicing and glorifying the Lord. The crowd began moving in, congratulating her and excitedly recounting the episode among themselves.

"How is it that you healed this woman on the Sabbath?" came a voice.

Jesus turned to see the local ruler of the synagogue standing next to two priests. With them, and unseen by them, were several religious spirits who were fanning the flame of their indignation. They were smirking at Jesus, safe in their assignment among these men whose hearts were hard. The ruler spoke loudly to the people.

"Do you see what this Man has done?" he began. "God has given six days out of the week for such things to be done. This Man healed this woman on the Sabbath! Why could He not have waited until another day? You are a law-breaker!"

"And you are a hypocrite!" Jesus answered. "You are upset with Me for delivering this woman, who has been in the grip of Satan for all these years? You yourselves will take care of the needs of your animals on the Sabbath! Isn't it more important to take care of the needs of a human being?"

The ruler had no answer for Jesus. The people were nodding in agreement with the words spoken, talking among themselves. And the woman who had been healed was weeping with great joy. The ruler looked at the priests and then motioned for them to leave. They had been shamed and melted away. The spirits accompanying them cursed Jesus as they left. And all of the people rejoiced.

"Here He comes," said Jerzeel.

The delegation of Pharisees waited for Jesus to come nearby. Peter looked ahead and saw them standing, motioning for Jesus to come to them. He growled at the others, "Get ready." But Jesus walked over to them, blessing a child as He went.

These were a group of Pharisees who were sympathetic to Jesus. They had spoken with Nicodemus and believed the words Jesus spoke. As Jesus neared them, they coaxed Him into the side door of a small building. Jesus indicated that all was well and told the disciples to wait for Him outside.

When He entered the room, the Pharisees were at first silent, making sure the room was sealed and there was no one else around. Finally, a young priest spoke up.

"Master, we heard You were coming to this region and that You might possibly be going to Jerusalem," he said.

Jesus nodded. He drank some fresh water offered to Him by another priest.

"We wanted to warn You," the man continued. He looked about as if he was going to be pounced upon at any moment by some secret agency. "The Herodians are plotting against you. Herod himself has heard of You."

"It is dangerous here and in Jerusalem," said another. "Herod will surely try to have You killed—just as he did Your cousin John."

Jesus looked kindly at the men, gratified at their compassion for Him. He realized the great risk they took in speaking with Him, let alone warning Him. He thanked them. He then added: "Do not worry about Herod."

He stood with a smile and a twinkle in His eye and said, "You go and tell that fox, Herod, I will continue My ministry just as it is— healing people and casting out devils. I'll be doing this today and tomorrow and on the third day I will be perfected!"

The priests understood His resolve and it saddened them. They knew He intended to continue on to the Holy City. Jesus walked over and looked out a small window that faced toward Jerusalem. He turned back to them.

"You know, it is not fitting that a prophet should die outside of Jerusalem." Looking back out the window He lamented, "Oh Jerusalem! Jerusalem! The city that kills the prophets and stones the very people sent to help you! How I would have loved to gather you up like a mother hen gathers her chicks! But instead you shall become a place of desolation and shall not receive Me until the day you are shouting, 'Blessed is He that comes in the name of the Lord'!"

"Oh, Jerusalem! Jerusalem!"

Jesus could hear the mocking of hundreds of devils screeching the very words He had just spoken to the priests. He looked up and, through the dark cloud of foul spirits, could see the innumerable Host overhead, like a shield of light above. He smiled at the thoroughness of His Father and the loyalty of the angels.

"Jerusalem…!"

Suddenly a dazzling light swooped in from the north and began breaking up the demons, scattering them in all directions. It was Michael, who, with several hundred angels, moved in and totally confounded the demons who had been sent there by Kara to taunt the Lord in this hour of decision.

As the dark cloud of wicked angels lifted, Jesus continued on His journey, resolute in His determination to travel on to Jerusalem. He gathered the disciples around Him and said, "Let's continue doing the work of the Kingdom while it is still light. For soon it shall be dark, when no man can work."

Great multitudes of people followed Jesus outside of the small cities and villages where He and the disciples were preaching. Many of the people came because they were ill; others were curious to see a miracle performed; still others were hungry and hoping to be fed. Jesus understood these things and made it clear that following Him meant more than receiving a day's meal or a healing of an illness. He began speaking to them as they seated themselves.

"Listen to Me! You come to Me and say that you want to be My disciple. But have you considered the cost as these men have?" He indicated the disciples. "If anyone comes to Me and does not hate his father and mother, his wife and children, his brothers and sisters—yes, even his own life—he cannot be My disciple. And if you are unwilling to carry your cross and follow Me you cannot be My disciple."

"I think I could learn to hate my wife!" someone yelled from the back. Several of the men around him began laughing. As Jesus continued speaking He pointed at a watch tower nearby.

"Suppose one of you wants to build a tower. Will you not first sit down and estimate the cost to see whether or not you have the resources to complete it? Otherwise you'll lay the foundation and then run out of money and be ridiculed for having begun something you were unable to complete. In the same way, any of you who does not count the cost cannot be My disciple."

Jesus saw a group of Pharisees listening to His words. They were muttering that this was a bunch of sinners and tax collectors—the same sort of people He broke bread with. Jesus only shook His head at them and continued.

"Suppose one of you shepherds has a hundred sheep and loses one of them. What would you do? Let it go? Or go after it? Would you not leave the ninety-nine in the open country and go after the lost sheep until you find it? And after you found it wouldn't you rejoice with your neighbors that the lost sheep was found?" He looked directly at the Pharisees and said, "I tell you that in the same way there will be more rejoicing in Heaven over one sinner who repents, than over ninety-nine righteous persons who do not need to repent."

"The sickness must be fatal and it must be quick," Rugio instructed. "I know how you like these things to linger, but this is a case that calls for a decisive illness."

The spirit of infirmity, Brusial by name, whose specialty was breathing disorders, nodded that he understood. He followed along with Rugio until they came to a small city far below them. Circling it, they lighted on the roof of a larger house on the outskirts.

"This is Bethany," he said. "And this is the house of Lazarus."

Brusial looked pleased.

"I don't need all of them sick, you understand," Rugio continued. "Someone must remain to be a witness to Jesus' inability to save the life of His dear friend. This is quite an important assignment."

They entered the house. Lazarus was seated with Mary and Martha. They were in the same room Jesus had occupied only a few weeks earlier. Rugio walked over to Lazarus and, taking out his sword, lifted it over the man's head and then cut through. Lazarus immediately lurched forward and began to cough violently. His sisters rushed to his side as he finally regained control.

"Not sure what brought *that* on," he said. "I'm alright. No fuss now."

Rugio smirked at the man, speaking to him.

"Lazarus, you fool! You don't even know what is about to be brought upon you." He turned to the spirit of infirmity. "Tonight you will strike a blow both at both faith and friendship!"

"Thank you Master," said the man.

He was holding his now-well daughter of six, who was instantly healed by Jesus from a very high fever.

"Do not thank Me," said Jesus. "Thank your Father in heaven!"

The crowds had been pouring out of Jerusalem for weeks now. The disciples, exhausted as usual, maintained a close watch over their Lord and tried to help as many people as they could. Jesus sat down for a moment in the shade. The crowds continued pressing in, although the disciples managed to put some space between them and their Lord.

"Jesus!"

"Who is that?" asked Jesus, turning to the direction of the voice.

"One of many calling You," said Peter, wiping his sweaty brow.

"Jesus! Please! I have a message from Bethany!"

Jesus ordered Peter to let the man through. It was a young man Jesus recognized from his time in Bethany. He was the son of a local priest there. The boy ran to Jesus and fell to his knees.

"Good master, the man You loved in Bethany—Your friend who is brother to Mary and Martha—is sick. Very sick. They are asking that You come immediately and help him. They said You are their friend."

"Don't worry, boy," said Jesus, putting a hand on the young man's shoulder. "This isn't a sickness of death. This is a sickness that will give glory to the Lord and to the Son of God!"

Peter was standing off to the side and could not make out what the boy was saying. He turned to Thomas who shrugged that he couldn't understand it, either. Jesus nodded at the boy and stood, motioning for His disciples to gather around Him.

"We will stay here for two more days," He said. "Tell the others to make the necessary preparations."

The boy could hardly believe his ears. He had just told Jesus that Lazarus needed Him urgently. Instead of responding immediately, Jesus was going to remain where He was for two more days. He started to leave, thinking about what he would say to Mary and Martha. Jesus stopped him as he left.

"Remember what I have told you," He said. "And be encouraged. This is not a sickness unto death."

The boy nodded that he understood. Suddenly his face lit up. So that was why He was waiting. Lazarus wouldn't die after all! He could tell the sisters that Jesus was delayed because He knew Lazarus would be alright until He got there. He thanked Jesus, and headed back down the road toward Bethany.

When the two days of ministry in that region were complete, Jesus brought the men together. They wondered where they should go next. Back to Galilee perhaps? Down to Jerusalem? They hushed their speculation as Jesus began to speak.

"We will be returning back to the countryside of Judea."

The men were surprised. Peter was visibly disappointed and Judas grunted a noise of disgust at the prospect of returning back to the little towns in that region. He was anxious to get to Jerusalem. They questioned Jesus' decision.

"My Lord, the Jews have already tried to stone You there," said Matthew. "If we return there they shall surely kill You."

The others joined in a chorus of protests, trying to dissuade Jesus from returning to the hinterland of Judea. He looked at them with great compassion.

"We must return to Bethany."

The men looked at each other.

"Our friend, Lazarus, is sleeping and I must return there and awaken him."

Peter scratched his head and spoke out, saying, "Lord, if the man is asleep, why wake him? He has been ill. Let him sleep."

Several of the disciples agreed with Peter.

"You don't understand," said Jesus pointedly. "Lazarus is dead. I'm glad we were not in Bethany before this so that you may believe what will soon happen there. Come. Let's go to him."

The group ambled off, picking up their things and heading northward once more toward Bethany. In the rear of the group, Thomas was speaking to the others. "Ah well. Let's go with Him that we might also die with Him!"

The house seemed so empty now. Having been filled just a few days earlier with friends and neighbors from Bethany who were comforting Mary and Martha, the mourners had all but left, leaving only two friends. The women had thanked the people, recounting numerous times how Lazarus had struggled for breath until he could no longer take in any more air, and how he died before their friend Jesus could arrive.

"I appreciate their concern for us," said Martha to Mary, when they were alone in the kitchen… "But I will be glad to have the house back to ourselves."

Mary nodded in agreement.

"I cannot believe our brother has been dead these four days," she said. "Just four days ago he was alive. And now…"

She began weeping.

"If only Jesus had come in time," Martha said, holding her sister close. "Then perhaps our brother would have lived."

At that moment somebody began pounding on the door. Martha, exhausted as she was, did not want to receive company right now. She opened the door to find the boy she had sent to find Jesus, standing there excitedly.

"He's coming," he said, pointing his finger. "Jesus is coming up the road!"

Martha rushed in and grabbed her scarf and ran down to meet Jesus. Mary stayed behind and thanked the boy for his hard work. She invited him in for some of the food left by the mourners. The two remaining guests motioned for him to come and join them.

CHAPTER 15

"Lazarus, come forth!"

"Jesus!" she called out when she saw Him in the distance. "My Lord!"

She embraced Jesus, then pulled back from Him.

"Why didn't You come sooner?" she asked. "My brother might have lived. The boy told me You decided to wait two days—and now he is dead."

She looked at the men with Him. They somehow felt ashamed— as if it were their fault they had delayed and that this woman had lost her brother. Some of them averted their eyes at her gaze. She looked back into the eyes of Jesus.

"I know God gives You whatever You ask," she said hopefully.

Jesus smiled at her.

"Your brother will rise again," said Jesus. "I promise."

"I know, Lord. He will rise again in the resurrection at the last day."

"Martha, I am the resurrection and the life. Whoever believes in Me, even if he is dead, shall live. And whoever lives and believes in Me shall never die. Do you believe this?"

She was wiping away her tears now and nodded.

"Yes, Lord. I believe You. I believe You are the Christ, the Son of God!"

She left to tell Mary that Jesus was coming into their house. She hurried into the room, motioning for Mary to come with her into the kitchen. When they were alone, she told Mary, "The Master is calling for you!"

At that, Mary went into the other room, and, apologizing to their guests, hurried out the door. The guests agreed among themselves that she was headed to the grave to weep in private. A few followed her.

Mary found Jesus at the same spot where Martha had indicated. She had a mixed feeling of happiness and disappointment: Happiness because she loved Jesus; disappointment that He had not arrived in time. She fell at His feet and began weeping.

"If You had been here on time my brother would not have died," she said, crying as she spoke. "Jerusalem is such a short distance away!"

He looked up and saw some of the Jews from the house with her. They were weeping for the loss of Lazarus whom they all loved. A few, who had heard of the raising of the widow's son at Nain, muttered that He should also have saved Lazarus. Upon seeing all these people crying, Jesus Himself wept.

"Jesus crying?" said Rugio, who stood in front of the tomb of Lazarus. "Finally we are beginning to see some results!"

The angel thanked him and hurried back to continue his assignment with Jesus. Rugio looked at Kara.

"It seems you were right," Rugio admitted. "Jesus is beginning to break under the strain of losing first John, and now Lazarus."

Rugio walked over to the tomb and knocked on the large stone which sealed it shut. The tomb was typical of stone sepulchers, although larger. Lazarus had built the tomb for his father who had recently died. As it turned out, he requested burial near his father's tomb in Hebron. And so the tomb lay empty...until now.

"You still in there Lazarus?" Rugio asked. He then stuck his head through the rock and into the tomb and quickly pulled back out. "Yes, he is still there, albeit changed in form!"

Kara snickered. "When this is all over I suspect Jesus will have changed a bit Himself!"

"Still, I wonder..." Rugio mused.

He called for Nathan, who was standing by. Nathan, one of Rugio's most loyal warriors, appeared before his commander.

"I want more angels on this tomb," he ordered. "I'm not sure what Jesus might have in mind. But I don't want any chance of His trickery. This tomb must remain shut."

Nathan nodded and vanished.

"Having doubts?" purred Kara. "Not like a warrior."

"Just careful, Kara," answered Rugio. "Jesus is quite a different problem to deal with—as you have found out so many times!"

Before Kara could answer, Nathan reappeared with several dozen warriors, who stationed themselves in and around the tomb.

"The tomb is sealed," Nathan reported. "Nothing will get in there short of the Most High Himself!"

"That's what concerns me," said Rugio, as he saw Jesus approaching the tomb.

As Jesus neared the rocky place, Nathan commanded his angels to beware any tricks of the enemy. They were so thick by that time that to Jesus they appeared as a black fog ahead of Him on the path.

"Here they come," he shouted, noticing an increasing number of holy angels descending upon the area.

Lucifer stood to the side of the tomb, along with Kara, Rugio and Pellecus. They were all interested in how Jesus would handle the situation. Opposite them, on the other side of the tomb, were Crispin,

Michael and Gabriel. They, too, had heard what was taking place and came to observe.

"Your test seems to have attracted much attention, my prince," said Pellecus, noting the great number of angels coming in. "They have all heard about Lazarus."

"There seems to be a sense of urgency among the Host," said Kara, looking at Crispin and the other holy angels. "Perhaps even a bit of doubt?"

"Perhaps," agreed Lucifer. "I told you this should prove a most interesting dilemma for the Messiah. If He unseals the door and enters the tomb, He shall become unclean. We shall see where the loyalties of Jesus lie—with His friend or with His Father!"

"Where did you place him?" Jesus asked, recovering from His distress.

"That one there," one of the men of Bethany replied, pointing to the large sealing stone which blocked the entrance of the tomb. "We sealed it ourselves."

Jesus looked at the stone for a moment and then turned to the crowd which had followed Him. He saw the teary eyes of Mary and Martha looking back at Him. Someone in the crowd remarked that Jesus surely loved the man.

"Yes," agreed another. "But if He truly could heal a blind man why couldn't He have saved Lazarus?"

One of Crispin's aides looked at his master. Crispin looked back at him and noticed that there were several angels with the same puzzled expression on their faces

He smiled in anticipation of their question.

"The human poses an interesting question, hmm?" he asked.

The angels nodded. Michael and Gabriel turned to see how their former teacher would handle the question which was on all of their minds: *Why did Jesus not arrive earlier and save Lazarus?*

"I have an answer for you," said Crispin. "But I'm afraid you won't like it. The answer is—I don't know."

The stunned angels looked to him for more.

"It's true," he continued. "I could speculate as to why the Most High does what He does. I can only tell you that whatever He does and whenever He does it—He is always right! No matter what the outcome, no matter how He does it; no matter what He does, the Most High is always right. It is foolishness and vanity for the creature to question the Creator."

Michael gave Gabriel a knowing look.

"You mean to say it was right for Lazarus to die?" asked one of the angels.

Crispin looked at the angel.

"I am saying the Most High's actions are not to be questioned by His creatures," Crispin said. "That He allowed Lazarus to die is obvious. It is the result of a fallen world driven by fallen natures. Now, if you are asking me why He permitted this to happen, I'm afraid I am back to ignorance. I can only say, again, that the Most High is always right and that His will shall ultimately prevail."

"A good question," interjected Michael, who enjoyed watching Crispin challenged in matters of knowledge. "Perhaps 'Why?' is one of the greatest questions in Heaven!"

Crispin nodded at Michael.

"True, Michael," he said. "But there is an even greater answer to a creature asking 'Why?' of his Creator."

"And what is that answer, good teacher?" asked Gabriel, taking the bait.

"Simple," said Crispin smiling in a sly way. "The answer is…Because!"

"Remove the stone!"

The astonished crowd stared in disbelief. Martha looked around at the others then stepped out and approached Jesus, who stood in front of the tomb. She took Him aside and whispered to him.

"My Lord, I know you loved Him," she said. "And he loved You. But do not do this thing. It will be offensive. He has been dead four days!"

Jesus looked at her with compassion.

"Martha, I once told you your sister was looking for something glorious while you were busy with the distractions of this world. Again I tell you: If you only believe, you will see the glory of the Father."

She looked into His eyes and stepped back. Turning to the crowd she ordered, "Do as He says. Open the tomb!"

"Here it comes," said Nathan. "Be ready!"

Nathan's angels prepared to hold the tomb door in place. Rugio also joined them in the effort, determined not to allow the seal to break.

"No! No!" commanded Lucifer from where he stood." Rugio! Allow the seal to be broken! Give them all a glimpse of their rotting friend!" He turned to Kara and Pellecus. "Perhaps the odor of their recently departed friend will convince them that the fragrance of life Jesus offers them is not as sweet as He has preached!"

The angels moved away from the entrance as the men of the community broke the seal and rolled the large, flat stone away. Everyone watched Jesus, curious as to what He would next do. Would He actually go into the tomb? Wouldn't that violate the Law by exposing Him to a dead body? Jesus looked up to heaven and began praying aloud:

"Father, I thank You that You have heard My words. I know You always hear My words, but I wanted these people standing here to hear My words as well. I want them to hear Me call You 'Father,' so they might also believe!"

"HE IS GOING TO RAISE HIM!" shrieked Lucifer.

"Rugio! Nathan! Hold Lazarus! Get on him. Jesus intends to raise him!"

In a flurry of orders, Lucifer commanded his angels to move into the tomb and hold back the power that was to oppose them. Rugio and Nathan entered the tomb, followed by hundreds of demons. They surrounded the body of Lazarus, whose burial linens were still fresh and tightly wrapped around his body.

"LAZARUS"

Upon the booming voice of Jesus, the demons were rocked as if shaken by an invisible earthquake. They held fast to Lazarus, determined not to allow him to respond.

Rugio and Nathan stood by his head, holding it down with all their might.

"LAZARUS!"

The place shook again, this time more violently, tossing several demons around the tomb. But they would not relent and came to order immediately. Rugio barked orders at them: "Hold him! We still have him!"

"COME FORTH!"

Upon these words a tidal wave of power, like circles of light crashed through the cordon of demons, scattering them throughout the tomb. Rugio and Nathan noticed that the eyes under the linens were beaming lights, and that a brilliant glow could be seen piercing the linens and lighting up the tomb.

Outside the tomb the people gasped in astonishment as the darkness lit up in a brilliant white light. Some fell to the ground in fear. Mary and Martha held on to each other. They watched as Jesus said once more:

"COME FORTH!"

Rugio and Nathan could no longer contain the power that was surging around them and the body suddenly began to move and sat upright. Rugio cursed at Lazarus, but was powerless as he and the other demons watched the man, who a second ago was dead and rotting, sit up and slide his feet onto the ground.

"Here he comes!" someone called out.

The people could not believe what they were seeing: a man dressed in burial linens slowly coming out of the tomb. Mary and Martha ran to their brother. Jesus ordered that the bandages be removed.

"It really is Lazarus," said another, as the face was uncovered. The people crowded around, praising God and celebrating the return of their friend. Mary and Martha could only embrace their brother, who didn't seem to remember much at all.

"Glory to God!" someone cried from the crowd.

"Welcome back!" said another.

Lazarus looked up, dazed and confused.

"Welcome back?" he asked. "Have I been gone?"

The crowd burst out in laughter and tears.

Lucifer watched the demons scattering in defeat. He looked at his commanders. All of them were silent. Finally Rugio managed to join the group and explained that the power was so compelling it was impossible to contain.

"Then how can we ever stop the power that Jesus possesses?" asked Kara.

Lucifer watched as Jesus and the crowd escorted Lazarus back to his home. He looked at the bandages which once imprisoned the body of Lazarus lying on the ground. He picked up a single piece of linen and held it in his hand.

"Jesus has the power to heal the sick," he said, tearing off a strip of bandage.

"He can make blind men see, the deaf hear."

He ripped the linen once more.

"He can dispossess our spirits from humans, and teaches a message of love and Kingdom. And He can raise the dead!" he ripped off a final piece, leaving a single strand in his hand, which he held up in illustration.

"These funeral bandages represented death's hold on Lazarus, and now he is free. It occurs to me we have played this the wrong way all along."

"How so?" asked Pellecus. "What are you suggesting?"

"I am suggesting that perhaps this burial cloth was on the wrong man all along. I am suggesting that once we remove the Healer, the sick will perish. I am suggesting that once we remove the Deliverer, our angels need not fear being cast out. I am suggesting that once we remove the Teacher, the Kingdom will have no voice."

He dropped the linen to the ground.

"I am suggesting it is time for another burial," Lucifer said, a reddish tinge in his eyes. "But this time a more permanent one!"

Chronicles of the Host

Dark Plans

And so it was that many of the Jews who had come to visit Mary, and had seen what Jesus did that day, put their faith in Him and the power of the Kingdom of which He spoke. But others, driven by a dark desire to perpetuate the power of human reason and religion, went to the Pharisees and told them what Jesus had done. And so the chief priests of the nation, along with the leading Pharisees of the Sanhedrin met to discuss the growing threat they perceived in Jesus...

"What are we accomplishing, meeting like this?" a Pharisee named Bazael asked. "Here is this Man Jesus performing many miraculous signs. It makes us look like fools to oppose Him. And yet, if we let Him go on like this, everyone will believe in Him, and then the Romans will come and take away both our place and our nation!"

"It always comes down to Rome with you, Bazael," snapped Zichri. "We will survive Rome just as we have survived the Greeks, Persians and Babylonians. But we will *not* survive the destruction of our faith!"

Caiaphas, who was high priest that year, stood up and spoke. "My brothers. We cannot argue among ourselves. But Zichri is correct. I have tried to remain aloof from this matter. But now it is becoming increasingly dangerous to us all."

He looked at Bazael.

"You know nothing at all! You do not realize it is better for you that one Man die for the people than for the whole nation to perish."

Zichri smiled.

"And so He must die, my priest?"

Caiaphas looked at the men in the darkened room in his home in which they were meeting. The lamp gave an eerie glow so that only their faces shown in the light. He shook his head in dismay.

"This is a rotten business," he said resignedly. "But for the good of the nation we must find Jesus and have Him arrested and charges brought."

The group grunted in affirmation.

"I am appointing Zichri in charge of the effort," he continued. He looked at Zichri's black eyes. "Find a way, Zichri. But not until after the coming Passover! Otherwise there shall be a riot among the fools who love Him."

"Finding Jesus is not the problem," said Zichri. "One need only follow the crowds. He is even now in Bethany where a dinner is being given in honor of the great miracle there."

"Lazarus," muttered Caiaphas.

"Yes, Lazarus," said Zichri. "Ever since he was supposedly raised from the dead, many Jews have been going to Bethany to see for themselves. And many are believing."

The High Priest nodded grimly.

"Then perhaps it becomes expedient that two must die for the good of the nation," said Caiaphas. "As I said, this is a rotten business."

Zichri bowed his head in agreement.

"I will see to Lazarus as well," he said.

"Now—as to Jesus. I suggest we have our best opportunity immediately after the Passover," Caiaphas continued. "That is when they shall all be together."

"It's only Jesus we want," said Caiaphas. "He will come to Jerusalem for the feast. Once their Shepherd is killed, the sheep will scatter!"

"Yes! Find where they shall celebrate the Passover!" someone said.

"Set spies throughout the city," said another.

"Enough!" said Caiaphas. "Zichri will handle this discreetly." He turned to Zichri. "What will you need from us?"

"What we need is help from someone who knows Him," mused Zichri. "Someone who shares His meals. An intimate of His would be ideal."

"A traitor among the disciples?" said Bazael doubtfully. "They have declared their lives to Him."

"Yes," said Caiaphas. "But have we not heard a rumor of one who is perhaps disappointed with Him...One who is not quite with Him...someone who has borne His life but no longer bears Him love."

"Yes, my lord," said Zichri. "In fact, I have heard of such a one..."

"Rabbi?"

Jesus turned to see a group of Pharisees standing near a well off to the side of the road they were taking through the region of Ephraim. The disciples, weary from the trip and ready to get to

Jerusalem for the Passover, were not ready to be patient with these men. Peter turned to say something, but Jesus held His hand up to keep him quiet.

"Yes," answered Jesus. "What is it?"

"Rabbi, You honor us by moving through our land," one of them said. "We would ask You to further honor us by joining us in some refreshment."

"My Lord we must push on if we are ever to get to Jerusalem," said Judas, who had pushed through the other disciples to see what was happening.

"Be patient, Judas," said Jesus. "I shall arrive in Jerusalem in plenty of time for the feast."

Judas shook his head and resignedly sat at the side of the road. Jesus walked to the Pharisees and sat with them. After a few moments of bread and freshly drawn water, they began discussing points of His teaching. One of them, Shallah, an acquaintance of Zichri, finally stood, his black robe billowing in the wind.

"Rabbi, You speak of a Kingdom and yet we see no Kingdom," he began. "We too believe the Lord will one day restore our nation. But we know only God Himself knows when this shall be. May we ask when Your Kingdom shall come?"

Judas perked up at this question. His interest was not lost on Shallah, who had been told by Zichri to observe the peculiarities of the different disciples, especially the one called Judas. Jesus considered Shallah's question and then proceeded to answer him.

"Do you really believe that the Kingdom of God is something that you can observe with your eyes?" He asked them. "You cannot simply say, 'There it is!' or 'Over there!' No! The Kingdom of God is within you."

Jesus watched as Lucifer suddenly appeared with several demons, who began mixing in with the Pharisees, attempting to stir them up. Lucifer ignored the customary warrior angels who accompanied Jesus and the disciples, and instead wandered over near Judas. It was quite evident now to Jesus who His betrayer would be.

"I wonder the value of a Kingdom born from within?" Lucifer purred in Judas' increasingly frustrated heart.

Judas shifted uncomfortably. Jesus turned back to His disciples and continued teaching, loudly enough for the Pharisees and others milling around to hear.

"I tell you all, the time will come when people will search for the Son of Man but He will not be found! And just like these who are seeking a Kingdom of this world, people will run all about saying, 'Look! There He is!'"

Jesus shook His head.

"But don't you go after them. I promise you that the day of the Son of Man shall be like lightning that flashes in the sky lighting it up from one end to the other!" Turning to the Pharisees, He added, "But first He must be rejected by His own people and suffer much at their hands."

Shallah scoffed at these words.

"Look here," he said. "Either You are here to establish a Kingdom or You are not. Why do You deceive these poor men who follow You? Go home! All of you! You are wasting your time here!"

Judas looked up and saw only the fixed gazes of resolve on the faces of the disciples. His own face belied his true feelings.

"Enough of this Kingdom from within," Lucifer spoke, sitting next to Judas. *"The priests are correct. You are wasting your time with these unlettered men!"*

"When the Son of Man does come, it will be very much like it was in Noah's day," Jesus continued. "They were going about their business as usual—eating, drinking, buying, selling, marrying…"

"Doesn't sound so bad to me!" someone called from the crowd of onlookers.

The people laughed.

"Ah, but think about it," said Jesus, looking at the young man who had made the comment. "It was all well and good until the day

Noah entered the ark, and the flood came and swept all the people away. Same with Sodom. It was well with Sodom until the day Lot departed—and then the city was overthrown!"

He turned back toward His disciples.

"This is how it shall be when the Son of Man is revealed. Two people shall be in one bed, but one shall be taken and one shall not! Or two women shall be working together, but only one of them shall be taken. The other shall be left!"

"And where will this take place?" asked Shallah.

"Wherever the dead remain, that is where the vultures gather."

"He speaks in riddles as always," said Lucifer. *"He is leading you to destruction…"*

Judas stood to join the group as they continued on their way. Nathaniel waited for him and the two walked together behind the others.

"Where to?" asked Judas. "Jerusalem?"

"Not yet," said Nathaniel wearily. "Jericho."

"Ah, Jericho," said Judas sarcastically. "I wonder if the walls are still down?"

Nathaniel smiled at him and said, "Come on!"

CHAPTER 16

"Hosanna to the Son of David!"

Chronicles of the Host

Death Foretold

Jesus did indeed lead the disciples through Jericho, where they encountered a blind man by the name of Bartimeus. Moved by the man's plight, Jesus instructed him that his faith had healed him—and he was able to see again!

The Host always enjoyed Jesus working with the people who needed Him so desperately. One man, a rather nasty character named Zachaeus, actually climbed a tree in order to catch a glimpse of Jesus as He passed by. The Lord rewarded him by coming to his house for fellowship! Jericho was a wonderful time of watching the Lord at work. We could not have known, however, that in leaving Jericho, He would indeed begin His final journey north...to Jerusalem...

"How is your little task coming along?" asked Kara, as Lucifer followed the twelve disciples who moved up the road from Jericho. Judas, as usual, lagged behind the others. He preferred his own company these days and was seriously considering leaving the band of disciples altogether.

"Judas?" asked Lucifer. "See for yourself. He is increasingly vexed and withdrawn. But I have very little to do with this change of heart."

Kara and Lucifer continued walking along. From time to time a holy angel moved in close as if to ascertain their movements, and then pulled out again. Kara would scowl at or curse them.

"So Judas is a natural traitor?" asked Kara. "Interesting."

"As natural as anyone with freedom to choose his destiny," said Lucifer. "He grows weaker by the day in his love for Jesus. And I can feel his envy of the others for their closeness to Him. But mostly it is Jesus' own teachings that are driving him away."

"Thy Kingdom come, thy will be done," scoffed Kara. "Sounds as if Judas will not bend to that will!"

"Why should he?" asked Lucifer. "Judas has ambition to live. He follows a Man whose ambition is to die. Judas seeks position and prominence. His Master teaches humility and prudence. Judas seeks a Kingdom from without. Jesus promises a Kingdom from within."

"Quite a dilemma," agreed Kara. "But delightful."

"It is the talk of death that will push him over," said Lucifer matter-of-factly. "Just listen to the Man! How could anyone with even a spot of ambition follow such a depressing scoundrel?"

They listened in as Jesus continued speaking.

"Thus it must be," He said. "We shall go to Jerusalem and I shall be delivered over to the chief priests and the scribes and I shall be condemned to death."

The disciples looked at each other, but said nothing. They had learned long ago they didn't always understand what Jesus was saying. They comforted each other with the possibility that Jesus was speaking in parables once more.

"I will then be turned over to the Gentile rulers who shall mock and scourge Me and then crucify Me."

He stopped and turned to His disciples.

"But on the third day, the Son of Man shall rise again!"

"Rise again?" asked Kara nervously. "Is that possible?"

"Of course not," said Lucifer. "I believe the Lord has positioned Himself in a very compromising situation. No, Kara, Jesus will die. And when He does the dream shall die with Him." He laughed. "He saved others. But how could He possibly save Himself?"

"By God the Father, of course," said Kara.

"Exactly," said Lucifer. "And that is precisely the position wherein He has compromised Himself."

"How so, my prince?" asked Kara hopefully.

"I never really understood until Jesus said that He and the Father were One. And as you pointed out, the Father would most likely save the Son. There is, however, one major flaw with that possibility."

"And that is?" asked Kara.

"In this case, the Father *is* the Son!"

Kara nodded in understanding.

"So if Jesus dies…"

"Then the possibility of the Father saving Him dies with Him!"

"Judas!"

"Yes, my Lord?" Judas answered.

"Do not rebuke Mary," Jesus said.

"But Master, this perfume is very expensive. It might have been sold and the money given to the poor! Instead she has wasted it by drenching Your feet with it!"

Jesus gave Mary a reassuring look. He turned back to Judas. They were in the room of Lazarus' house where they had met for a celebration. Bethany was situated close enough to Jerusalem that Jesus had decided to stay there during the week. He knew the Jews in Jerusalem were watching for Him, and preferred to stay away from the Holy City during the evening.

"Judas, Mary is anointing Me as one would anoint a person for burial. The poor shall always be here. But I will not!"

Judas stood silently, excusing himself from the room. He walked outside, where he saw a group of men talking. He had become weary of the gawkers and beggars—somebody always wanting something. That was how he justified his own stealing of the funds from the ministry. In fact, the reason he was upset with Mary was that he had hoped to sell the precious perfume and take some of the money for himself.

After all, why shouldn't he? Jesus had not come through with His promise. Where was the Kingdom He spoke of? Three years he had followed this Man; sleeping on the cold ground; going hungry at times; being persecuted by his countrymen.

And for what? So they could wander from place to place in search of a door that would open to them for the night? He was more than justified in stealing some of the money. He looked at it as earned rather than stolen.

"Such a waste of money," came a voice. *"All of that perfume wasted on His feet when you might have taken your rightful share."*

Judas groaned under his breath.

"What difference does it make if Jesus only lives to die?"

Judas walked down the path away from the city to where Lazarus' now empty tombs was. He looked at the tomb. Jesus was certainly an extraordinary Man.

"Jesus, You are wonderful," Judas admitted out loud, speaking toward the tomb. "I must admit it. I have seen many miracles in my time with You. I came to You and You accepted me—something not too many people had done in my life. And You promised everything to us—though it cost everything. And we agreed!"

He was pacing in front of the tomb now as he spoke.

"And yet the Kingdom delays..."

"But where is the Kingdom You promised?" he asked aloud. "I would follow You anywhere, if You were truly headed to some glorious place. But You speak of nothing but death these days. Where is the glory in death? Are we to die as well?"

Judas looked down at his feet and saw evidence of the bandages from just a few days earlier. He picked one up and held it.

"Is it not time to put an end to all of this?"

Judas looked around, embarrassed at his thought, as if someone might have heard him thinking such a thing. And yet, he felt an odd agreement with the notion. Perhaps it was time he got out. Maybe he should return to his home...

"You could become a legend yourself...You could even profit by the end of this nonsense by serving a true kingdom—a kingdom of this world..."

Judas dropped the linen binding and tried to shake off the feeling he was having. He trembled as he thought about the possibility of being used as an instrument for the destruction of Jesus. Could it be? Was it better for the nation that Jesus perish and His false hope of an invisible Kingdom perish with Him?

"If He were truly God, would not the priests be in agreement with Him?"

That was it! Perhaps the chief priests would have an answer for him. Perhaps he should seek them out for counsel on how he should dispel this whole business. Was it not prudent to seek the counsel of the custodians of the faith?

"Seek out the priests and see a true kingdom arise..."

"Judas! Come along!" Andrew called out.

"Coming," said Judas.

He looked about him as if he wanted to make sure he was quite alone even though he had spoken to no one. He then trotted up the path to join the others.

Berenius and Kara were standing near the tomb. Lucifer stood on top of the rocky opening. Kara was nodding his head in approval at Berenius' performance.

"Very good, Berenius," he said. "I think you captured his mind magnificently."

"True," said Berenius. "But it will be up to Lucifer to capture his heart."

"All in due time," Lucifer said. "For now, we must develop a way for Judas to meet with some of Zichri's scouts."

He glided down to the entrance of the empty tomb.

"I assure you both this tomb shall host Lazarus' rotting flesh again. Only this time there shall be no Messiah to interfere." He smiled at them. "I would say this should prove to be a most interesting Passover!"

Jesus had decided on Bethany as the place from where He would journey to Jerusalem each day during the Passover Week. Situated on the far slope of the Mount of Olives, He was comfortable with the place where Mary and Martha lived and where He raised their brother and His friend, Lazarus, from the dead.

It was also in keeping with tradition, as well as by order of the security-conscious Romans, that pilgrims attending the annual feast should only remain in the city during the day. In the evening they were to spend the night in outlying cities or in the hills. That first morning of the week, Jesus set out toward the Holy City. His journey brought Him, along with His disciples, over the top of the Mount of Olives and then down its western slope leading to the great city below. The view of the ancient city, that had played so long in the hearts and minds of the people of Israel, was spectacular!

Directly below was the Necropolis—the "city of the dead"—a graveyard that had been in place long before Jesus was on the earth. The disciples could not help but feel uncomfortable surveying the vast cemetery in light of Jesus' insistence He would soon die at the hands of the chief priests and the Gentiles.

From here they continued on through the groves of olive trees and down into the Kidron Valley leading to a great wall—the platform built by Herod the Great called the Royal Porch, which encircled the Temple. It was here, on the eastern side of the city, through the gate called Beautiful, that Jesus would make His entry into the city.

A.D.33

Monday, the Last Week

The Temple

"Hosanna to the Son of David!"

"Blessed is He who comes in the name of the Lord!"

The crowds lined the streets to see the entrance of the Man from Galilee of whom they had heard so much. Filled with the faithful who had journeyed to Jerusalem for the Passover Week, the city welcomed Jesus as their hero. Many of them gathered near the road leading through the Beautiful Gate and lay palm branches down—symbols of joy and celebration. But not all of Jerusalem celebrated.

Zichri stood on the Royal Porch with several other high ranking priests watching Jesus enter the city. From time to time he looked at people rushing toward the throng with palm leaves and shouting, "Hosanna!" He gave a look to the others and walked off. They followed him along the porch and entered the Temple. Walking through the outer courts, he brought them to the Court of Priests, where they could talk in private.

Unseen by them, Berenius, under strict orders from Kara to keep the pressure on these men to destroy Jesus, followed along.

The whole court was abuzz with priests excitedly talking about the stirring in the city. Zichri was disgusted by what he saw in his fellow priests. He was also alarmed as he heard activity in the Antonia, which suggested that soldiers were being dispatched to keep order.

"This Fellow is going to see all of us destroyed," he said, as a priest hurried by to catch a glimpse of the Miracle Worker. "And these fools want to see who He is!"

"Caiaphas is aware, of course?" Zechar, one of the priests, asked.

"How could he not be?" Zichri snorted. "The time for action is rapidly approaching. Caiaphas is convening a meeting with some of the Herodians to determine if there is something we can do jointly."

"The High Priest and the Herodians?" asked Zeruiah, another priest. "Quite an unlikely alliance, isn't it?"

"These are unlikely times," said Zichri. "But a bit of good news in all of this is about to be reported, I believe."

He indicated Shallah, who had just returned from gathering information on the disciples. He joined the group in the inner court. Zichri smiled as Shallah approached.

"Tell us the news, Shallah." demanded Zichri.

"As you can hear, the city has opened its arms for Him," said Shallah. "The Man is immensely popular with the ignorant and unlettered. And his disciples are completely supportive of Him. That is, eleven of them..."

"Is it the one we have heard of?" asked Zichri.

"Yes," said Shallah. "You can report to the High Priest that if there is any disciple who is ripe for betrayal, it is the man Judas. He is different from the others. And seems to be nearing the end of his patience."

"How so," asked Zeruiah.

"I have planted men in various places to speak to him when he was off by himself," Shallah continued. "It seems what was once love for Jesus has turned to disappointment in Him. He is ready to bolt—but lacks the proper...motivation."

"Motivation?" asked Zichri.

"The man is greedy beyond belief," Shallah continued. "He has even stolen from the group's treasury. I think he can be bought."

Zichri considered the words for a moment. Just then another shout of "Hosanna!" could be heard echoing throughout the inner court. Zichri looked up resolutely. He placed his hand on Shallah's shoulder.

"See to it," he said. "As for charges brought against the Man, we shall have to meet with Caiaphas. I know he will want to move, but at the proper time. If we move too quickly the people will tear us to pieces."

"Very well," said Shallah. "I shall see to Judas."

"And I shall see to Jesus," said Zichri, smiling.

Berenius could only shake his head in utter disbelief at the vanity of humans. "And I shall see to all of you," he said, vanishing to speak to Kara.

"GET THESE THINGS OUT OF HERE!"

Jesus' words echoed throughout the Court of Gentiles where the moneychangers had set up their tables in order to sell sacrificial elements to pilgrims from all over the world. They were astonished to see Jesus for a second time turning over their tables and railing about the Temple being "My Father's house!"

"I told you this is a place of prayer—not a place of commerce and thievery!"

The last of the moneychangers scrambled away as the crowds watched in astonishment. The priests, on the other hand, were amazed at His brazenness. Jesus dropped the whip and sat down.

The priests, huddled as usual, discussed what to do. Suddenly, Zichri emerged from the shadows, ready to confront Jesus for His behavior. It was one thing to enter the city and have a crowd of fools think He was a god. It was quite another thing for Him to come into the Temple and *act* like one.

"He is only providing the evidence we need," said Zichri quietly to an aide, before moving over to Jesus. "Then we shall have Him."

"Why not take Him now?" questioned the aide.

"Not now," cautioned Zichri. "Not before the Passover. Be patient. Three more days and He shall never be heard from again!"

"Why is it your Lord insists on such drama?" asked Kara.

He was speaking to Gabriel, who had recently arrived at the Temple. Most of the higher ruling angels were beginning to descend upon Jerusalem. They all knew something out of the ordinary would happen during Passover. Gabriel turned to the angel who once served with him in Heaven.

"You speak of drama?" he asked. "Your master is the inventor of theatrics."

"Perhaps you will find this latest drama amusing," Kara sneered, looking at Zichri who had reached Jesus and was speaking to Him. "And deadly."

"Listen here!" began Zichri. "By whose authority are You doing these things?"

The other priests grunted in agreement. Jesus looked up at the angry men who stood next to Him. Dressed in their dark garments, they looked every inch the part of leaders of the covenant. Yet Jesus knew what was in their hearts.

"And who gave You this authority?"

Jesus stood and brushed the dirt off His hands. He turned to the men and answered. "I'll tell you the answer to that question, provided you first answer a question."

The men looked at each other suspiciously. But they were not willing to let this chance slip past them and agreed to hear the question.

"Very well, Rabbi." said Zichri, cautiously.

"The baptism of John," said Jesus. "Was it from Heaven or was it from men?"

Zichri was dumbfounded. When one of the younger priests was about to blurt out an answer he silenced him. The priests huddled together to discuss their answer.

"He's a crafty one," said Zichri. "We cannot answer Him. If we say John's baptism was from Heaven, He will condemn us for not having believed. But if we say it was from men, the people who regard John as a prophet will be against us!"

Zichri finally approached Jesus with his answer.

"We cannot tell You."

"Then neither shall I tell you by what authority I do these things," answered Jesus.

"Good question," said Gabriel, who had watched the encounter. "Wouldn't you agree, Kara?"

Kara gave Gabriel an icy stare.

"Riddles are not going to save Him, archangel!" he fumed and vanished.

Gabriel could not help but laugh.

"Don't go away just yet," continued Jesus. "Let Me tell you a story."

The priests agreed to hear Him.

"Tell Me what you think," He continued. "There was a man who had two sons. He went to the first and said, 'Son, go and work today in the vineyard.'

'I will not,' the rude boy answered, but later he changed his mind and went.

Then the father went to the other son and asked him to go into the vineyard and work as well. Now this boy answered, 'I will, sir,' but he did not go.

Which of the two did what his father wanted?"

"What is the trick here?" asked Zichri suspiciously.

"No trick," said Jesus.

"The first boy," someone answered. "Obviously".

Jesus nodded His head and said to them, "I'm telling you that tax collectors, prostitutes, and others whom you despise are entering the Kingdom of God ahead of you. You see, John came to show you the way of righteousness, and you did not believe him. But the tax collectors and prostitutes and those whom you abhor believed."

Incensed, the priests began to walk away. Jesus stopped them one more time to relate another story.

"There was a landowner who planted a large vineyard. He fully developed the property. He put a wall around it, dug a winepress in it and even built a watchtower. Then he rented the vineyard to some farmers and went away on a long journey. His plan was to send his servants to collect the fruit when it came into season.

"But the tenants abused his servants; they beat one, they killed another one, and stoned a third. So he sent other servants to them. Only this time he sent more along. But they, too, were mistreated. Finally, he decided to send his own son, believing they would respect the owner's son."

Jesus glanced at the cold eyes watching Him.

"Go on," said Zichri.

"Instead, they said to each other, 'This is the heir. If we kill him we can share in his inheritance!' So they took him and threw him out of the vineyard and killed him. Now here is My question: what will the owner do when he returns?"

"He will bring those ingrates to a wretched end," they replied, "and he will find other tenants who will respect his property and serve him."

Jesus asked, "Have you never read in the Scriptures where it is written, 'The stone the builders rejected has become the capstone; the Lord has done this, and it is marvelous in our eyes?'"

"What about it?" asked Zichri, becoming increasingly agitated.

"Listen to Me," continued Jesus. "The Kingdom of God will be taken away from you and given to a people who will respect its rule. He who falls on this stone will be broken to pieces, but he on whom it falls will be crushed."

Zichri looked coldly at Jesus.

"You are speaking of us, of course," he said.

"I say we take Him here and now," someone whispered.

"No," said Zichri, turning away from Jesus. "His time will come. But not here and not now unless you wish to deal with these fools who fawn upon Him."

He watched as Jesus made His way across the court, moving around the tables He had turned over. "His time will soon be over and He will be forgotten like all the others who have come to this Temple to disturb it."

"Master?"

Jesus turned to see a party of Herodians standing nearby. These men, political allies of the Herods, kept a wary eye on anything that might disturb the peace of the realm—and usually this meant the Temple. They kept their power through bribery and cunning, and had become increasingly interested in this miracle-working Nazarene. Some of them had been conferring with the Pharisees, and Zichri was nodding vigorously to the lead official Achish, one of Herod's envoys to Jerusalem. Achish ambled over to where Jesus stood.

"Greetings, good Rabbi," Achish said, bowing his head slightly.

Jesus said nothing to the man.

"I don't understand this hostility toward You," he began. "We know You speak the truth and that You teach God's ways. We also know You are partial to no man or group."

Jesus listened silently.

"You defer to no one because You are so wise," Achish continued. "We therefore have a question to put to You."

Jesus gave no response.

"After all, as custodians of the peace and as liaisons with Caesar, it is important that things of a delicate political nature be resolved reasonably."

"Here is the question," Zichri burst in. "Is it lawful to pay tax to Caesar or not?"

"The poll tax of course," added Achish, disturbed by Zichri's intrusion.

Jesus looked at both of them.

"Why do you persist in provoking Me?" He asked. "Why are you testing Me, you hypocrites? Do you have one of these coins?"

An aide to Achish produced a denarius and handed it to Jesus. Jesus held out the coin for both men to see. Zichri looked at Achish uncomfortably.

"Whose image and inscription do you see here?" Jesus asked.

"Caesar's, of course," said Zichri.

"Then pay to Caesar the things that belong to Caesar. But give to God those things that belong to God!"

Achish, although preferring to have cornered Jesus in some legal entanglement, nodded and was satisfied with the answer. Zichri was astonished. Jesus handed the coin back to Zichri, who threw it to the ground and walked off. Achish signaled the men with him that it was time to leave.

CHAPTER 17

"How goes the matter with Judas?"

"Twice today Jesus has bested the opposition," said Crispin, who had just joined Gabriel in the Temple. "This is quite a day."

"True," said Gabriel. "They are getting more and more impertinent with Him."

"With humans that means they are getting desperate," cautioned Crispin. "Better keep quite alert." He scanned the area and saw a number of unholy angels about. "These loathsome fellows have been here for some time. Ever since Jesus began His ministry some three years ago."

Gabriel looked at the religious spirits whose place of power was in all places of human worship. Their task was to do anything and everything to keep men's eyes and minds off the One True God.

"I'd say they have been here much longer than that, Crispin," Gabriel said.

"Kara, what are you doing with that rabble?" asked Pellecus.

He discovered Kara at the Temple among the Sadducees, whose allegiance was more to Herod than the Lord. He had crafted in their minds a foolproof question to trap Jesus. They were even now on their way to find Him.

"They are on their way to find Jesus," he said proudly. "My little visit with Gabriel reminded me we'll need more than the Pharisees and Herodians to bring Jesus to account."

"Jesus. He is in another part of the Temple," said Pellecus. "He just made fools of the priests *and* the Herodians. Again."

"Easy enough," said Kara. "The Pharisees are so bent on being right they do not know how to be subtle. And the Herodians simply want to keep their grip on the throne. But *these* fellows—they are crafty and jealous of the Temple. I hope they will prove a powerful adversary."

Pellecus scoffed at the notion. He had seen Jesus in too many instances where His answers completely humbled any opposition. Pellecus' pride had been injured as well, since he had promoted the Pharisees all along as the intellectual response to Jesus' murky gospel. But he followed along with Kara and the Sadducees who were determined to avenge the moneychangers as well as the honor of the Temple.

The Sadducees, more political than religious, were perfectly suited to Kara's manipulations. They were bent on seeing Jesus destroyed, not because of His offense to the faith, but because of His threat to the peace and their position as wardens of the Temple. The ever-present threat of Roman intervention kept the Sadducees on a precarious perch balancing between submission to Rome and loyalty to the cult.

The Sadducees emerged during the bloody and confusing times when the Maccabees controlled Judah. They took their name from Zadok, the high priest of David, from whom they claimed descent. They were involved in the political life of the Jews and were closely associated with the Temple.

Their ambivalence to Jesus began when His cousin John called them "a brood of vipers" as they came to watch him baptize in the Jordan. Their claim, "We have Abraham as our father," was met with John's stunning rebuke, "God is able, from these stones, to raise up children to Abraham!"

They were also aware that Jesus was warning people to stay away from the teaching of the Sadducees. He said His followers should bewar, and have nothing to do with their teachings. They did not believe in the resurrection of the dead, and believed that angels were simply fables. Thus, they now approached Jesus, with Kara's encouragement, to trump His knowledge with a question of their own.

"The Pharisees certainly haven't shown themselves any threat," admitted Pellecus, "at least not on an intellectual level. Still, in the end, it is religion and not politics that will destroy Jesus."

"I suspect a little of both," sniffed Kara. "But who knows? Perhaps the common threat of Jesus will bring these two together to destroy Him."

Pellecus smirked and added, "Jesus did come to bring men together, did He not? I would say He is successfully uniting His enemies even now!"

Kara laughed.

"They marveled that only Jesus could bring a Simon the Zealot and a Matthew the Tax Gatherer together under one cause! But what would they say about His ability to bring the Sadducees and Pharisees together to destroy Him?"

<hr />

"Teacher!"

Once more Jesus looked up to see a group of men approaching Him. This time it was the Sadducees. He looked about and—yes—lingering in the background were several Pharisees in the company of Zichri.

"Another question?" Jesus asked wearily.

A couple of His disciples snickered.

Ignoring Him, Zereth, the lead priest among this group, spoke up.

"Rabbi, as You know, Moses told us if a man dies without having children, his own brother must marry the widow so that she might have children in his name."

"Yes?" responded Jesus. "That is what the Law says."

"Good," Zereth continued. "Now here is an interesting puzzle. There were seven brothers. The first brother married and soon after died. Rabbi, since he had no children, his brother stepped in as the Law required."

He looked around as he told his story, noticing a crowd gathering. He raised his voice.

"And so the same thing happened right down through all the brothers—to the second and third brother, right on down to the seventh. And then the woman died! Now then, at the resurrection, whose wife will she be of the seven, since all of them were married to her?"

Jesus could only shake His head in disbelief. Zichri had moved in and was urging the crowd on, repeating the question and acting as if it were all very serious.

"You who do not believe in the Resurrection are asking Me this question?" Jesus asked.

Zereth looked uncomfortably at Zichri, knowing the Pharisees did believe in a resurrection. He looked back at Jesus.

"First of all, you are in error because you do not know the Scriptures or the power of God. So how can you possibly ask an intelligent question or deliver a truthful answer? But I will tell you."

Jesus spoke not only to the Sadducees but to the crowd around them. Zichri, by now, had stopped working the crowd and was preparing to arrest Jesus as soon as he uttered a heresy.

"At the resurrection people will neither marry nor be given in marriage," He said. "In that regard, they will be like the angels in Heaven."

He turned sharply to Zereth and the other Sadducees.

"But about the resurrection of the dead—have you not read that God Himself said, 'I am the God of Abraham, the God of Isaac, and the God of Jacob?'"

"Of course we have," said Zereth, as if defending himself in front of the people.

"So God is not the God of the dead but of the living," said Jesus.

The crowds began muttering, astonished at His teaching and wisdom in so many things. Zereth and Zichri looked at the people's faces, and could tell they believed Jesus' words. The Sadducees remained silent, unable to respond.

Not about to let Jesus get by with this, Zichri signaled and a Pharisee by the name of Eli, an expert in the Law, came forward.

"Teacher, which is the greatest commandment in the Law?" he asked.

Jesus quickly replied: " 'Love the Lord your God with all your heart and with all your soul and with all your mind.' This is the first and greatest commandment of them all. And the second is like it: 'Love your neighbor as yourself.' All the Law and the Prophets hang on these two commandments."

Before they could question Him further, Jesus addressed the Pharisees.

"What do you think about the Messiah? Whose Son is He?"

Zichri hushed the crowd so he could hear the question. They conferred a few seconds before deciding the answer, "The Son of David."

"Very good," Jesus said. "But how is it that David, speaking by the Spirit, calls Him 'Lord'? As you recall, he says, 'The Lord said to My Lord: Sit at My right hand until I put Your enemies under Your feet."

Jesus turned to the people and asked:

"If, then, David calls Him 'Lord,' how can He be his Son?"

Zichri was enraged. He looked at the others and was so beside himself he could not speak. A few of the Pharisees made a weak suggestion here or there, but they were otherwise silenced by the authority of Jesus' answer.

Kara and Pellecus watched as the three groups of bested men—the Pharisees, the Herodians, and the Sadducees—murmured among themselves. The crowd in the outer court of the Temple was pressing in to hear Jesus.

"These fools will never defeat Jesus with words," remarked Pellecus. "Look how the people hang on His every word. It's obvious they believe Him."

"It is not by twisting words that the Son of Man will be destroyed," came a voice. "It is by twisting minds."

"Ah, my prince," said Kara, as Lucifer walked over. They stood under one of the porticos in the outer court of the Temple. "How true. These men have proven that words are useless with Jesus."

"Nevertheless, you will continue fanning the passions of these men," Lucifer said, looking at Zichri. "In the end they will serve us well."

"How goes the matter with Judas?" asked Pellecus. "Has he turned yet?"

"As I have taken over that assignment personally I can assure you he is very close to 'turning'," snapped Lucifer. "I should think in the next day or two he shall be paying a visit to the high priest. It has already entered his mind."

"You mean, it was introduced into his mind," said Kara smiling.

"Yes and no," said Lucifer. "What Judas does is of his own free will—just as every other crime committed by humans. I am merely expediting what is already in his heart. I am appealing to his greed, you know. And while normally we can allow men to run their lives with little interference, as long as they are not in covenant with the Most High, in the case of Judas I will leave nothing to chance. Thus I am personally seeing to it."

"And then?" asked Pellecus.

"Then we shall see what the life of Jesus can be bought for," said Lucifer.

Jesus began walking in a circle, speaking to the crowd. When He came to the Pharisees and Sadducees, He stopped. He gestured toward the religious leaders, then spoke to the crowd.

"These men, these teachers of Israel," He began, "they sit in the seat of Moses and have great learning and wisdom. And so you must obey them and do everything they tell you."

Zichri and the other priests looked at each other as if they were trying to figure out just what Jesus was saying. Several of them nodded in cautious agreement.

"But do not do what they do, for they do not practice what they preach!"

"Here now, Rabbi," protested Zichri. Jesus ignored him and went on.

"These men create heavy loads and put them on your shoulders And yet they themselves are not willing to help you carry the burden they impose upon you."

The crowd murmured. Zichri sent his priests throughout the crowd to begin quelling some of the passions that were brewing. The Sadducees simply listened, hands folded, faces as smug as ever.

"Everything...everything these men do is done as a show—to be seen of other men. Have you ever noticed how they love the place of honor at banquets and the most important seats in the synagogues? Have you ever seen them in the marketplaces being greeted by the people and loving it so? Oh yes—they especially love it when you call them 'rabbi'!"

Several people in the crowd, as well as a few of the disciples that were with Jesus in the Temple, laughed aloud. Zichri shot a sharp glance in the direction of one of those in the crowd. The man stopped immediately.

"Rabbi, a word please," pleaded Zichri.

"Woe to you, teachers of the law and Pharisees, you hypocrites! You are shutting the Kingdom of Heaven and the hope of ever entering into it in the faces of men who are seeking it. At least move out of the way and let others enter into the Kingdom which you yourselves shall never enter!"

"How dare you say..."

"Woe to you, teachers of the law and Pharisees, you hypocrites! You work very hard to convert someone over to your way of thinking. And in the end that poor fellow becomes twice as hell-bound as you yourselves!

"Hell-bound? Really, Jesus..."

"Woe to you, blind leaders! You strain out a gnat but swallow a camel whole!"

Laughter again.

"Woe to you, teachers of the law and Pharisees, you hypocrites! You clean with great diligence the outside of the cup and dish to keep from being unclean. Don't you see that on the inside there is greed and self-indulgence? You blind Pharisee! Clean first what is inside, and then the outside shall become clean!"

Zichri and his men were slowly becoming more and more enraged at Jesus' accusations. But they dared not touch Him in the Temple.

"Woe to you, teachers of the law and Pharisees, you hypocrites! You are like freshly scrubbed and whitewashed tombs that are beautiful on the outside. Yet consider the rot and corruption housed within. So it is with you—looking fine and polished and righteous on the outside—yet on the inside you are full of hypocrisy and wickedness."

"Enough!" sputtered Zichri.

"You snakes! You vipers! How will you escape being condemned to hell?

But because of you, I am sending prophets and wise men and teachers. And yes—you will kill some of them, and harass others, and persecute many. You will hunt them down from town to town. But it shall be on your own heads that righteous blood shall be shed—just as has always been the case from Abel to Zechariah whom you murdered in God's Holy Temple!"

"Blasphemy!" shouted Zichri, who turned and stormed out of the area. The Temple guards were standing ready to make sure the crowd did not riot. Zichri could hear Jesus crying out as he left.

"Oh, Jerusalem! Jerusalem! You are the city that kills the prophets who are sent to save you! How often I have longed to gather your children together, as a hen gathers her chicks under her wings. But you are stiff-necked and unwilling. And now you shall become desolate."

Jesus turned back to the people and looked at them with compassion. Some of them were disturbed by His words; others had simply gathered to see what was going on; still others pondered this Man's ability to get the better of the Pharisees.

"I tell you all now, you will not see Me again until you say, 'Blessed is He who comes in the name of the Lord'!"

Lucifer turned to Kara and Pellecus following Jesus' address.

"That was it," he said. "He has just signed His own execution order. Mobilize the Pharisees and see they carry out the evil plans festering in their hearts."

Kara nodded with understanding.

"You, Pellecus, shall wait until the Romans are brought into this. That fool Pilate will have to give the order. These priests are supremely hypocritical, you know. Rather than a dagger in the back in some alley, they will want this to be done publicly and legally. But Pilate is a vacillator by nature—he may need shoring up."

Pellecus nodded.

"And I shall visit Judas," said Lucifer. "The matter is drawing to a close in his mind now."

His eyes lit up with a reddish glow. He turned his back on the two angels, looking in the direction of the Most Holy Place.

"And so our little adventure is coming to a close," he began. "One way or another, for good or bad, this week shall decide the fate of Jesus, ourselves and humanity. There is much blood to come, be sure. But I never demanded blood. I would have settled for a resolution long ago if the Most High were not so stubborn. But He has determined we play out our little game to the bloody end. And so we shall." He smiled. "Wait and see. As I said before, Jesus will bleed like any other Man!"

A.D. 33

Tuesday, the Last Week

Mount of Olives

"Our Lord certainly loves this place," said Nathaniel, resting his aching feet.

Bartholomew nodded in agreement.

"Up and down, back and forth," interjected Thomas. "We must have been on this mountain a dozen times in the past few months!"

"And we'll go a dozen more if the Lord leads us here," said Nathaniel.

"A dozen more?" Judas asked wearily.

The men laughed.

The disciples had left Jerusalem and stopped at the Mount of Olives, a few hundred yards from the Temple Mount. Only two miles long, the Mount of Olives is a low ridge rising over two hundred feet above the Kidron Valley. Some of the disciples recalled numerous events in their nation's history that had taken place there.

David fled over the Mount of Olives to escape his son, Absalom. King Solomon built pagan altars there. Later, the reformer-king Josiah destroyed them. The prophet Ezekiel had a vision of the Lord there; and in Nehemiah's time, the people came bearing olive branches for the renewal of the Feast of Tabernacles, which they had not celebrated since being taken into captivity.

The disciples were personally familiar with the place, as it had become their route between Bethany and Jerusalem during Passover Week. Enjoying a light breeze on the gently sloping hillside, they rested from their long days of ministry. How far away it all seemed right now—the pressing of the crowds; the venom of the Pharisees; the burden of not completely understanding, and yet trusting in the Man who had led them these past three-and-one-half years.

"I wonder how it will end," came a voice.

"What?" asked Peter, looking around.

"I wonder how it will end for Jesus. And for all of us."

It was James.

"You know as well as I do," said Peter. "Jesus has promised that we are to be a part of His Kingdom."

"A Kingdom not of this world," said Judas with a bite of sarcasm. "How practical."

Peter began to object to Judas when Thomas stopped him.

"It's a fair question," he admitted. "Judas is only speaking what all of us have thought. I mean...where does it all end?"

"Let me tell you," said Jesus, walking into their midst.

"My Lord, I was not doubting You," said James, now regretting he had given voice to his thoughts.

"Don't worry, James," said Jesus. "I know you all are wondering what is to come." He sat down and the men drew in. "You know what is to come of Me. Now let Me tell you what is to come of this world."

He then began to teach the men what must happen.

"Now you'll get some answers, teacher," said Serus.

Crispin stood next to a large olive tree near where Jesus sat with His disciples. He only nodded and grunted an affirmative. Not his usual demeanor.

"What is troubling you, Crispin?" asked Serus.

Crispin looked at Serus as if he were surprised that Serus had picked up on his mood. He walked over closer to the men.

"It occurs to me we are very near the end of this ministry," he said. "I was thinking back to all we have witnessed; all that has been done on behalf of these humans; all that has transpired since Eden. And now it is drawing to a close."

Serus smiled.

"But of course it is," he said. "It had to come to an end one day."

"Yes," Crispin admitted. "But I am beginning to see that the end coming is very different from the one I had envisioned."

"What do you mean, teacher?" asked Serus.

"I mean, that the love of God is beyond the capacity of even angels to understand," he said, marveling. "And I believe I am beginning to understand what Jesus means when He speaks of dying at the hands of men."

"He has been talking about that for some time now," said Serus. "Most of the angels believe He intends another meaning—something cryptic."

"Do they now?" mused Crispin.

Serus looked sharply at Crispin.

"You mean to say that you really believe that Jesus—the Most High—intends to be taken by men and killed?"

Crispin looked at Jesus, then turned to Serus.

"No, Serus. I never said I believe Jesus will be taken by men. I said I think He will give Himself to them."

"Master," said James. "Will you tell us what we might expect at the end of the age? What will be the sign of Your return?"

"First of all, be watchful that nobody fools you. There will be many claiming to be Me, who will come in My name. And many will be deceived! Many things must happen before the end comes. But be watchful! There will be talk of wars and much violence throughout the world. People will rise against other people, countries shall go to war against other countries. Not only that—the earth itself shall suffer violence with earthquakes and famines occurring all over. But these are like birth pains and not yet the end."

"But what about us?' asked Thomas. "Here and now?"

Peter turned and glared at Thomas. But Jesus waved Peter aside.

"A fair question, Thomas," He said. "And here is the answer. You and others in the future who come after you, will suffer persecution and death and all manner of hatred because of your love for Me. In fact, the intense persecution will cause many to falter in their faith. Some will betray the truth, testifying against their brothers and turning them in to the authorities for fear of them. False prophets will emerge and lead many people astray. And love in those days shall grow cold as wickedness increases."

"Is there any hope then?" asked Andrew.

"Yes, Andrew," said Jesus, encouragingly. "For he who stands firm to the end will be saved. What's more, this good news of the Kingdom you now preach shall be preached to all the nations of the world—only then will the end come."

"But when shall this be?" asked James. "How shall we know?"

"I'll tell you," said Jesus. "Though it is a mystery. When you see standing in the Holy Place 'the abomination that causes desolation,'—you know, the one spoken of by the prophet Daniel—then you should be prepared for the end. Those who are in Judea should flee to the mountains. Don't worry about going back for things. I pity the women who are pregnant in those troubling times.

"I tell you that there is coming a time of great travail that has never been witnessed before in this world—nor shall it ever be witnessed again. But because of you who know the Father, those awful days will be cut short—or else no one would survive them. And so you see I am telling you all these things ahead of time."

"So we may look for Your coming?" asked Bartholomew.

"Yes!" said Jesus. "But beware. There will be many people claiming to be the Christ. Some will say, 'He's out there in the desert'. Others will say, 'no, He's over here'."

"But do not believe it. Let Me describe how the coming of the Son of Man shall be. It is as I described before: just as lightning that comes from the east is visible also in the west—that is how My return shall be."

Jesus stood, looking into the sky as He continued speaking.

"The sun will be darkened, and the moon will not give off its light; the very stars will fall from the sky, and the great heavenly bodies will be shaken. The nations will mourn because they will know the time of the Son of Man is at hand. And then they will see the Son of Man coming in the clouds of the sky, with power and great glory. And a loud trumpet will signal the holy angels, and they will gather those who love His coming from one end of Heaven to the other!"

"But when, Master?" pleaded Andrew. "When shall these things happen?"

Jesus smiled at Andrew.

"I don't know, Andrew. No man knows—nor angel. Only the Father in Heaven knows the hour of the Son's return. But this much I can tell you: No one knows about that day or hour. Remember how it was in Noah's days? That's how it shall be. Nobody expected the Flood to come crashing down on them, and so they continued their normal lives—eating, drinking, raising their families—until that day when the ark was shut and the Flood came. That is how the return of the Son of Man shall be."

"So what are we to do?" asked Thomas.

"As I said you must keep watch. You don't know when the Lord might return—so you must be ready at all times. Think of it this way: If the owner of the house had known what time of night the thief was coming, he would have kept watch and would not have let his house be broken into. You see? You must also be ready for the return of the Son of Man—just like that thief coming at some unknown hour.

"I tell you though, the Lord shall be returning for the servant who is looking for His return. You know, a faithful servant takes care of his master's place when the master has gone away on a long trip. He keeps things in order so that when his master returns all will be in place. But a foolish servant thinks while the master is away he can do as he pleases. The master will return unexpectedly and condemn him."

Jesus looked at the men with deeply concerned eyes, as if seeing all that He was describing in his mind's eye. "And he will cut the foolish servant to pieces and assign him a place with the hypocrites, where there will be weeping and gnashing of teeth."

Crispin was silent for a while after Jesus finished speaking. He was grasping the enormity of these things. He realized Jesus' ministry on earth was only the beginning of something far greater, something far more glorifying and terrible that must happen in the future. It would be a difficult and dangerous but rewarding destiny for the humans who knew the Lord!

CHAPTER 18

"We need to settle this before the Passover."

A.D. 33

Tuesday Evening, The Last Week

House of Caiaphas

The light in the room was dim, just enough to make out the faces of the several men around a large table. They had gathered in the house of Caiaphas, to discuss the final disposition of Jesus. Kara and Berenius were in the room as well, silent, dark shadows unseen by the men and enjoying the final fruits of their labor.

"You know why we are meeting," Caiaphas said. "I had hoped it would not come to this. But this Jesus is causing the people to lose confidence in us. Therefore, the good of the nation must supercede the life of this Man."

"The Sadducees have assured us of their cooperation," said Achish. "And we already know Herod will not stand in our way."

"It's a dirty business having to consort with such men," said Caiaphas. "But we have to act."

"When shall we strike?" asked a priest.

"We *never* strike," said Caiaphas. "It is the Law that shall strike. We will only fulfill the requirements of the Law that a blasphemer be put to death."

"The Romans shall never agree to that," said Achish. "Pilate thinks little enough of our religious controversies."

"Perhaps," said Caiaphas. "But he thinks a great deal of his position. You leave Pilate to me. If he sees Jesus as a potential threat to the peace of this region which he governs, then he will take an enormous interest in our 'religious controversies'."

"Greetings all," came Zichri's voice, as he entered the room.

Achish watched as his master walked over to the table. Zichri glanced at Achish with a look that told him he had been successful.

"I have met with the man," Zichri said, whispering. "He is willing to give Jesus up. But he insists on meeting with you."

"What?" cried Caiaphas. "That is out of the question. Make the deal and be done with it!"

"I beg your pardon, my priest. But he will not deal with us unless he can first speak with you." Zichri smirked. "I think the man wants to clear his conscience before he violates it!"

"Very well," Caiaphas said. "Tomorrow night. But tell him to be discreet about it. We need to settle this before the Passover."

"It shall be done," said Zichri.

"Did he name a price?" demanded Caiaphas.

"He did," said Zichri.

"I suppose we can draw it from the treasury," said Caiaphas, looking at his aide to make the arrangements.

"Oh, no bother with that," Zichri said. "It's a small sum."

"Indeed?" asked Caiaphas. "How much does he want?"

"Only thirty pieces of silver," said Zichri, laughing.

The men snickered at the thought of such a paltry amount.

"I had no idea betrayal came so cheaply," said Caiaphas. "Otherwise I would have bought him a long time ago!"

The men left the room.

"Well done, Berenius," said Kara. "But I don't think Caiaphas will find the betrayal so cheap in the end."

A.D. 33

Wednesday, the Last Week

Bethany

Philip watched as a group of men, Greek according to their dress, approached him. He looked about to see if there were any of the other disciples nearby, but they had gone into Bethany. He nodded to them. It was not unusual to see people from all over the empire around Jerusalem during the Passover. Many made pilgrimages here at least once in their lives. Perhaps these were Greek Jews, or maybe Gentile seekers.

"You are one of the men of Jesus?" they asked.

Their accent was definitely Greek.

"Yes," said Philip "But He is not here right now."

"We have come to worship at the feast," said one of them. "My name is Aristobulus. My father owns property on the coast. He is a merchant."

He was speaking in a halting manner as if he were unsure of how to approach Philip and assure him that he was genuinely seeking the Lord. He looked back at his fellow Greeks who urged him on.

"But my father has not forgotten the Lord who has blessed him. And so we have come to honor the Lord in Jerusalem. We are staying nearby."

"What can I do for you, my friend?" asked Philip, relieving the discomfort of the man with his reassuring manner.

"We came to see Jesus," he said. "We have heard of Him, how He works miracles. And that He is perhaps the hope of Israel."

Philip sized the men up. Normally he was careful to protect Jesus. But he felt a sincerity in the man and excused himself.

"Wait here," he said. "I will look into it for you."

Philip raced into town and found Andrew. He explained the matter to him and the two of them went to the house where Jesus was staying, telling Him there were some Greek Jews who wanted to see Him. Jesus' face was intent—His eyes looking forward as if in deep thought. He listened to the explanation and then, gathering His disciples around Him, began speaking to them.

"I cannot go to all men," he said. "But take Me to those who seek Me. The hour has come that I should be glorified."

The disciples looked at one another with puzzled expressions. Andrew and Philip led Jesus and the other disciples to the spot where the Greeks waited. Several others had joined them now. Peter began to speak but was silenced by Jesus' hand. Jesus looked at Peter with great compassion.

"Yes, it is time. But I have to tell you My soul is troubled by it all."

He looked at the men whose faces He knew so well after three years of living, working, playing and serving together. He then looked at the men who sought Him out. "But this is what I came for. Shall I now say, 'Father, I don't want to do this?' No. I say rather, 'Father, glorify Your Name!'"

Suddenly a burst of thunder echoed through the Mount of Olives and down the Kidron Valley into Bethany. A Voice spoke from the thunder, shattering the air:

"I have both glorified Your Name, and shall glorify it again."

"Was that an angel?' asked someone.

"It was just thunder," said another, noting that the sky was clear.

Over the past few days, angels of both camps, wicked and holy, had begun descending upon Kidron. They all understood that a great contest ensued, although none clearly understood its meaning. Lucifer and several of his angels stood near the place where Jesus was now speaking. Holy angels were also present in greater numbers.

"Why does He not simply get to the point," fumed Kara. "He is always speaking to these fools in terms that humans cannot possibly grasp!"

Lucifer turned to Kara, whose smug face belied his own ignorance of the matter.

"And suppose you teach us what this all means," said Lucifer. "I had no idea you were so wise."

"The Man is going to die," said Kara defensively. Rugio and Pellecus enjoyed his discomfort. "I am simply wondering why He doesn't say so!"

"He has told them often enough," said Pellecus.

"I, for one, would like to be there when He takes His last breath," snarled Rugio.

"You will, Rugio," said Lucifer. "You will."

Jesus looked past the men, in the direction of Lucifer. Their eyes locked and Jesus continued speaking.

"Now is the judgment of this world upon us," He said, looking squarely at Lucifer. "And now the prince of this world shall be cast out."

The words had a paralyzing effect upon Lucifer, momentarily. He continued looking at Jesus, not so much in defiance but as an animal who has been mesmerized by a predator. He shook it off.

"We'll see who casts out whom," Lucifer managed.

Pellecus and Kara nodded eagerly. Rugio remained impassive.

"I leave you with this," Jesus continued. "For just a little while longer the Light will be with you. Walk therefore in the Light and become children of Light by believing."

He then left the area. Many people called after Him and some attempted to follow. But He managed to elude them all, and hid from the people for the remainder of the day. The Greeks thanked Philip for bringing Jesus to them and went back to the place they were staying for the Passover.

As the disciples walked back to the home of Simon the leper, where Jesus was staying, they saw a pilgrim. He was a man coming to the Passover. With him was his young son, who was holding a little spring lamb. Philip looked at the boy, remembering the time his own father had taken their lamb to be offered in sacrifice to the Lord. How difficult it was—but what a lesson about the price of sin.

Philip nudged Andrew as the father and son walked by.

"The lamb to the slaughter," he whispered. "Remember those days?"

Andrew nodded, remembering his own childhood when they were given a lamb to offer on Passover. He caught up with Jesus and recounted the conversation he had just had with Philip.

"Many a lamb will give its life in Israel in two days, eh Master?"

Jesus said nothing.

Andrew looked back and then, with a strange expression on his face, asked:

"Where is Judas?"

+⊫⸻⊨+

Judas had slowly dropped back from the others and was now half-way to the city. He had an appointment to keep with the high priest. As he walked, he wrestled with himself over the whole idea. Clearly Jesus was steering them all to disaster and had to be stopped. But should he betray Him? Or should he simply walk away? He stopped at the edge of the slope of the Mount of Olives leading gently down the Kidron Valley.

"What should I do?" he agonized aloud.

"What indeed?" said Lucifer, who had followed him.

Judas sat on the edge of a hill, looking over the twilight of Jerusalem. He could still make out the magnificent Temple, as well as parts of the Antonia fortress. Somewhere in that massive building sat Caiaphas and others who were interested in meeting him. Should he keep the date or not?

"Jesus has made a fool of you all," hissed Lucifer, who had seated himself next to Judas. A few holy angels watched from a distance, but as Judas' will had become increasingly accommodating toward Lucifer, they could not interfere. Lucifer ignored them and continued speaking to Judas' mind.

"He has betrayed the cause that originally brought you to Him "

Judas thought back to the early days of the ministry when Jesus had promised a Kingdom! Now all He offered was hardship and the prospects of being seen as a common criminal, a heretic or both.

"You could be a great man in Herod's eyes..."

Judas didn't care for the priests. He disliked dealing with them. But perhaps they could promote him to Herod as the man who helped put an end to a rabble-rouser. It was worth investigating. Of course he didn't *have* to make the deal tonight. He was just going to talk to them.

"Judas, it is not you who is the betrayer...it is Jesus..."

"Jesus," he whispered. "Why? Why did You lead us to this point?"

"You must lead them back, Judas...you must save your people...you must take the step to end this nightmare once and for all..."

He looked defiantly at the Temple below.

"It will cost you, Caiaphas!" he said. "And much more than the thirty pieces of silver I bargained for!"

Lucifer smiled as he felt Judas' will slipping into complete resolution. He took his hands and grabbed Judas by the skull and spoke the words,

"Now Judas...do what is in your heart to do..."

Judas stood as if on command and, taking one look back toward the direction of Bethany, turned and headed down the mountain toward Jerusalem. Lucifer smiled as he felt murder enter into the heart of Judas at last.

A.D. 33

Thursday, the Last Week

Passover Day

"Master, the Passover lamb is slain," said Peter. "But where shall we prepare it?"

Jesus looked at Peter, carrying the freshly killed and cleaned lamb in a bundle. He called John over to where they stood.

"Both of you shall go into the city," Jesus told them. "Once you are there a man carrying a pitcher of water shall meet you and take you to a house. Tell the owner that your Master has need of his house for the Passover. He will then show you to a room that will be ready to receive us. That is where you shall make preparations."

Peter looked at John and the two turned to leave.

The other disciples sat about anxiously. This Passover promised to be especially eventful, given all the recent tension in the city. Simon the Zealot carried a sword just in case. He planned to tuck it under his robes to use if the need arose. As Peter walked by with John, he saw the sword.

"And what are you planning to use that for?" Peter asked good humouredly. "The lamb is already slain."

"This?" said Simon. "This is for Roman lambs."

Peter took the sword from him.

"You have no need for this," he said. "Your hot-headedness will only get us all in trouble. I'll keep it for you until after the Passover."

Peter then tucked the sword under his own robe.

"Zealots!" he said.

Everyone laughed.

Chronicles of the Host

Passover

All of the cities surrounding Jerusalem were alive with the traffic of the faithful, heading into or around Jerusalem, preparing for the Passover feast. For many, this would be their first celebration in the Holy City. For some, it would be their last...

Just as Jesus had said, Peter and John were shown a room and made ready the Passover. Before the sun went down the others arrived, and they all sat around a large carpeted table where they could recline and enjoy their meal.

The Host, knowing that a supreme hour was imminent, surrounded the place where Jesus had gathered to prevent the enemy from interfering. The disciples enjoyed the meal as befit their custom, and all seemed to progress uneventfully. Until...

"One of you shall betray Me tonight."

The conversation stopped. Dead silence.

"What was that, Master?" asked Peter.

"One of you shall betray Me this very night."

"Betray You?" asked Peter astonished. "But who? Is it I?"

Others followed Peter's lead, asking who it was and then the lingering refrain, "Is it I?"

Lucifer saw the many angels surrounding the house in Jerusalem where Jesus was, at that very moment, announcing His betrayal. Several angels saw him and sounded an alarm. Michael himself was standing at the door of the house.

"Lucifer, how dare you show yourself here?" he said.

"Just collecting on what is due me," Lucifer said. "Now move aside."

"You shall not pass through this place, Lucifer," said Michael, his sword beginning to glow an icy-blue.

"Indeed?" he countered. "You had better confer with your brother archangel."

Michael looked up to see Gabriel, who had just appeared. Michael was happy to see Gabriel, until he read his face.

"You see, Michael," there is one in there who is begging for me to come in," Lucifer said. "So stand aside."

"What does this mean, Gabriel?" asked Michael.

Gabriel was in despair. Looking at his old friend, he said, "It means you must allow Lucifer in."

"What?" asked Michael, incredulously. "We cannot simply…"

"Lucifer has the right," said Gabriel. "It has been given to him by the Most High. We are not to interfere this night."

Lucifer smiled at Michael.

"Well, well. It looks as if my star is rising once more," he said. "And once I have finished with Jesus, you shall see it permanently in place back in the heavens where it belongs—and off this wretched planet. Now out of my way."

Michael watched as Lucifer moved past him and entered the home. He looked at Gabriel, who could not bear to look back at the archangel. Other angels were arriving, all sensing something extraordinary hung in the balance.

"We are not to interfere at all?" Michael pleaded.

Gabriel only shook his head.

Jesus saw Lucifer enter the room and stand behind Judas. Lucifer, though feeling his strength, dared not look Jesus directly in the eyes, at first. Instead, he stood next to Judas, making sure of his resolve to follow through on the betrayal.

Jesus looked at Lucifer, who for the first time felt compelled to look at Jesus.

"What you are about to do," He said to Lucifer. "Do quickly."
Lucifer sneered at Jesus.

"Judas is only the first to turn," he said. "I have also set my mind upon Peter. He, too, shall betray You in the end. As will the rest. And then Your dream of kingship will die with You!"

Judas got up and looking back only once, left the room. The others thought Jesus had sent him for more money from the treasury. Lucifer lingered for a moment and then, nodding his head at Jesus, vanished.

"Take this bread and eat it," said Jesus. "It has been blessed. It is My body."

The men took the bread and ate. Peter looked at his brother Andrew, wondering what this was all about. But they had come to expect such extraordinary behavior with Jesus, and ate it with the other men.

"Now drink from this cup," Jesus said. "It is the cup of remembrance. It is My blood…"

"Blood?" the men wondered. Though some recalled Jesus' words over a year ago when He said they should eat His body and drink His blood.

"It is the blood of the New Covenant that has been shed for the remission of sins for many," Jesus continued. "As often as you drink of this cup, do it in remembrance of Me and what this New Covenant means."

Peter offered the cup to Jesus, who refused at that point.

"No Peter," he said. "I shall not drink of this cup again until I drink it new with all of you in My Father's Kingdom. Now, before we leave here, I have one more task I wish to do…"

"You're certain He shall be at Gethsemane?" the officer asked.

"Yes, of course," said Judas, looking around nervously. "That was the plan. He will be there and I shall direct you to Him."

Judas had met the arresting officer and his men at the pre-arranged location. Together they had mapped out the plan to over-take Jesus. It would happen after the Passover feast in a garden called Gethsemane on the Mount of Olives. Caiaphas liked the plan—it was quick and it would happen in a remote place. Judas could see a priest standing in the shadows but could not discern who it was.

"How shall we know which man is Jesus?" the officer asked.

"The man that I greet with a kiss will be Jesus," said Judas. "And then your master can do with Him as he wishes."

As Judas turned to leave, the bag of silver under his robe banged noisily against a pot which stood nearby. He felt the bag—filled with coins—and wondered if perhaps he should have asked for more. He then hurried off into the night.

The officer turned to the priest.

"He seems quite willing," he mused.

"And useful," said Zichri, removing the robe covering his head.

Jesus stood after washing the feet of every disciple. All of them were amazed at His humility, and had been quite uncomfortable watching the Man they loved do such a menial task. And yet He had taught them an example of serving one another. His robe was wet in front from the washing.

"One more thing before we depart from here," Jesus said, gather-ing His things. "All of you will scatter tonight because of Me. But do not fear. I promise after I am risen I shall see you all again in Galilee."

"Enough Lord!" Peter exclaimed. "I will never leave. Though the rest of these flee Your side, I shall always be with You—even to the end! I will never deny You!"

Jesus put a hand on Peter's shoulder.

"Dear Peter," He said. "Do you know Satan has targeted you so he might sift you like wheat? But I have prayed for you that your faith will not fail you. Yet, I promise you, before the rooster crows you will deny Me three times."

CHAPTER 19

"Is this how you betray your Master?"

Pontias Pilate looked over the balcony of the Antonia Fortress where he had arrived only a few hours earlier. He preferred the coastal city of Caesarea, but found it prudent to be present during these troublesome Jewish religious festivals. He also found it prudent to bring the three thousand soldiers stationed with him at Caesarea and to position them in and around the city to ensure the peace.

Gazing at the Temple, he could only wonder at the minds of such men who could build a magnificent complex such as this, dedicating it to an invisible god. Still, as long as they kept their nonsense to themselves, he could live with their zealous faith. Besides, the emperor was counting on him to keep this rebellious nation subdued, and religion might prove his greatest ally.

Pilate, a man in his forties, owed his appointment as procurator to Sejanus, the real power behind the emperor in Rome. He was a merciless man, not at all above demonstrating Rome's hold on the Jews. At one point he caused a riot when he placed images of Tiberias in the city. In addition, he had also ordered the massacre of several

Galileans who had revolted due to his placing of offensive symbols in the region.

Tiberias was not pleased with these events, and ordered Pilate henceforth to keep the peace—at all costs. Thus he was predisposed this Passover night to allow the Jews to worship their god and to leave them alone—so long as they worshiped quietly.

From inside the palace he could hear his wife, Claudia, tossing and turning in her sleep. At one point he had gone in to see to her. Now her servant was headed to the room with a hot liquid to help her sleep. Poor Claudia. She dreamed of being a great lady in Rome. Instead she was consigned to this backwater of the empire. Still, it was a ladder that could be climbed—even from Judea.

"Governor," came a voice. "The report."

Pilate put his wine down and took the daily briefing from his aide. The report always updated him on the most recent arrests, executions or other occurrences in the city which was under Roman authority. Pilate read the document.

"Who is this Jesus?" he asked curiously, as he read.

"Just another religionist," said the aide. "A Galilean who entered the city for the Passover like the others. He seems to hold the people in some sort of spell."

"Seems there was a disturbance of some sort reported by the priests in the Temple," Pilate continued.

The aide laughed.

"There is always some sort of disturbance in the Temple, Excellency. Especially during one of these holy days."

Pilate thought for a moment. As he did, he could hear his wife moaning in her sleep. The aide glanced in the direction of the hallway. Pilate folded the document and handed it to his secretary, standing nearby.

"Nevertheless, double the guard around the Temple gates and make sure of the watchmen," he said. "And send for my physician. My wife seems to be ill."

"I have many things to say to you," Jesus said. "But you cannot bear them right now. I will tell you I am about to leave you. And where I am going you cannot go. But when the Holy Spirit comes— He will guide you in all truth. So do not be troubled. In the Father's house there is much room. I am going so I can make a place for you. Then I will return for you."

"We believe you, Master," said Andrew. "We believe in all You have told us."

"Do you?" asked Jesus. He looked over the faces in the room that flickered in the dim light of the oil lamps. Then His eyes dropped to the center of the table. "The hour has come. The prince of this world has been judged. You all say You believe me. Yet I assure you, that you will soon scatter and leave Me alone—except that I can never be alone for the Father is always with Me."

The disciples stared at each other in consternation. They thought again of Jesus' words about a betrayer among them. Was this what He meant? Jesus pulled His cloak up around His neck.

"Let us go. But remember these words: I want you to be in peace. In the world there will be times of great stress and tribulation. But you can be of good cheer. I have overcome the world!"

"My dear you might at least look like you are religious," said Herodius. "After all, these festivals only occur a few times a year."

Herod was bored. He hated coming to Jerusalem. In his father's day there was at least a measure of respect for the king—if only motivated by fear. Herod Antipas felt the people neither respected nor feared him. And though he was a Jew, he believed the religious obsession of his people had become unhealthy in view of the Roman presence. Still, he made his way each Passover to the Hasmonean Palace where he could be officially present.

"More wine," was all he could manage. He smiled at his wife, with eyes half-closed from the wine. "It's the only way I can get through this endless parade of fawning and fake embassies." He scoffed as he read through a pile of communiqués that had been delivered to his room. "Even the high priest sends his blessing!" He sneered. "Caiaphas! I should have that man removed some day." He drank his wine.

"It is important your people see you on these occasions," Herodius continued.

"Your presence inspires them."

"My people?" Herod retorted. He slammed his goblet on the table. "They were my father's people! He had them in the palm of his hand!" As he said this he picked up a bunch of dark purple grapes from a small bowl and crushed them in his hand. The juice dripped around his fingers and on to the floor. "But one day they will fear me!"

"They fear you now," Herodius said soothingly. She brought a towel and basin to him and began washing his fingers. "They fear you now. And they love you."

"Their love I will never have, my pet" he said, looking at his wife. "And they fear only their faith. They fear any fellow with some sort or new revelation or trickery. Like John. Or that man Jesus."

"Jesus?" Herodius said. "John's cousin?"

"Yes," said Herod, gritting his teeth. "That miracle-working Holy Man who claims to be the Son of God or some such nonsense. That is the sort of Man that preys upon the minds of my simple people." He began to wave his goblet around as he spoke. "They want miracles. Signs. Wonders." He sniffed. "And I'm afraid I can offer only majesty."

Chronicles of the Host

Gethsemane

And so it was on that dreadful Passover night, the Lord led His disciples back to the Mount of Olives, to a little garden spot called Gethsemane. He intended to pray there and requested three of His own—Peter, James and John—stay close by while He called out to the Father.

The Host remained alert and nearby as well—daring not to interfere, but desiring to put an end to this episode, should the Most High command it. Michael stood by, intent on spoiling the plot of those who would destroy the Lord. He watched...he waited...but the command to deliver Jesus never came...

A.D. 33

Early Friday Morning, The Last Week

Gethsemane

"Father, I know this is the reason I came," Jesus prayed. "I know the plan is a good one..."

He looked at His arms where sweat beaded with droplets of blood ran down to his hands. His entire body was wet with perspiration mixed with blood—so great was His distress. He looked up toward Heaven and continued in prayer.

"Do you see that, Kara?" asked Rugio. "He's breaking, I tell you!"

"So is Michael," said Kara. "Have you noticed how this prayer has disturbed him? Wouldn't it be ironic if, having come all this way, the ridiculous Man died of His own stress, here in the garden?"

"Stress or cross, it's all the same to me," growled Rugio. "So long as He dies!"

Michael looked at Kara and Rugio for a moment—penetrating them with his deep, dark eyes. He then turned his attention back to the Lord.

"Poor Michael," chuckled Kara, mockingly. "How frustrating it must be for an archangel to be so impotent at such a time."

"Wait until his Master hangs on the cross," said Rugio. "Then we shall see what this ruling angel is made of!"

The angels, making an impregnable wall around Jesus, stood in silent, reverent positions. Huddled together, they formed a shimmering shield of light, the likes of which had not been seen since they had appeared to the shepherds near Bethlehem 33 years earlier.

Gabriel and Michael stood by Jesus' side, feeling helpless to do anything for the Lord they served. Above and around them, thousands of howling demons, cursing and blaspheming Jesus, told Him the humans He was to die for did not love Him and were not worth His life.

"You have been betrayed by Your Father!" shouted one.

"Death...slow and painful...and for what?" came another.

Jesus bowed His head low, scraping up against the rock which had become His altar. "Father, if there is any other way to do this...If there is another way, then do not have Me drink from this bitter cup..."

Every angel—wicked and holy—stopped as if frozen. What were these words coming from the mouth of the One sent from the beginning of time? Michael and Gabriel stared at each other in shock. Could this be?

"What did He say?" asked Kara.

"He wants out!" shouted Rugio. "I told you He was breaking!"

"Nevertheless..." continued Jesus.

"Wait, He's still praying," cautioned Kara.

Every angel hung on the words that held the plan of the ages in the balance. Since Eden, the Seed had been promised, and through years of blood and strife it had finally arrived in the Person of Jesus. Now the mysterious plan the Most High had decreed seemed precariously close to falling apart. And yet...

"Your will be done in this matter, Father," He said. "And not Mine."

The angels cheered their Lord, drowning out the harassing words of the demons. Kara and Rugio were infuriated. As for Michael and Gabriel, they looked with great compassion and respect at their Lord. What a God they served! Michael suddenly knelt down next to Jesus.

"Michael, what are you doing?" Gabriel asked.

Michael placed his hand on Jesus shoulder to strengthen Him.

Lucifer stood next to Judas as the men waited in the darkness of the garden. He had completely won Judas over by now, although he could sense some remorse on the part of the man who would soon betray Jesus. Several warrior demons accompanied the group of brutes that Zichri had assembled to bring Jesus in for a speedy trial.

"Remember," said the officer in charge. "The man he greets is the Man, Jesus. He is to be arrested and taken alive. If there is any trouble from His followers, you are at liberty to deal with them."

"Here they come," said Judas. "Quiet now!"

Jesus and the men and decided to move near the Kedron brook. Peter and John had made a secret covenant that they would see Jesus through to the end even if it cost them their very lives. As they came to a clearing, Judas moved out to greet them. The disciples saw him and waved him in. Ignoring them, he went immediately to Jesus. Lucifer stood behind him the entire time.

Judas came to Jesus, who looked at Judas and then at Lucifer. Judas greeted Jesus with a kiss exclaiming, "Master! Master!"

Looking at Lucifer, Jesus said the words: "Is this how you betray your Master? With a kiss?"

Lucifer only looked back into Jesus' eyes.

Suddenly, a rush of men emerged from the darkness, uncovering their torches. The disciples jumped to Jesus' side, and Peter felt for the sword he had taken from Simon earlier that evening. Jesus looked over the men who had come for Him. He then stepped away from His disciples and stood in front of the band of men.

"Who are you looking for?" Jesus asked.

"Jesus of Nazareth," said the officer, holding a writ in his hand.

"I am He," said Jesus.

Upon these words, the men fell over backwards and tumbled onto the ground. Judas fell as well. Even Lucifer fell back. Gathering themselves, the men repeated their demand that Jesus come with them.

"All this time you could have taken Me in the Temple, or in the city," Jesus said, preparing to go with them. "Yet for fear of the people you must take Me in darkness. But I will go because it is the Father's will."

Peter suddenly grabbed the sword and came down hard, slicing off the ear of Malchius, servant to Caiaphas. The man bent down in agony. The others made a move to take Peter but Jesus held up His hand and they stopped.

"Peter, you cannot do this by the sword," He said, rebuking him. He then touched Malchius' ear and healed him, restoring it. "This shall not be overcome with violence." He turned to the men who were to take Him. "Although, if I wanted, I could command twelve legions of angels to destroy you with great violence!"

Michael and Gabriel stood nearby, watching it all.

"Can't we do anything?" Michael asked. "Will the Lord simply give up?"

"He knows we are here," said Gabriel. "But His is a greater mission than that which would involve mere angels."

The disciples followed the arresting party down the mountain. They were silent and devastated. Only Simon the Zealot managed to say to Peter, "And you thought I would use my sword heatedly?"

Peter didn't say a word.

A.D. 33

Early Friday Morning

Caiaphas' House

"I ask You again, are You the Son of God?"

Jesus looked at the high priest. In the room were several of his high-ranking priests and Pharisees. Jesus was bound at His wrists, and showed signs of bruises and cuts from having been handled roughly on the trip to the home of the high priest. One of the men present, a priest named Ethan, who was a friend to Nicodemus, was concerned about the highly irregular nature of the proceedings.

"I have told you," said Jesus, panting for breath. "I sat with you in the Temple; I taught in the open. I did nothing in secret. Everything I have said you have heard. What more do you want of Me?"

Jesus' answer was met with a stinging slap from one of the priests.

"How dare You answer the high priest like that?"

Lucifer, Kara, and Berenius were in the room watching it all with great delight. They were amazed at how quickly things had gone badly for Jesus. The slap echoed loudly.

"Slapping the Most High," said Kara. "Now that is something unheard of!"

"They hate Him," said Berenius. "I have been with them a while now. They are jealous of His hold over the people. There will be more than a slap in the face before this is all over."

"I'm counting on it," agreed Lucifer. "The religion of all men eventually degrades into law and death. It is how this game will be won.

The chill air of the evening seemed even colder as Peter stomped his feet to warm himself. John actually managed to go into the house with Jesus, but Peter preferred to stay outside. He stood near the gate of the house of the high priest. From time to time, he could hear raised voices coming from within.

"You there," came a voice. It was the girl who kept the door for the high priest.

"Yes," said Peter.

"Aren't you one of the men who came with Jesus?" she asked.

"Of course not!" said Peter, walking away.

"May I have a word with you, Zichri," said Ethan.

"What, now?" said Zichri, trying to hear the interrogation.

"It is urgent."

Zichri sighed, moving to the other side of the room. He never trusted Ethan. He found him too agreeable with the populace. Besides, he was a friend of Nicodemus, whose loyalties were going to be investigated as well, once the matter of Jesus was settled. Zichri bowed his head courteously.

"Zichri, I know you have nothing in your heart except for the good of our nation," Ethan began.

"Of course," said Zichri, as another slap across the face sounded in the room.

"For the record, I am concerned about the...legality of these proceedings," Ethan continued. "The nature of this is extraordinary. A trial at night? Clearly a violation of law! There is no legal mandate here. And these proceedings were instigated through the efforts of this fellow, Judas. That clearly violates our rabbinical tradition that every detail of such an arrest be handled by us..."

"Ethan, my friend..."

The men, warming their hands at the fire, whispered among themselves as they looked at Peter. He was sitting there, finally getting warm on this long night. He noticed the men looking at him but said nothing.

"What is He like?" asked a man stirring the coals.

"What is who like?" Peter responded, suspiciously.

"Jesus, your Master."

"He is not my Master!"

"You came in with Him, didn't you?" asked another man.

"No!" said Peter, standing up. "I am not one of His men!"

"There was no lawful warrant in the hands of the arresting officer," Ethan pleaded, "only that piece of paper on which he had scratched the name of Jesus. He has not been arraigned before the Sanhedrin; no formal charges have been lodged…"

A few of the priests in the room could hear Ethan talking and had turned their heads to listen. Zichri ushered Ethan out of earshot.

"Even these dubious witnesses cannot agree on their story," he continued. "One fellow says he overheard Jesus say He was able to destroy the Temple. The other said that He *would* destroy the Temple. The testimony does not agree…"

"Ethan…"

"I order You by the Living God," boomed the voice of the high priest. "Tell me if You are the Son of God!"

"And that!" said Ethan pointing. "The High Priest is supposedly a protector until the charges have been proven. He is not to prosecute."

"Are you the Son of God?" Caiaphas demanded.

"Yes," said Jesus. "It is true. Just as you have said."

"Blasphemy!" cried Caipaphas, turning to the others in the room. "He is guilty of blasphemy and therefore has condemned Himself to death!"

The other priests agreed with the verdict.

"Wait!" shouted Ethan. "The law provides that we wait one full day before pronouncing judgment! This Man cannot be sentenced lawfully."

Caiaphas and the others looked at Ethan. Zichri turned to the man and coaxed him along. "Come with me Ethan."

"These are desperate times, Ethan," said Caiaphas. "They require extraordinary measures. Zichri will explain all this to you."

Zichri nodded and took Ethan, still protesting, away from the council.

"And now, what do we do with Him?" asked Achish.

"The law prescribes stoning," said a priest.

"Yes," said Caiaphas. "Our law does require that. But Roman law requires that all death sentences be cleared through them."

He considered for a moment.

"We haven't much time," he said finally. "We must settle this before the Sabbath. I don't want to hold Him any longer than needed in this city. He has too many friends here. Take Him to Pilate. Zichri!"

Zichri came back in without Ethan.

"Ethan understands now why this trial was necessary," he said. "I explained to him, should Jesus be allowed to live, it was quite possible the Romans would bring an end to us all—including our families."

"Forget about him," said Caiaphas. "Take these charges and this blasphemer to Pilate. Tell him we await his instructions."

"At this hour?"

Zichri took the charges in his hand.

"And tell him we will be grateful for a speedy disposition of the matter."

Zichri nodded and motioned Ashich to follow him. The guards hustled Jesus outside.

Caiaphas watched as they left. On the floor were drops of blood from the cuts on Jesus' face made during the questioning.

"Get that filthy mess off my floor," he ordered a servant. "I will not have the blood of a blasphemer staining my house!"

Peter had moved to the side of the house, near a seldom-used entrance. A man followed him into the alley. He was scrutinizing Peter in the dim light of the early morning sun, just breaking over the horizon.

"You are one of them," declared the man. "You were in the garden with Him when my cousin Malchius was attacked!"

"I DO NOT KNOW THE MAN!" Peter swore.

At that moment, he looked back and saw Jesus, bleeding from the face, and being led by the guards out the side entrance. Jesus looked at Peter just as a rooster crowed. Their eyes met for an instant.

"Come on, You," said a guard.

Jesus was hustled on by the men. Peter began weeping bitterly and ran off.

"Poor Peter," sneered Lucifer, as they watched him run. "Just as I told the Lord last evening. The man is absolutely hopeless!"

"Where is Berenius?" asked Kara. "He would enjoy this."

"He is presently on another mission," said Lucifer. "With Judas."

CHAPTER 20

"Crucify Him!"

33 A.D.

6 AM Friday Morning

The Antonia Fortress

"The high priest has sent a delegation at this hour?"

"Yes, excellency," said Lucius, Pilate's aide. "They said it is most urgent. A matter of state."

"Nothing in this province is urgent," grumbled Pilate. "Let them wait a while."

"Excellency, Caiaphas himself has sent a letter," Lucius offered. He handed over the document to Pilate, who laughed as he read.

"These pious hypocrites, who will not defile themselves by entering my home, are trying to have a Man put to death for some offense against their religion. For this I was roused from my bed?"

Pellecus had maintained a vigil at the home of Pilate ever since the entrance of Jesus into the city. He had done all he could to stir up

Pilate's vanity regarding the Jews. He hoped that by the time the matter of Jesus was brought before him, Pilate would agree to anything just to get rid of them.

He walked with Pilate to the front of the house and out onto a court of the Antonia. The Temple loomed off to his left. Down below was an assembly of official-looking men from the priest's office, and some soldiers dragging a beaten, bloodied Man bound at the wrists. Pilate descended the stairs. Pellecus joined Lucifer and Kara.

"I see the other side is not missing any of this," said Lucifer, noting the presence of Michael, Gabriel and Crispin. They stood near Jesus, watching the proceedings. Jesus remained silent, His eyes lowered.

Pilate scanned the face of the Man standing before him. He was a young Man. Too young, he thought, to be condemned for violating the pride of the priesthood. But he would reserve judgment for the moment. He walked around Jesus, examining Him, noting the places where He had been beaten.

"He is obstinate," assured Zichri.

"I am sure," said Pilate, bitingly. "So unlike the priests."

Zichri glanced at Achish uncomfortably.

"Well, what are the charges here?" sighed Pilate, whose official robe had been brought out to him by his servant.

"The charge is blasphemy, excellency," said Zichri. "A crime most heinous to our people, and punishable by death."

The priests noted that several squads of Roman soldiers had begun to close in. An adjutant came and whispered into Pilate's ear and then stood by at attention. Pilate looked at the man who was charged.

"Blasphemy, is it?" he said in mock seriousness.

"Yes, excellency."

Pilate turned to Lucius, his aide.

"You know Lucius, if we Romans ever put to death everyone who had blasphemed the gods, there would be none of us left alive!"

Lucius laughed.

"If He were not guilty, we would not have brought Him before you," said Achish.

Pilate sneered at the men.

"You bring this Man to me because He is guilty of violating some idiocy involving your religion, and expect me to condemn Him? Judge Him according to your own law!"

Zichri looked at the men.

"Excellency, as you know, it is unlawful for us to put a man to death."

Kara moved over to Achish and spoke into his mind.

"The Man is a menace to Caesar..."

"Of course blasphemy is only an offense against our people," said Achish. "He is also guilty of treason against Rome."

"Really?" inquired Pilate. "How so?"

"He calls Himself a King," said Zichri, picking up on Achish's reasoning. "He says He is King of the Jews, and He forbids tribute to Caesar!"

With the matter of Caesar brought up, Pilate was forced to take action. He ordered Jesus brought into the palace where he could question Him further. When they were in private, Pilate began speaking.

"Look, You, I know these men are vile and petty," he said. "They are wanting to kill You for reasons I think are ridiculous. But they have now implicated You in treason. Now, we both know Caesar is king. What do You say? Are You a King? Answer me and I'll have them flogged and end this nonsense."

"Did they tell you to ask Me this?" Jesus asked. A droplet of blood ran off His cheek and fell on the floor between them.

"Am I a Jew?" Pilate mocked. "It is Your own people who brought You here. What have You done?"

"The Kingdom of which you speak is not of this world," Jesus said, looking through Pilate.

Pilate was confused.

"So You are a King then?"

"I am a King, if you say so," said Jesus. "But I command truth. And all who hear Me hear the truth."

Pilate was getting frustrated with it all.

"What is truth?" he asked.

"What is truth," Berenius whispered into Judas' ears.

Judas stopped up his ears as if to shut down the voices speaking into his mind. Ever since the betrayal he had fallen into a deep despair. Now he felt completely abandoned by everyone, including himself. He had even returned the money to the priests, casting it at their feet, and confessing to them he had condemned an innocent Man to death.

Now he was condemning himself.

"You shall never be able to live with yourself..."

"Stop it!" Judas shouted, hitting his head with his hands.

He wandered through the early morning, like an animal uncaged for the first time and unsure of where to go. He could not find solace anywhere...in any place...in any face. He was a man separated from life itself.

"Why prolong your condemnation? End it..."

"End it," Judas said under his breath. He saw a rope nearby.

"End it..."

He began crying and picked up the rope, looping it over the branch of a tree, and climbing on a stump. Taking one last look toward the city, he tied the other end of the rope around his neck. In the distance he saw the temple, shimmering in the morning sun now. With a shuddering sob, Judas threw himself forward.

When Pilate emerged from his conference with Jesus, he shouted at Zichri.

"This is nonsense! I find the Man innocent!"

The priests began protesting vehemently, spurred on by Zichri.

"His teachings stir up the people throughout our land, from Galilee to this very city! He is guilty of sedition!"

Pilate turned to Lucius.

"Did they say Galilee?"

"Yes, excellency. Jesus is a Galilean."

Pilate smiled.

"Your own king, Herod, is in this city for the Passover," he said. "He is ruler over Galilee. My judgment is that you take this Man to Herod to be tried by him. He has the legal jurisdiction, not I."

"But excellency," pleaded Zichri, glaring at the men who had brought up the fact Jesus was from Galilee.

"Enough!" shouted Pilate. "Take Him to Herod. And get out of my sight!"

33 A.D.

7 AM Friday Morning

The Hasmonean Palace

Herod still smelled of wine when Jesus was brought into the entrance of the Hasmonean Palace. Herodius, who had always been curious what the famous cousin of John looked like, watched from the shadows. Herod groggily read the charges that were brought before him.

"Apart from all these things, sire," continued Zichri, "this Man…"

"This is the One who performs miracles, isn't it?" interrupted Herod, who was suddenly more alert. "Herodius! Come and see! This is Jesus of Nazareth; the One that John went on and on about." He looked almost embarrassed and added. "Oh, I am sorry about Your cousin. But when a king makes a vow…"

"Perhaps He will do a miracle for us," suggested Herodius.

"Really, sire," stammered Zichri. "This is neither the time nor the place…"

"I will say what is what in my own palace!" shouted Herod.

Zichri bowed his head and backed away.

"This is quite astonishing," said Kara. "This Herod must be absolutely mad."

"Not really," said Lucifer. "He is simply a fool trying to be a king. Like every other human ruler. Ah, Berenius!"

Berenius appeared and walked over to Lucifer, bowing his head. Kara was annoyed at not knowing what assignment Berenius had been on.

"It is done?" purred Lucifer.

"Yes," said Berenius. "It is finished. Judas has taken his own life."

"Good," smiled Lucifer. "The rest of them shall also be rounded up and killed or scattered into oblivion. Either way, this Kingdom dies with their King."

Jesus refused to answer Herod. Herod plead with Him to perform a miracle of some sort—but Jesus remained quiet. The priests were becoming unnerved by it all. Zichri was moved to impatience.

"They say You are a king," Herod said. "A king of the Jews. I thought I was king of the Jews. Are you King, Jesus?"

No answer.

"They have brought You here so I may judge You. I will release You if You will only answer me and perhaps perform a miracle to prove who You are."

No answer.

"A king should always look his best for his subjects," said Herod. "Bring me my robe—the one that is for special occasions."

An aide ran out of the room.

"I'm afraid I cannot help You, Jesus," said Herod. "But I can do something for You. They brought You here a King looking like a clown," he said. "I shall send You back a clown looking like a King."

He then ordered the robe placed upon Jesus. The officers made a great show of it, bowing low before Jesus and enrobing Him as if for a coronation. The priests watched the charade impatiently.

"Take Him back to Pilate," Herod finally ordered. "I find nothing to charge this Man with. Farewell, King of the Jews."

He looked Jesus in the eyes.

"I envy the people's love for You, Jesus," he said quietly, so that only Jesus could hear. "Just as these men are jealous of their love for You. And so I release You into the custody of God. I only hope He will have more mercy upon You than His priests."

After they were gone, he noticed a spot of blood on a tile near the doorway. It was still moist. He ground it into the tile and retired to his chamber.

33 A.D.

8 AM Friday Morning

The Antonia Fortress

"You have brought this Man to me twice now, as One who perverts the people. And yet having examined Him before you I find no fault in Him. No, nor does Herod find anything worthy of death. I will scourge Him and release Him."

Lucifer was becoming increasingly agitated at the priests' inability to get a charge. He ordered his angels to begin moving in and out of the gathering crowd to stir them to demand Jesus' life. Pilate ordered more guards into the area.

"He is a traitor to Caesar!" one of the priests screamed.

Rugio and his troops arrived and began whipping the crowd into an angry mob. Thousands of angels poured into the area, gripping people by the eyes and mind and inciting them to perverse and violent notions.

Pilate held up his hands to subdue the crowd. While he had no reservations about brutalizing this mob, he did *not* want word to get back to Tiberias of yet another disturbance in Judea. When they were quiet he told them:

"I know you have a custom in this land to release a prisoner at the feast," he began. Zichri was already shaking his head 'no'. "I shall release to you this Jesus of Nazareth; after He has been scourged, of course."

The crowd exploded once more in opposition to Jesus. Where did all of this come from, Pilate wondered. Then a name was called out from the crowd.

"Barabbas! Release him instead!"

The people began voicing the name of 'Barabbas' over and over. Pilate wondered at a crowd who would allow a known murderer to be freed, while an innocent Man would be condemned. What should he do?

In his cell, not far from where the trial was taking place, Barabbas could hear his name being called out. He began fearing for his life believing they intended to take him by force and kill him. But he knew he was guilty and he was prepared to die. He only hoped death would come quickly.

"My love!"

Pilate turned to see his wife, Claudia, in the entryway. He walked over to her and escorted her back inside.

"What are you doing?" he demanded. "This crowd is nearly in riot!"

"I have not slept my darling," she said. "Because of that Man."

"Nor has any of Jerusalem, it seems," Pilate answered, stroking her hair.

"No! You don't understand," she continued. "I have suffered terrible nightmares because of Him. You must have nothing to do with Him or else there will be a tragic consequence for us."

"Nurse!" he shouted.

He ordered the nurse to take his wife back to her room. She was still crying as she left. But the crowd only grew louder…

"BARABBAS!"

"BARABBAS!"

"BARABBAS!"

Lucifer had not been so confident since the first days of the war after the fall of A'dam. He looked with approval at his angels working the crowds over, causing them to rave about Jesus and asking for His blood. He saw Pellecus standing with Pilate firming up his resolve. There was Kara with the priests, encouraging their mischief.

"Well, Most High," he said, looking past the scene and up into the heavens, "It has come to this moment. In a few short earth hours it will all be over. And all of Your prophets and laws and covenants and messiahs will have been for nothing. I told You man's free will would be Your downfall. I told You Your love would watch Your Son die! And so You shall!"

"Take Him in and scourge Him," ordered Pilate.

His soldiers removed the white kingly robe Herod had given Him, and lashed His back the prescribed 39 times. They then fashioned a crown made of thorns and placed it upon His head. Not wanting to end the drama Herod had started, they threw a purple robe across His back, so that the blood would not be quite as evident. After the scourging, they led Him out once more.

"Behold the Man," proclaimed Pilate. He then muttered to Lucius, "Perhaps seeing some blood on this Fellow will feed their appetites for execution."

Lucifer, watching the drama, continued to foment a riotous and bloodthirsty attitude among the crowd.

"Drive them!" he ordered his angels. "Make them demand His blood!"

Rugio and Kara had, in the meantime, instigated a new chant in the minds of the priests and the people:

"CRUCIFY HIM!"

"CRUCIFY HIM!"

Pilate was astonished at the stubbornness of the crowd. He held up his hands again and told them, "You crucify Him yourselves. I find this Man innocent of the charges you have brought!"

Zichri walked over to Pilate, and bowing his head spoke.

"Sir, we are not trying to be troublesome to you," he began. "But we have a law requiring the death sentence if someone proclaims himself to be the Son of God."

"What?" said Pilate, shaken by this latest statement. He hurried to the entryway where Jesus had been removed, lest the crowds rush Him.

"Where are You from?" he demanded, sweat beading down his face.

Jesus said nothing.

"Don't You see I am trying to *help* You"? he asked. "Don't You see I have the power to release You or to have You killed?"

Jesus looked up at Pilate, the dried blood caking one eye.

"The only authority you have over Me is that which was given you by My Father," he responded. "But those who delivered Me into your hands are guilty of a greater sin."

Pilate returned to the throng outside. The day was already beginning to get warm, though it was only about eight. He addressed the people again.

"I will release this Man!"

Lucifer had positioned himself next to Zichri and spoke into his mind. At that moment, Zichri spoke up:

"If you release this Man, then you are no friend to Caesar. For whoever makes himself out to be a king, speaks against Caesar's authority!"

Lucifer smiled at the incredulous look on Pilate's face. He turned back to Lucius, who only shrugged as if to say he didn't know what to do. Pilate looked at the angry crowd, the jealous priests and the bloody Man he was about to condemn to die.

"Very well," he said, ordering Lucius to bring him a basin of water. "But first I am washing my hands to show you I am innocent in this Man's blood."

Zichri and the other priests awaited the final word from Pilate. The crowd had grown quiet. Lucifer and his angels waited on one side of the court, while Michael and his angels waited on the other.

"This reminds me of when we were in Eden," observed Kara. "Waiting for Eve to take the bait from the serpent."

"True," said Pellecus. "Only this time the bait is the Lord Himself!"

"It won't be long, my brothers," said Lucifer, as Pilate prepared to speak. "Then we shall have a taste of real freedom!"

"Let Him be crucified!" said Pilate.

Chronicles of the Host

Bloody Seed

The shame of knowing...the horror of seeing...the pain of watching the Son of the Most High God; it is something no holy angel will ever fully recover from. All our hopes in a victorious crown of gold faded in the blood of a crown of thorns. We watched as they led Jesus through the streets, mocking

Him and forcing Him to carry the instrument of His death on His beaten shoulders. They took Him to the outskirts of the city, to the place of execution called Golgotha.

The enemy was ecstatic, wildly dancing about as if they themselves had allowed this crime to occur. And yet, we wondered why it had occurred at all. Was this part of a larger plan unknown to angels? Or did the Lord truly succumb to the ignorance and faithlessness of men? The answer would be evident in three days. But the waiting seemed to last forever...

33 A.D.

9 AM Friday Morning

Golgotha, the Place of the Skull

THUD!

The sound of the cross dropping into the ground behind Jesus followed by His agonized scream was a macabre backdrop to the unfolding drama. The Romans in charge of the execution took Jesus' arms and bound them to the crossbeam on which He lay. They offered Him wine mixed with vinegar to diminish the intensity of the pain, but He refused.

Looking at the crowds of people who had followed Him up the pathway, He could distinguish some of His family, including His mother, Mary. Above and unseen by them, He could also see thousands of unholy angels, covering the sky like a swarm of locusts, jeering and celebrating the death of the Lord.

CLING!

A streak of pain shot up Jesus' arm, unlike any He had ever experienced. It moved through His whole body like fire and he cried out in pain.

CLING!

CLING!

CLING!

He looked to His left and saw the hammer raised to nail the other arm into place.

CLING!

CLING!

CLING!

The Romans, professionals all, went about their business routine deftly, hardly speaking to one another. They knew their job. And they were doing it well. They lifted Jesus up with ropes, and positioned Him above the hole where they would stake the cross. Just as they were about to let it drop, an officer stopped them.

"Hold on there," he said. "Pilate ordered this placed above His head."

He handed the soldier a placard, inscribed in Hebrew, Greek and Latin:

JESUS OF NAZARETH
KING OF THE JEWS

Then with a violent thud that shook Him to His very core in agonizing pain, the cross dropped into the ground and was positioned upright. Jesus hung there for a moment in shock, trying to collect His thoughts. Nearby were scores of people weeping and watching. Several of the high priest's men were also watching.

CLING!

CLING!

CLING!

The crowd gasped at the horror of the scene as the Romans fastened His feet to the cross with one more heavy iron nail, completing their duty. Jesus cried out once more as the weight of His body was forced upon the nails through His feet.

The Romans' gruesome work was finished—now they simply had to wait for Him to die. Jesus' struggle was just beginning as He strained to live.

Kara and Pellecus watched Jesus squirming on the cross, trying to position Himself for just a tiny relief of the pressure on His torn body. But His muscles would soon give way and the full weight of His body was again forced upon His feet in wrenching pain. Kara noted the priests moving up to the cross.

Berenius had moved in with them and created a spirit of cruel mockery which they were now exhibiting with relish.

"Well Jesus," said Achish. "You promised You would send legions of angels down upon us!"

"Yes," said another. "And what about destroying the Temple in three days!"

"You saved others," Achish said, indicating some of the crowd. "Yet You cannot save yourself?"

"Enough!" admonished Zichri. "We are priests, not butchers. Achish, you will stay here until it is over. The rest of us need to return to the Temple." He walked over to Achish, pulling him aside. "Remember, He must be dead before the Sabbath. Pay them if you must, but see to it."

He glanced down at the iron bar used to break the legs of the prisoners in order to hasten their deaths.

"Father, forgive them!"

Zichri turned to look at Jesus.

"Did He say something?" he asked Achish.

"Father they do not understand what they do."

"As you say," said Achish uneasily. "I will see He is dead before Sabbath!"

"Jesus."

Jesus turned His head to the right. He saw the man condemned to die next to Him watching Him with interest and wonder.

"All these people, these priests," he marveled. "You must be the One they say You are."

Jesus said nothing.

"Please take me with You into Your Kingdom."

Jesus opened His dry, blistered mouth and spoke to the man, "I promise you today, that you shall be with me in paradise."

CHAPTER 21

"The stone is moving!"

33 A.D.

12 Noon Friday

Golgotha

"My Lord! My Lord! Why have You forsaken Me?"

Michael and Crispin stood on the hill watching Jesus die. They had been asking themselves this very same question. The jeering demons and Lucifer's proud leadership had begun to enrage Michael. He was ready to fight—yet he was compelled to hold his peace.

"What good can come of all this?" despaired Michael. "It will only serve to encourage Lucifer in his efforts."

"Michael, I cannot answer you," said Crispin. "Except to say these are things God's own prophets wanted to look into and were forbidden. If He withheld such things from His prophets, do you think He would reveal them to mere angels?"

"Then we are to wait upon the Lord's command to rescue Him?" asked Michael.

"Yes," said Crispin. "Should it come. But remember, Michael, the Lord said He would die. This is exactly what He is doing."

"But I thought that was a story—a fable to teach men," said Michael. "I did not think the Man, Jesus would truly die."

"You must trust the Most High," said Crispin. "Though Jesus die the Seed can never die. The Seed can never die…"

By three in the afternoon, darkness began to descend. The Romans were becoming increasingly nervous as people told them about Jesus, and what a crime this act was against God. Achish studied the darkening sky. Perhaps a storm was brewing? It was all very odd.

Lucifer peered into the black sky. He could sense death closing in on Jesus. He ordered his angels to encircle the cross as close as they could so they could witness the death of the dream.

Michael and Gabriel could only watch in disbelief as Jesus suddenly cried out one last time in the darkness:

"Father! Into Your hands I commit My Spirit!

"Wait—I think it is done," cried Lucifer.

"It's over," said Michael.

"Those words were His benediction," Achish said to his aide.

IT IS FINISHED!

"Break His legs!" ordered Achish. "We have Pilate's permission."

The soldier, not given to taking orders from priests, looked past him to his commander. The commander nodded and the man shrugged, picking up the heavy iron bar. He went to the first man, the one to whom Jesus assured would be with Him in paradise, and with a hard swing, brought the bar across the man's legs. They snapped in two and the man began to die. He repeated the process with the second man.

He waited until the last to break Jesus' legs simply to agitate the priest further. But when he reached Jesus, he found the Man already dead. Achish walked and examined Him.

"You had better make sure," he said. "Pilate personally ordered this Man's death."

The centurion picked up a spear and thrust it into Jesus' side. When Achish saw both blood and water spurt out, with no reaction from Jesus, he knew He was indeed dead. He left to report the news to Zichri, walking past Mary as he went. It was just as the old prophet Simeon had said—a sword had pierced her heart.

"Was that another earthquake?" asked Pilate.

Lucius came into the room where Pilate was eating with Claudia. Lucius brought in a report of strange occurrences and rumblings throughout the city that included graves opening, long departed holy men and women appearing to people, and flashing bolts of lightning.

"I told you to have nothing to do with that Man!" Claudia shouted. "You have profaned the Hebrew God!"

Pilate walked away from the table, clearly upset. Lucius followed him. They entered the front room where only hours before Pilate had questioned Jesus.

"I have given orders to the soldiers to form fire brigades where some houses have caught on fire," Lucius said. "And I have ordered more security at the execution site until the body can be safely moved."

"Good, good," muttered Pilate, whose eyes were fixed on the floor.

Lucius walked over to him and looked at the ground where Pilate had stationed his eyes.

It was a drop of dried blood.

"It is done, teacher," said Zichri.

Caiaphas nodded his head in approval. He looked at Achish for confirmation.

"I saw the body being taken down myself," he said. "Pilate has doubled the guard so that there can be no chance of His followers stealing it."

"Good," sighed Caiaphas, relieved. "Such a dirty business. But it had to be done for the good of the nation."

"There is still the matter of Lazarus," said Zichri.

Caiaphas stared coldly at him for a moment. He then nodded silently.

"See to it," he agreed.

"For the good of the nation," Zichri reminded.

"Master! Master!" came a voice from the hallway. Ethan appeared excitedly in the doorway, bearing important news.

"Rabbi...the veil of the most Holy Place!"

"What about it?" he asked.

"It has torn in half."

Caiaphas looked at Zichri and Achish with great perplexity.

"How could that be?" Zichri asked, mystified. "That fabric is so thick. It would take the strength of one hundred men to tear that veil."

Ethan stood looking at the blood stain on the tile in Caiaphas' floor. The stain had not come up.

"Or perhaps, the strength of a God," he mused, as thunder loudly exploded around them.

Lucifer's gathering of his ruling angels was the greatest celebration he had allowed since being cast out of Heaven. Every angel of any rank or order was there. They met in celebration of the death of the Seed and to toast each other in congratulations.

The raucous angels spoke hopefully of their future, something heretofore unmentionable. Kara, Pellecus and Rugio sat closest to Lucifer. Next to them were their chief aides, Berenius, Nathan and the like. The looming question was, of course, what now? With the Messiah gone, the Lord would have to reason with them. Now perhaps

He would leave them in peace. Perhaps some of them could even find their way back to the Kingdom.

Lucifer had convened the meeting on the very spot in the Garden of Eden where the two trees once stood: the Tree of Life, and the Tree of the Knowledge of Good and Evil. Both were long gone, as was the garden. But it was a satisfyingly symbolic place to meet. He stood to speak.

"Some time ago, I stood before many of you on this very spot. I must admit at the time it was a very different place!"

The angels laughed.

"It was Eden. The garden of the Most High. And there were two trees here that became a symbol of the Lord's hold over the humans that lived in the garden. I swore I would build my throne here one day. I have returned to this place to declare that what was once a dream has now become reality."

The demons cheered and howled at Lucifer's declaration of victory.

"The war we waged was a good one, and not without cost. Much human blood was shed in defense of this rotten world. I never wanted it that way. It was the Most High who insisted we duel in the minds of men. As it turned out, the mind of humans responds more favorably to our side than to His."

More cheering.

"And so we wrestled against a relentless enemy. We fought His Word, His Covenant, His Prophets. We had to deal with His cunning and treachery in changing the rules of engagement whenever He desired. Finally, we had to struggle against that infernal Seed—the likes of which we never understood until It finally arrived.

"And yet we dealt with the Seed when It came. Just as we dealt with the Law and the Prophets and all the rest. Moses came and went. David came and went. And now Jesus, the hope of the world, has died. And with Him, the dream of an empire on earth for the Most High.

Wild cheers.

"Nevertheless, after war comes the diplomacy. It is my pledge to you that I will negotiate for us a peace that will ensure our authority on this planet forever, and we will then demonstrate to the Most High, once and for all, that angels can rule from on high.

"I will make the following appointments which will be part of the new kingdom we are establishing: Kara, shall be the Chief Elder among you, Pellecus shall head up our own Academy of the Host, so that the truths we espouse will not only be promoted among angels, but among men as well. Rugio, my valiant warrior, shall be Commander of the Host.

"These three shall make up the ruling authority in our kingdom. Some of you shall rule with them. Others will be assigned to more fitting positions."

He looked down to the earth far below, a star in the distance.

"But the kingdom we now establish, built upon the back and blood of a broken Messiah, shall forever reign on earth!"

"You have secured the tomb of course," said Lucifer to Rugio as the celebration continued. "I want nothing to disturb the place—be it spirit or human."

"Yes of course," he said. "Pilate has posted a guard and the tomb is sealed."

"Remember what happened with Lazarus," said Kara.

"That was different," said Rugio. "At that time Jesus was on the outside wanting in. This time it is He who is on the inside!"

They laughed.

"Then it is done," said Lucifer. "I must admit I was fearful the Lord would call angels down before He died, but He did not."

"But why did He die?" asked Kara. "I still don't understand."

"I suspect He died of a broken heart," said Pellecus. "Once He realized the frivolity of men and their wandering ways it must have shattered Him."

"Still, I wonder about a God who can die," said Kara. "Is it possible?"

"Would you like to see the tomb?" asked Rugio, smiling.

"Yes," said Lucifer. "Why don't we all venture to the tomb and have some conversation with Michael. I'm sure it is safe now. After all, it has been three earth days."

Michael and Gabriel walked along the garden path following the two women. They were listening to their conversation, touched by the tender regard they held for Jesus. It was Mary Magdalene and Mary, the sister of Lazarus. They had visited the tomb for the last two days to honor the Lord and bring fresh flowers to place at the entrance. Today they brought spices and oil, hoping they could prepare the body and anoint him. But the tomb was tightly closed with no way to enter.

Lucifer thanked his attendees and began to excuse himself from the assembly. Kara had already departed for the tomb to begin negotiations with Michael. The other angels scattered as well—some to their assignments on earth, others to await their king's next command. Lucifer liked what he saw. He finally felt like a king.

"Berenius!" Lucifer shouted.

"Yes, lord," said Berenius, standing in front of Lucifer.

"I have not forgotten the many services you have rendered me," he said. "I am appointing you prince over all of the region promised to Israel."

"I thank you, my lord," he replied, bowing his head.

"Rather fitting that the terror of Jerusalem be made its shining new governor," Lucifer smirked. He then turned his attention outward and asked, startled, "Who is that?"

Everyone turned to see a bluish streak streaming toward them from earth. It was Kara, looking quite frantic. He found Lucifer and immediately attempted to speak.

"Did you find Michael at the tomb?" asked Pellecus pointedly.

"Yes," said Kara, half out of his mind. "But the tomb..."

"Stop stammering you fool," said Lucifer. "What about the tomb?"

"The stone is moving—but no human hand is moving it!"

Lucifer charged the tomb as the earth was quaking all around it. He stood in front of it, not believing what he was seeing. The stone was indeed beginning to move! He ordered Rugio and his angels to stop the tomb from opening. Kara and Pellecus joined in the effort, ordering all of Lucifer's angels to keep the tomb sealed.

Michael and Gabriel's angels fought with Rugio's warriors above the tomb. Lucifer kept an eye on the tomb, which was guarded no longer by Roman soldiers but by a Holy angel. A sharp blow came across Michael's head as Rugio brought his sword down hard. Michael responded with a hard thrust of his own.

"This is long in coming, archangel," sneered Rugio.

"The Lord has won, Rugio, " said Michael.

Then Michael's sword began to glow with a blue-white aura as he swung hard at Rugio. The devil managed a shriek before Michael's sword sent him spinning far into the heavenlies. Gabriel went after Kara, who stood atop the rock, shouting frantically to his angels. Upon seeing Gabriel's advance, Kara yelped and landed on the ground. He shot Lucifer a grim look and vanished.

Infuriated, Lucifer manifested his reddish aura to its fullest brilliance and decided to get satisfaction by killing the two women standing by the tomb. His face contorted and his features began transforming from fallen angel to a hideous dragon. Baring his teeth and claws, he roared and lunged at the women.

Suddenly an unmistakable sound echoed throughout the cosmos...it was the sound of the rock moving.

"NO!" shrieked Lucifer, who turned from the women to watch the stone being pushed aside by angels.

When the tomb was opened, a blinding light caused every angel to fall to the ground. The stone rolled away and waves of brilliance fanned out of the entrance. By the time the angels could see, they perceived a figure standing on top of the tomb. It was the Angel of the Lord!

The demons began scattering in every direction. Pellecus vanished with a defiant look at Michael. Lucifer, still in the form of a red dragon, looked up and saw the Angel staring at him. He roared in defiance, his dragon eyes shooting fiery flames, and lunged at the Angel with a mighty thrust.

The Angel used his shield like a weapon and swung it hard across Lucifer's chest. The impact was so terrific that the earth shook around the area for several seconds with a thunderous crash. Lucifer, enraged out of his mind, charged once more. The Angel of the Lord brought his weapon down hard once more and it crashed through the dragon's skull, spewing reddish light everywhere.

Michael and the other angels, having vanquished the remaining devils, watched as Lucifer recovered for a final attack. He lunged toward the Angel of the Lord, charging past him to the tomb itself. As he touched the entrance he was suddenly hurled back with a brilliant blast of white light. Lucifer vanished in a fiery red cloud, shrieking and cursing as he disappeared.

Michael and Gabriel bowed low to the ground as the Angel of the Lord himself settled upon the very stone He had just rolled away. The women, Mary Magdalene and Mary, the sister of Lazarus, were frozen in terror at the sight of the angel and of the two unconscious guards.

"Don't be afraid," the Angel said. "I know you are looking for Jesus who was crucified. But He is not here; He is risen! Go and tell Peter and the others that Jesus has risen. He is alive!

Chronicles of the Host

Epilogue

And the Angel of the Lord said, 'He is alive!'

There is, of course, much more to the story, and much yet to be written. We all await the day of the Most High's return to earth where Lucifer, though defeated at the resurrection of the Lord, still retains a measure of authority over the minds and hearts of men who are unwilling to turn to the Truth.

That Jesus did as He promised is a matter of record. That we, the Host, never understood until it was finally revealed to us, demonstrates both the wisdom and nature of our Lord. To men God has revealed His places, for it was for men He came and died. The greater puzzle, indeed, is not that the love of God brought Him to earth to save it; but that men still refuse to receive the Love spilled out for them on that agonizing day in Jerusalem.

And so it is, Most High Lord, that I humbly submit these Chronicles of the Host into Your keeping. Until the glorious day of Your return, I therefore submit these records that they may bring to Your Name Glory forever and ever.

Respectfully submitted,

Serus

Chronicles of the Host 4: Final Confrontation Study Notes

The fourth book of the Chronicles of the Host series takes us from the birth of Jesus to His Resurrection. Well, not quite. If you remember, the third book ended with the actual birth of Jesus. But this book begins some time later as the Magi—wisemen from the east—are ending their journey to Jerusalem in search of a king who was foretold by a star.

To the angels, it is not theology—it is simply God working in his mysterious and wonderful, if not difficult to understand, ways.

Here are a few questions to think through as you enjoy the book. May God continue to bless your journey with Him.

1. Think about it. The conflict of the ages waged between Lucifer and the Lord of Creation became prophetic in Eden. Re-read Genesis 3 and focus particularly on the Lord's penalties upon Adam, Eve and the Serpent. Notice the Earth is also included as a part of Adam's sin.

What are the judgments pronounced on each?

Adam

Eve

Serpent

Earth

What was the difference between the judgment on Adam and Eve and that which the Lord spoke upon the Serpent and upon the Earth?

2. Over the years, Eve has been blamed for the downfall in Eden. In speaking to the angels, Crispin places the responsibility squarely on Adam's shoulders.

Do you agree with Crispin's assertion that Adam bears the responsibility for sin's entry into the world? Why or why not?

Check out Genesis 2:15 as a part of your answer.

3. How do you feel about God using astrologers and mystics from a pagan nation to bring gifts to the Christ Child? What does that tell you about God?

4. Lucifer and his crew are not very impressed with the men Jesus chose as disciples.

Why do you suppose Jesus gathered such a hodge-podge of personalities instead of going straight to the best and brightest of Israel?

What does that say about our Lord?

5. Read John 6:26-65. Crowds of people followed Jesus around for all sorts of reasons—curiosity, food, healing, etc. but when He takes them into deeper teaching, some begin to leave Him. He even asks His disciples if they will also leave Him.

Do you know people who follow Christ to a point and then seem to dwindle away at the point of hardcore commitment?

How far does your level of commitment go? Are you ready to follow Christ no matter what the cost?

6. The book of John is organized around seven "I AM" statements by Jesus. (I AM...the bread of life...the light of the world...the door...the gate...the Good Shepherd...the Resurrection...the true vine). He also told the Pharisees, "before Abraham was born, I AM."

What do each of those declarations mean to you?

Is there a connection between Jesus' use of I AM and Moses' encounter with God at the burning bush? (Exodus 3:14)

7. *In the book, the religious leaders were often susceptible to demonic suggestion and influence.*

How could such learned and religious people be open to spiritual oppression? Are Christians open to such suggestions from dark spirits?

What do you believe is the greatest crime against God that people commit in the name of religion?

8. *Matthew 17:1-13 records the Transfiguration of Jesus on Mt. Tabor and His meeting with Elijah and Moses.*

What is the significance of this event?

Why Moses and Elijah?

9. *In answer to a question posed to Him about paying tax to the occupying authority, Jesus tells a Jewish leader that they should "give to Caesar what is Caesar's and to God what is God's." Look at Matthew 17:24-27 for a similar incident.*

What does this say to you about Jesus?

Why does God demand that we respect earthly authority? Check out Romans 13 as part of your answer.

How far must we go in obeying government if the authority is wicked?

10. *As Jesus is being paraded around at His trial, the players react to Him differently. Read Matthew 27:11-32, Luke 22:66 - 23:25, and John 18 and 19.*

What is going on in the minds and hearts of:

The Priests
Pilate
Herod

Why do you suppose that Jesus doesn't answer Herod but spoke to Pilate?

The trial was illegal according to Jewish law for a number of reasons. How do you think the high priest justified this murder?

11. *In the book, as Jesus dies on the cross, he is being cajoled and cursed by humans and devils alike. Read all four of the accounts of Jesus' death on the cross (Matthew, Mark, Luke, John); they record different statements made by Jesus and/or others.*

What was Jesus feeling and thinking during His agony?

What were the humans (friend and foe) thinking?

12. *At the Resurrection, the devils attempt to hold off the inevitable and keep the tomb sealed.*

Do you think they really believed they had a chance? Why or why not?

Think About It

Jesus was the Seed that finally arrived to deliver us all from the sinful natures we inherited from Adam's disobedience. It was a long time coming but Galatians tells us that "in the fullness of time" Christ came. Sometimes God seems to delay when we find ourselves struggling for a quick resolution. Many men and women of the Bible struggled with God's seemingly delayed answers as well. In the end, God's timing proved true and resulted in His greater glory.

Are you struggling with waiting on the Lord for something right now? Try this: think about past instances when God showed up just when He needed to. He doesn't keep us on pins and needles because He finds it amusing. He realizes that in our waiting He is producing something greater than the results we want—He is producing something positive in our character.

God is more interested in the long haul than in our momentary discomfort. It doesn't mean that He will not comfort us in our trials, but it might mean that He will walk alongside us rather than pick us up and rush us across the finish line.

Next time you are involved in an intense period of needing an immediate answer, step back and ask God what it is that He wants to produce in your life—then let Him produce it!

Chronicles of the Host series
by D. Brian Shafer

▬ BOOK ONE: CHRONICLES OF THE HOST

Lucifer, the Anointed Cherub, whose ministry in Heaven is devoted to the worship of the Most High God, has become pessimistic about his prospects in Heaven. Ambition inflamed, he looks to the soon-to-be-created Earth as a place where he can see his destiny realized. With a willing crew of equally ambitious angels, Lucifer creates a fifth column of malcontents under the very throne of God. Hot on their heels, however, is a group of loyalists, led by Michael and Gabriel, who are suspicious of Lucifer's true motives. In detective-style fashion, they slowly start to unmask the true nature of Lucifer's sordid plot. *Chronicles of the Host* is a fantastic novel of the beginning of all things. Follow Lucifer's deceptive plans to rule over Earth and his inevitable fall from grace.
ISBN 0-7684-2099-7

▬ BOOK TWO: UNHOLY EMPIRE

The prophetic clock is ticking. Lucifer and his army of "imps" search frantically for the prophetic "Seed of the woman." The memory of God's promise that this seed would rise up and bruise the serpent's head stirs them to shadowy demonic activity. *Unholy Empire* chronicles the duel between God and the fallen angels as both focus their attention on the Seed. The devils watch for any and every sign of the Seed in an all-out effort to stop, delay, compromise, or otherwise destroy this impending prophetic nightmare. If they fail they are all doomed.
ISBN 0-7684-2160-8

▬ BOOK THREE: RISING DARKNESS

The Chronicles' saga continues as Israel establishes herself in the land of promise, in spite of the unholy efforts of Lucifer. A satanic shift in strategy occurs as Lucifer forsakes the simple elimination of one family that *might* carry the Seed. Now he is determined to bring down the whole nation. He is obsessed in his efforts to prevent the appearing of this mysterious Seed. Kings, priests, prophets, and pagan nations are deceived into becoming cosmic chess pieces in this calculated war between light and darkness. From Jerusalem to Babylon and on to Rome, Lucifer believes he can destroy Israel in a deadly and delicate game of power politics…and he must do so or the nightmare will only intensify—a nightmare that will eventually be realized one starry night in Bethlehem.
ISBN 0-7684-2177-2

▬ BOOK FOUR: FINAL CONFRONTATION

With the birth of the Seed, Lucifer and his demons are more determined than ever to win the war against God and His holy angels. Manipulating the murderous politics and religious fervor of the times, Lucifer and his evil minions plot to use God's own people to destroy the Seed and conquer humankind. The Seed must be victorious. But at what cost?
ISBN 0-7684-2174-8

Available at your local Christian bookstore.

For more information and sample chapters, visit www.destinyimage.com

Additional copies of this book and other
book titles from Destiny Image are
available at your local bookstore.

For a bookstore near you, call 1-800-722-6774

Send a request for a catalog to:

Destiny Image® Publishers, Inc.
P.O. Box 310
Shippensburg, PA 17257-0310

*"Speaking to the Purposes of God for This
Generation and for the Generations to Come"*

**For a complete list of our titles,
visit us at www.destinyimage.com**